THE SE

Mrs Cecily Massingham pulled the thin material closely about her hourglass figure, displaying to full advantage the swelling of her bosom, the smallness of her waist and the fullness of her backside. As she strolled about the room the delightful manner in which the generous cheeks of her bottom rolled under the negligee caused Monty and Selwyn to exchange a glance of indecent speculation.

Cecily turned suddenly on her heel and uttered a little exclamation of dismay – her left slipper had twisted from her foot! Before either of the men could help her, she bent over to replace the errant shoe. In doing so, the bowed posture caused the front of her negligee to fall open and her pair of plump white titties rolled out into plain view . . .

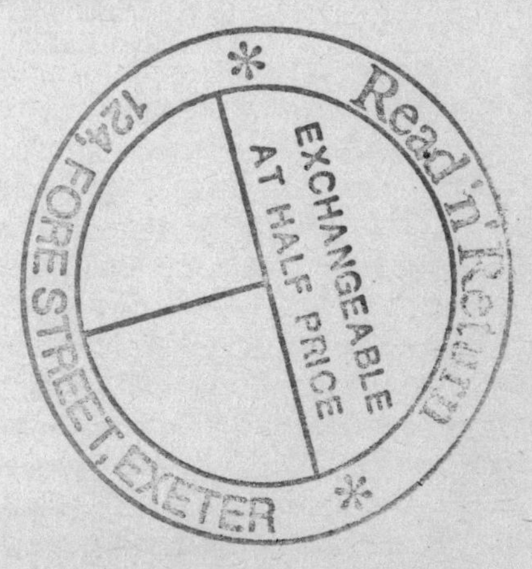

Also available from Headline

In the same series:
The Pleasures of Women

Venus in Paris
A Lady of Quality
The Love Pagoda
The Education of a Maiden
Maid's Night In
Lena's Story
Cremorne Gardens
The Lusts of the Borgias
States of Ecstasy
Wanton Pleasures
The Secret Diary of Mata Hari
Sweet Sins
The Carefree Courtesan
Love Italian Style
Body and Soul
The Complete Eveline
Sweet Sensations
Lascivious Ladies

The Secrets of Women

Anonymous

HEADLINE

First published in 1991
by HEADLINE BOOK PUBLISHING PLC

10 9 8 7 6 5 4 3 2 1

ISBN 0 7472 3626 7

Typeset by Medcalf Type Ltd, Bicester, Oxon

Printed and bound by
Collins Manufacturing, Glasgow

HEADLINE BOOK PUBLISHING PLC
Headline House
79 Great Titchfield Street
London W1P 7FN

PUBLISHER'S NOTE

As is normal for most Victorian erotic literature, the title-page of *The Secrets of Women* has neither an author's name or a date. The only designation is the initials *A.McK.H.* These are known to be the initials of Alexander McKenzie Hammond, a Scot resident in England, who was described by that greatest collector of erotica, Henry Spencer Ashbee, as 'a barrister in good standing.'

In the catalogue of his collection of underground Victorian classics, Ashbee says this of *The Secrets of Women*:

'The present work is certainly one of the most remarkable upon its subject, viz., physical love and its aberrations between persons bound by close ties of blood. We may fairly assert that this book is the most subversive of morality and unblushingly indecent of any we have read.'

CHAPTER 1

An Investigation Leads to a Curious Discovery

It is commonly accepted and thought commendable that when an author brings a book before the public he ought to write a few words by way of introduction. The present author humbly begs to be excused this unnecessary duty, having nothing at all to say about the characters of his most unusual story other than what is contained within the book itself. The gentle reader is asked to accompany the author to a house situated in Seymour Place, London, where Mr Monty Standish was comfortably lodged. This young gentleman had only recently celebrated the twenty-third anniversary of his birth, and had in fullest measure the spring and zest of youth.

The year was that in which Mr Gladstone promised to abolish the Income Tax and was so wretchedly disbelieved by the public that his party lost the General Election and he was forced to give way as Prime Minister to Mr Disraeli. On an afternoon in May of that year, at about four o'clock, Monty Standish was at home in his rooms in Seymour Place, enjoying a cup of tea and a slice or two of Madeira cake, and reading with much amusement a book he had purchased the day before in Greek Street,

Soho. The book was entitled *Lady Bumslapper's Boarding School for Young Ladies*, and was offered as a true and genuine account of some odd events in a Gloucestershire educational establishment.

True or not, the delightful and Sapphic events of which the book spared no detail had a marked effect on Monty, whose shaft was standing at full stretch within his trousers. Shortly after that his reading was interrupted by a creaking noise from the ceiling above him – a sound which forced itself into his reluctant awareness. He glanced up towards the source of the interruption, wondering what the top-floor tenant could be at. Not that it required more than a moment of Monty's vigorous imagination to supply the answer. He dropped his book and went into the bedroom that adjoined his sitting room, and found that he was standing directly underneath the origin of the creaking.

The sound was unmistakably that of a creaking bedstead, and there was only one human activity known to Monty that caused wooden bedsteads to creak in so regular a rhythm. The top-floor tenant was rogering a visitor on his bed – it could be nothing else! Monty sat on the side of his own bed and stared upwards to the white-papered ceiling above him and pondered how unusual and remarkable it was to be directly beneath a woman laid on her back with her legs parted and a strong shaft plunging into her pussy.

At this point it is expedient to give some small account of the household where this curious scene is placed. At 17 Seymour Place, only a step or two away from Edgware Road and a stroll from the Marble Arch and Oxford Street, stood a typical London house in a long terrace of such houses. The landlady was named Mrs Gifford, and who owned the property only she knew. The basement was given over to kitchen, laundry and other domestic offices; the ground floor was occupied by Mrs Gifford herself, there being no visible evidence that there was, or ever had been, a Mr Gifford.

Nor was one required, for the landlady's mode of life was to let out two floors of the well-furnished house to respectable gentlemen. The first floor up had been occupied for the past seven months by Monty Standish, a young man in sadly reduced circumstances who nevertheless contrived to exist comfortably without work, on an investment left to him by his grandfather. The floor above him was let out to Mr Selwyn Courtney-Stoke, a young gentleman with a position in the Board of Education, who had lived there for about three weeks. On the top floor of the house were the attics, where Mrs Gifford's two servants slept – the cook-general and the skivvy.

There could be not the slightest doubt, therefore, in Monty's mind who was responsible for the creaking over his head. It was Mr Selwyn Courtney-Stoke, rogering away for dear life. Monty's manly shaft had been fully hard before ever he moved into his bedroom to trace the sound overhead – this pleasing stiffness being the direct result of his reading about the unconventional teaching methods at the Boarding School for Young Ladies. After hearing what was taking place in the room above him, his shaft had become so thick and swollen and strong that it could not be neglected for another instant.

Monty slipped his hand under his waistcoat and down the front of his trousers without opening the buttons, and grasped his throbbing shaft to curb its leaping movements, which threatened to squander his resources if allowed to continue unchecked. He sighed in amazement to feel how long and thick his One-Eyed Jack had grown. He sighed again to hear the high-pitched squeak that had first attracted his attention now speeding up into a rapid and sustained groaning of wooden bedstead joints.

This passionate tattoo unambiguously informed the panting and agog listener below that his upstairs neighbour had reached the short strokes! There was a staccato rattle of bed-legs on the floor, and Monty gasped loudly in the realisation that this was the instant when the woman on her back above him was straining her belly upwards to have her pussy filled!

And while Monty had done nothing to provoke the bodily spasm, the crucial moment had also arrived for him. He was hardly able to breath, though his mouth was hanging open, and all his limbs shook fiercely in tremors that racked him from head to toe. His clasped hand gripped One-Eyed Jack tightly to hold him still, but that apoplectic gentleman refused to be restrained. He jumped ominously in Monty's grasp, rubbing his uncovered head quickly against the linen underdrawers that enclosed him.

At this sudden and unexpected sensation, Monty was undone. He ripped wide open his waistcoat and trouser buttons, pulled out his shirt, and let his shaft burst raging out into the light of day. Whilst he stared in alarm and dismay at One-Eyed Jack's shiny and swollen head, he gasped, *Down, Sir, down! I forbid you to . . .* but his command was never completed, for the pent-up desire inside his belly swelled to an uncontrollable explosion. His muscles clenched and he fell over backwards on the bed as, defiant and unbidden, One-Eyed Jack hurled the hot elixir of his passion in a raging flood up his belly, soaking the front of his shirt.

'You beast!' Monty was gasping out to each wet throb of his shaft. 'Stop it, I say! I forbid you to come off, you lustful beast!' but it was to no purpose, for One-Eyed Jack continued until he had fully satisfied himself.

When Monty recovered his senses, the creaking overhead had stopped and all was silence. No doubt Mr Selwyn Courtney-Stoke had withdrawn by now from the friendly pussy that had received his tribute. The lady had surely risen from the bed to attend to whatever precautions she took in order to evade the natural consequences of being poked – intimate ablutions at the wash stand, most probably. The image of a well-rogered pussy being washed was an interesting one, but even more interesting than that was the question of who the lady might be.

In the short time that Selwyn Courtney-Stoke had occupied the floor above, Monty had made his acquaintance in a casual way. They had introduced themselves to each other on the occasion of their first accidental meeting on the stairs. They exchanged a *good morning* and a *good evening* whenever they caught sight of each other, and Monty's inquisitiveness had led him to enquire of Mrs Gifford, and of the skivvy who cleaned his room, what more they knew of the new tenant. It was in this way he learned that Courtney-Stoke had come to London from Berkshire to take up an appointment in the Board of Education.

In person he seemed a somewhat diffident young man, of about five-and-twenty, very neatly dressed and handsome in a rather weak sort of way. He went out in the morning at nine and came back in the afternoon at three-thirty, the hours of work at the Board of Education being far from demanding. Monty knew this because, having no regular employment of his own, he had time to observe the household before he took himself out in mid-morning to meet his friends.

The problem that was now occupying Monty's mind, as he lay on his back in the pleasantly languid aftermath of his involuntary sexual emission was this – how could the general effeteness of the upstairs tenant's deportment be reconciled with the lusty rogering he had just engaged in?

Since Courtney-Stoke had moved into Seymour Place, there had been only one lady Monty had seen visit him – a dark-haired charmer in fashionably expensive clothes. Enquiries to the skivvy as to her identity had produced the information that she was a sister of Mr Courtney-Stoke who dropped in on him for tea when she was in town shopping. Other than her, there had been no female visitors at all upstairs, yet Courtney-Stoke had achieved a sufficient degree of friendship with someone to roger her in broad daylight!

His curiosity raging, Monty sat up and took off his trousers to mop himself dry. When he was presentable again, his clothes properly adjusted and his hair brushed, he moved back into his sitting room and stood by the door to the landing, to listen closely for sounds of movement. Five or six minutes later his diligence was rewarded by footfalls on the stairs, coming down from the floor above. He picked up his hat and waited until he heard footsteps right outside his door, then flung it open and stepped out onto the landing, exactly in time to come face to face with Courtney-Stoke and the dark-haired charmer.

'Good day, Selwyn,' said Monty very pleasantly, and bowing slightly to the lady at the same time.

'Good day to you,' Selwyn replied. 'You haven't met my sister – Mrs Fanshawe. She's in town on a shopping spree. Gwendolen, my dear, allow me to present Mr Monty Standish.'

Monty shook Mrs Fanshawe's gloved little hand and smiled at her in as charming a way as he could. He was sorely puzzled by the position – if Selwyn had rogered this pretty lady, then she very evidently could not be his sister. But if she truly was his sister, then Selwyn had not rogered her. So much was clear. The three of them descended the stairs together, while Selwyn explained that he was escorting Mrs Fanshawe to the railway station to catch her train home. Monty thought her delightful – in her face and form those features which suggested weakness in Selwyn were displayed as a most enchanting femininity, so that Monty was disposed to give some credence to the suggestion that there was a family relationship between the two of them. Perhaps Mrs Fanshawe was Selwyn's cousin, but why then pretend that she was his sister? Here lay a mystery to be unravelled.

Outside the house Selwyn steered Mrs Fanshawe towards where the hansom cabs waited, and Monty bade the two of them goodbye, raised his shiny top hat and walked the other way. He halted as soon as he was round the corner, and let a minute or two pass. When he turned back to the house, Selwyn and his friend were nowhere to be seen, and Monty strode swiftly through the front door and up the stairs, straight past the door to his own rooms and on up another flight to Selwyn's door.

Doors were never locked, for this was not a hotel or a common lodging house. Inside Selwyn's sitting room, Monty paused with his back to the door and looked round. He had been in this room many times before, when Naunton Cox had it, he having become a good friend before his misfortune. The room was almost as it had always been, furnished with comfortable heavy chairs and a settee. Naunton's rack of pipes was gone from the mantelpiece and his collection of walking sticks from the stand by the door. On the wall over the fireplace the new occupant had hung a large framed water colour of a village green with a cow up to its knees in the duck pond and a small church in the distance.

The real difference was that in Naunton's time the room was always redolent of the strong and manly smell of good tobacco – and that was gone completely. There was another and infinitely more interesting fragrance in the air – that of the expensive perfume Mrs Fanshawe was wearing when Monty was introduced. It was hard to put a name to it. Monty thought it might be a kind of patchouli, but it seemed more delicate than that, and it was certainly provoking to a man's fancies, no doubt of it!

He crossed the room with light and rapid step and went into the bedroom. What he had expected to see, he had no clear idea, but the sight of a perfectly made bed came as a surprise. It would have seemed more in keeping for the bed to be rumpled up if pretty Mrs Fanshawe had been vigorously rogered on it twenty minutes before. Yet the blue and yellow counterpane was as flat and smooth as if it had remained totally untouched since it had been made that morning.

Monty was beginning to doubt whether anything of interest had taken place on the bed at all that day – the creaking he heard might have had some other cause. To settle it one way or the other, he took hold of the bed clothes and with a sweep of his arm flung them to the foot of the bed – and there was all the evidence necessary! There on the bottom sheet was a damp patch which he knew from his own experience was caused by a wet pussy dribbling a little when a well-poked woman lay with her legs apart after the conclusion of the act.

There could be no doubt of it, Selwyn had given his

visitor a thorough rogering on this very bed. Therefore she was not his sister and he was lying – but to what purpose? Under the guise of shopping she gave her husband the slip and came to London to be pleasured by Selwyn. That was clear, and enviable too, for the truth was that Monty was much taken by Mrs Fanshawe. He had seen her for only a few minutes and exchanged no words with her other than the courtesies of a formal introduction, yet he had a great and throbbing desire to make use of her pussy.

He sat on the edge of the bed and contemplated the damp patch while giving himself the considerable pleasure of speculation on Gwendolen Fanshawe's pussy. The hair under her bonnet had been of a very dark brown hue that might be particularised as walnut by a man of a romantic trend – and it might well be imagined that the curls between her thighs were of the same rich shade. Monty had also observed during their brief meeting that she was a full-fleshed woman, ample of bosom and of hip – and from that he concluded that the Mount of Venus that so drew his thoughts would be plump and prominent.

Needless to say, these fervid imaginings as to the shape and colouration of Mrs Fanshawe's secret parts were inflammatory in the extreme to a nature so unrestrained as Monty's. Though only fifteen minutes had elapsed since he collapsed in convulsions of ecstasy to the furious spouting of One-Eyed Jack, his blood was again racing hotly through his veins and Jack was standing hard once more and making his presence felt by means of strong and impatient jerking inside Monty's trousers.

'No!' Monty said aloud. 'I refuse absolutely to be tricked yet again into an act of beastly self-pollution!' and while he was making his protest and stating his determination to control his passion, even at that moment he was undoing his buttons and easing out his twitching shaft to ease the unbearable pressure of his clothes on its swollen length.

What unseemliness might have transpired next on the bed with the damp patch if Monty had been left undisturbed can be only a matter for impure conjecture. What happened in fact was that in through the half-open door of Selwyn Courtney-Stoke's bedroom came Minnie Briggs, the sixteen-year-old skivvy, to find Monty seated on the bed and stroking his stiff shaft.

'Lord love us, Mr Standish – whatever are you doing?' asked the girl, an impudent grin on her face.

After the first shock of discovery, Monty's fears were quick to be calmed and he grinned back, for he was on friendly terms with Minnie. Some might have categorised the terms as much more friendly than was proper between a gentleman and a housemaid, for there had been many a time in the past six months when, with nothing else to occupy his attention for half an hour, he had given the girl half-a-crown to stroke his manly shaft while he felt her pussy. Beyond that he had never ventured to go with her, apprehensive of making her belly swell if he did.

'You know very well what I am doing, Minnie,' said he boldly, 'come here and take hold of my shaft and stroke it for me – and you shall have a silver half-crown.'

'You've got no conscience at all, the way you tempt and abuse a poor girl,' Minnie answered, and wiped her hands on her apron as she came across the room to sit beside him and take hold of his shaking length, 'oh my – it's wet and sticky already. You don't need me – you've done something naughty to yourself.'

'Not so,' said Monty, opening his legs, 'something unexpected happened to me, but it hasn't calmed me at all, as you see.'

Whilst Minnie treated his quivering shaft to a brisk stroke that would soon bring him off, Monty put his hand up her loose brown skirt and pushed her knees apart.

'What was it brought on this unexpected *something* that made you wet and sticky?' Minnie asked with a sideways grin at him. 'As if I couldn't guess what you've been up to – you've been reading one of the wicked books you buy – and reading it one-handed, I'll be bound.'

'No, it wasn't that,' Monty said, pushing his finger up into the girl's pussy, 'it was the creaking of this bed – I heard it down in my rooms and I knew that Mr Courtney-Stoke was rogering Mrs Fanshawe. She's very pretty, don't you think?'

'Ah, you want to give her a poke yourself, that's it,' Minnie said slyly, handling Monty's shaft very firmly, 'you're right out of luck there. You'll have to keep on dreaming of her, and fetch off in your hand when you hear the bed creaking.'

'What makes you so certain that Mrs Fanshawe wouldn't look at me?' demanded Monty. 'The ladies like me – why shouldn't I win the same divine reward as Courtney-Stoke has already, if I set myself out to charm her and win her esteem?'

'You've got no chance at all to get in with her,' said Minnie with a firm shake of her head, 'no more than fly to the moon. They're brother and sister and they're red-hot for each other. She's here twice a week to be poked by him.'

'That's ridiculous,' said Monty, his voice hardly more than a faint sigh, so delightful were the tremors that flitted though his belly from the girl's hand manipulating his engorged shaft, 'brothers don't poke their sisters – that would be a monstrous and unnatural act!'

'It must be different where you come from,' said Minnie, her tone filled with disbelief, 'but I was born in Hoxton and every girl in the street got poked by her brother.'

'This unspeakable depravity may be usual in the slums of the East End of London, perhaps,' Monty gasped, 'but Courtney-Stoke and Mrs Fanshawe were born into a family of means and education – how can you suggest for an instant that they would take part in practices so viciously degenerate?'

'You're a nice gentleman, but a bit simple,' was Minnie's impertinent reply, 'people with money aren't made different to us poor people. Mrs Fanshawe's got a hole between her legs just like me, and she likes it filled and her brother's got a shaft he likes to poke with. If you ask me, it's natural enough he's been sticking it up her ever since the day he could get it to stand up straight.'

The girl's words and the image they summoned of Gwendolen on her back with her legs spread apart, for a poke by her brother, was more than Monty could stand. It was a matter of the utmost desperation to get his shaft up a pussy and relieve himself of the letch that burned through his body and mind. The true object of his desires was miles away, but Minnie was at hand, and she was stroking One-Eyed Jack, who stuck so boldly up out of his open trousers.

At once Monty seized on the opportunity by snatching his hand away from the girl's pussy to take her by the hips and turn her to face away from him. Before she had time to protest, he had a hand on the nape of her neck to push her down on the bed, until her knees were on the carpet and her belly lay on the rumpled bed sheet, her backside to him.

'What are you doing?' she demanded, and before he

answered, Monty flipped up her skirt and underskirt to reveal her baggy drawers and her legs in coarse black stockings.

'You, Minnie,' he said, 'I'm going to do you, and afterwards you shall have five shillings.'

One-Eyed Jack twitched in delight when Monty pulled open the rearward slit of Minnie's drawers and beheld the twin cheeks of her bottom. Below, in the join of her thighs, her girlish and sparsely-fledged pussy awaited his pleasure. He pressed two of his fingers into it and rubbed her button, to make it grow wet.

'Oh, Mr Standish,' said she, 'if you're going to poke me, be quick about it before Mr Courtney-Stoke comes back and finds us at it on his bed!'

'Not much fear of that,' Monty assured her, 'he's taking Mrs Fanshawe to the railway station – I heard him say so. You'll be well rogered, my girl, and your pussy as slippy as a buttered bun, before anyone disturbs us.'

With that, he put One-Eyed Jack to Minnie's pussy and pushed. He expected her to be tight and difficult to pierce, but he sank into her with ease – right in, until his belly was flat against her backside, and he went at her briskly.

'You're a wicked gentleman, you are, Mr Standish – poking me on the same bed where Mrs Fanshawe's only this minute been given a pussy-full by her brother!' Minnie cried out as she jerked her hips back at him to meet his strokes.

'And now it's your turn for a pussy-full!' Monty gasped, his voice failing as the passion rose so strongly in him that he was like to faint with sensation.

'You've never wanted to poke me before,' said Minnie, 'though you've made me fetch you off with my hand times enough. Are you going to want to do this to me again?'

'Daily,' he sighed as he rammed away into her wet slit, 'not a morning goes by but I wake up hard-on like an iron bar – from now on I'll have you when you bring the morning tea.'

At that instant he hardly knew what he was saying, so intense were the emotions that held him in their grasp. He had no real intention of making promises to the housemaid that she might seek to hold him to later on. He had untied the bow behind her back that held her long apron, and thrust his hands up inside her loose and ill-fitting clothes, to grasp her bare titties. Faster and faster he plunged into her slippery pussy, a vivid picture of pretty Mrs Gwendolen Fanshawe behind his closed eyes – Gwendolen on her back, on this very bed, undressed down to her chemise and drawers, her creamy thighs wide apart to offer him her hairy slit.

'Oh, oh, oh!' Monty sighed, imagining himself lying with his trousers down round his knees and his shirt turned up to bare himself, his belly on Gwendolen's, whilst One-Eyed Jack thrust deep into her.

As Monty's frenzy mounted, he was unaware that he was ramming against little Minnie's bottom, and ravaging her wet pussy with a ruthless strength that shook her thin body under him. He was lost in his imagined rogering of Gwendolen, and he stabbed ever more fiercely, until at last the floodgates burst open in his belly and his hot tide of desire gushed into her.

Minnie cried out *Oh my*! and the bare cheeks of her backside battered against him. She, too, was in the very throes of coming off, the muscles of her belly contracting to grip his shaft and suck out the last drop of his spurting essence.

CHAPTER 2
Secrets Observed Through a Spyhole

Three days after the stirring events so far related, Monty was awakened at half past eight o'clock, as was his customary way, by a sharp tap at the door of his bedroom. Equally customary for him was the condition in which he awoke, with One-Eyed Jack fully rampant under his nightshirt. Monty was pretty sure that he had been dreaming about Gwendolen Fanshawe, although sadly he was unable to remember the details of what he had dreamed he was doing to that dark-haired charmer.

The knocker at the door who had woken him up was Minnie, the little skivvy bringing his morning cup of tea. She set it down on the night table beside him, and whilst she was at the window to raise the blind and draw back the curtains, he half sat up and wriggled his back against the soft pillows, to make himself comfortable.

'Good morning to you, Minnie,' he said, and he threw back the bedclothes to uncover himself. Minnie turned from the window and, seeing him lying in his nightshirt, her eyes alighted at once on the long bulge where his stiff shaft twitched strongly beneath the thin linen. The faintest of grins touched her mouth and Monty returned an encouraging smile, while he hauled up his nightshirt to his belly button and exposed his condition.

Minnie put her hands on her aproned hips and stared down at One-Eyed Jack, nodding up and down under her gaze, as hard as a brush handle. Although Monty had told the girl, when he poked her on Selwyn Courtney-Stoke's bed, that it was his intention to make daily use of her pussy, he had not done anything of the sort. She was, to his way of thinking, a plain little thing and none too well-washed, if the truth were told, and he had poked her only because she happened to be available at a moment of extreme need.

Other than that, he had no particular use for her, his needs being very thoroughly catered for on a regular basis by a dear friend – Mrs Cecily Massingham, a young widow who lived in St John's Wood. But now that he had awoken this morning in the grip of a strong letch – an aftermath of his dream of beautiful Gwendolen – Monty decided that he would make use of Minnie's pussy for a minute or two.

With his hand he gestured that she should sit down on the bed beside him, and he asked her to pull up her clothes and let him have a feel of her commodity. She sat on the side of the bed, facing him, but to his disappointment, her skirts remained down about her ankles and nothing of her body was shown to him. She handed him his cup of tea, to keep his hands busy, and stared thoughtfully at One-Eyed Jack, who was straining upwards in the hope of being handled by her.

'None of your nonsense, Mr Standish,' she said, 'I've no time in the mornings for all that – I've got my work to do and Mrs Gifford will be after me if she thinks I'm not hard at it.'

'At least hold my shaft in your hand,' Monty

suggested, 'only for a minute, and I'll give you a half-crown. It won't take any longer than that, Minnie, and a kind-hearted girl like you will never leave me in so desperate a plight!'

'Looks to me as if you've been holding it in your own hand,' she retorted. 'Get along with you!'

All the same, she clasped Monty's hot and hard shaft in the palm of her hand and jerked it up and down a time or two.

'That's it,' Monty sighed, his eyes closing in pleasurable anticipation of having his physical tension expertly relieved, but Minnie soon ceased her manipulation of him.

'I'll tell you what, Mr Standish,' said she, grinning at him as his eyes opened in surprise at her failure to continue the manual treatment she had begun, 'as you're so hard-on for Mrs Fanshawe, what would you say to seeing her given a good poking by Mr Courtney-Stoke? You'd have to stay very quiet, but you'd get a good look at her bits and pieces, if that's what you want – and you'd see her pussy being filled. What about it?'

His shaft answered for Monty by jumping in the girl's hand so fiercely that she giggled.

'Cost you ten shillings,' she said. 'Are you on?'

'When?' he asked, hardly able to believe his luck.

'This afternoon. She's coming to see him – I know because he told me when I took his morning tea and he ordered an extra cup and a whole fruit cake for four o'clock.'

'Can you really put me in a position to see what they do?' asked Monty doubtfully.

'I've watched them myself,' said Minnie. 'Is it yes or no? Do you want to see Mrs Fanshawe on her back with her legs open and her pussy wide open for her brother to shove his dolly-whacker up her?'

'Yes!' Monty exclaimed, his own dolly-whacker jerking hotly in the girl's hand. 'But how can this be achieved?'

'Never you mind how,' said Minnie, 'just leave that to me. You'll give me ten shillings for the peepshow, you promise?'

'Willingly! You shall have the cash before you go!'

'I trust a gentleman's word,' Minnie assured him. 'I'll take it this afternoon. Be ready and waiting for me at four o'clock, and I'll be here to lead the way.'

'You're a good girl, Minnie,' Monty exclaimed.

'Yes, I'm a good girl, I am,' she agreed with a grin, 'except when a gentleman pushes money into my hand. Then I'm a bad girl for him, I am. Now what do you want me to do about this hard-on you've been flashing about ever since I brought your tea?'

Monty drank his cooling tea and set the cup out of the way on his night table.

'What would you suggest, Minnie?' he asked her with a grin. 'I wake up every morning of the week and find it in this stiff-necked mood.'

'Stuck up, is it?' said Minnie. 'There's only one way to go then – it'll have to be taken down a peg, to learn it not to be so cocky.'

'I'm sure you're right,' Monty sighed, 'a touch of strictness is the only thing for it in this state. I'm too soft-hearted, that's my trouble – I let it do as it likes.'

'You leave it to me,' she said briskly, 'and I'll soon knock the stuffing out of it. You'll have no more trouble from this hairy monster this morning, I'll see to that.'

With this promise, she started to rub firmly up and down the straining shaft she held, whilst meanwhile, her other hand was groping between Monty's spread thighs to take hold of his soft knick-knacks and roll them in her fingers. Monty lay back at his ease against his pillows, breathing faster and more irregularly as his passions were raised, and mindful that at any moment now he was going to fetch off in a spectacular manner.

'Your dolly-whacker's shaking like a leaf,' Minnie announced, the rapid movement of her fingers sending such thrills through Monty that he gasped aloud and his belly twitched wildly, 'it's had about all it can take, if you ask me, and in a minute it'll come to a sticky end.'

Monty cried out in a frenzy of sensation and his legs jerked spasmodically as his thick white essence came gushing out in long jets like a fountain.

'Lor' love you, Mr Standish – just look at that!' Minnie exclaimed in awe to see how high the spurts flew and the force with which Monty was spraying the front of his nightshirt.'

'Oh, oh, oh!' Monty moaned to his delicious spasms.

'I've never seen anything like it,' said Minnie in admiration as the last creamy drop of sap hung trembling from One-Eyed Jack, 'you won't get another rise out of your diddler for an hour or two after that effort – it'll be on the slack for the rest of the morning, mark my words, Mr Standish.'

She was grossly underestimating Monty's admirable powers of recuperation. He had another nap after she'd wiped his belly dry with a corner of her long apron, and when he eventually got up, at about ten o'clock, he was much refreshed. He dressed and went out for lunch in a chophouse nearby, with a glass or two of porter, to prepare himself for the treat that he had been promised that afternoon. By three he was back in his own rooms, and to pass the time pleasantly he brought out from a drawer of his sideboard the book he had been reading when first he heard the bed creak upstairs that drew his attention to the rogering of Gwendolen Fanshawe by her brother, Selwyn.

Monty settled himself comfortably in his arm-chair and opened *Lady Bumslapper's Boarding School for Young Ladies* at the page where he had left off and proceeded with his investigation of teaching methods in this most unorthodox establishment.

. . . by the order of Her Ladyship, the offending girl was made to lie on the ladder that leaned against the study wall, while the two female servants secured her to it, with her arms and legs well stretched out. Her Ladyship had always preferred the use of the short ladder to the whipping-horse or whipping-post, declaring that the spaces between rungs made it easier to get at the vulnerable parts of the victim.

'Now, Harriet, my dear' said she to Miss Jarndyne, 'you see this wicked girl, Millicent, prepared for her punishment. Take up the instrument of chastisement and show me how briskly you are able to wield it.'

Whips and birches were never made use of in Lady Bumslapper's establishment, for she thought it a monstrous cruel spoiling of female loveliness to break the skin of a white young bottom and draw blood. The weapon with which miscreant young ladies were made to understand the errors of their ways was a whalebone strip, pulled from a worn-out pair of corsets. It was light and flexible and made a great crack across a bottom, stinging most fearfully, but without doing damage.

Miss Harriet inspected the lashings that pinioned Millicent's wrists to the ladder above her head, and her ankles to the rung first off the ground, then crouched underneath her to examine the bonds from below and test with her hand that they would hold firm, however much the victim writhed. The frightened girl stared at her through the rungs of the ladder with a pale face, pleading in a whisper to be pardoned.

Without deigning to reply Miss Harriet ran an immodest hand up under the girl's loose chemise to squeeze her plump titties, and pinched their rosebuds with cruel fingers, hard enough to bring tears to Millicent's innocent eyes.

'Oh, Miss Jarndyne,' said she faintly, 'I must ask you not to touch me on that portion of my person.'

Her tormentor laughed at her and deliberately increased her agony of mind by putting both hands up her chemise, to handle her titties freely. Then, satisfied that she had asserted her authority, she fetched a cushion from the sofa and pushed it between the girl's bare belly and the ladder – not as might be thought to protect her from bruising against the wood, but to force her bottom outwards for the lash.

The servants had pinned Millicent's drawers to the sides, to present her nether cheeks prominently, and had tucked up her chemise under her arms. All was ready, the victim awaited her dread Fate – yet with the cruelty implicit in her nature, Miss Harriet kept her in suspense a while longer. Laughing harshly, she passed a searching hand over the terrified girl's bottom.

'Excellently plump,' said she with relish, 'soft and delicate flesh for the lash! Ah, how I am going to make you sob, Millicent!'

'Have mercy,' the hapless girl pleaded, her face stained with tears, 'forgive me, I beg you, and I will never offend again.'

'It is too late to ask for pardon now,' said Miss Harriet. 'You have bitterly offended Her Ladyship, who is here today to witness your punishment. There will be no

pardon until these young cheeks have blushed under the sting of chastisement. After that, we shall see.'

Whilst she was adding to her victim's sufferings by her hard words, Miss Harriet's scornful hand roved over her uncovered bottom, and slipped down below the cheeks, to probe shamelessly between the girl's thighs and touch her secret furry place.

'A cut or two here would serve to teach you better manners in future,' said she, and her finger pried into Millicent's lower lips, 'well, I shall think of a use for your girlish plaything when the punishment is completed. I shall make you shriek out a second time while I have you bound to the ladder, though it will be for a different reason.'

'Not that! Spare me, I implore you!' gasped Millicent. 'You may beat me all you will, Miss Jarndyne, but do not outrage my maidenly modesty! Lady Bumslapper – I throw myself on your mercy to save me from violation at the hands of Miss Jarndyne.'

'Tush, girl – hold your tongue and take your punishment,' Her Ladyship replied. 'As for the rest, it is my earnest intention to give your pussy a good tousling myself, after Miss Harriet has had her fill of it. You'll be carried to your bed senseless from coming off, when I've done with you.'

'By George!' Monty exclaimed, astonished by the methods of discipline in use in female boarding schools. His shaft was standing at full stretch in his trousers, despite the exercise it had undergone that morning at the hands of the skivvy. Soon after four o'clock he heard footsteps go past on the stairs outside his door, and knew that Selwyn had brought his sister to his rooms for tea. In another five minutes he heard more steps and guessed it to be Minnie taking up their tea tray. He put away his book and sat impatiently waiting.

A light tap at his door and in came Minnie, grinning and with a finger pressed to her lips to enjoin silence. Monty nodded to her that he perfectly understood and, when she beckoned to him, he rose from his chair and in complete silence followed her out of his rooms and up the stairs. They went up past Selwyn's door and on to the attic stairs, which Monty had never seen before. They were uncarpeted, narrow and steep, so that as Minnie led the way up, her bottom was not far from Monty's face.

With a merry grin he slid his hand under her skirts and up between her legs, to the slit of her drawers, until he had hold of her pussy. She squealed in surprise when he gripped her, but suppressed her outcry quickly, and went the rest of the way to her room bow-legged, Monty's hand preventing her from closing her legs properly.

Her room under the roof was small and cramped, with a window let into the slates. There was a small iron-framed bed, a chair with a split seat, and a washstand that looked rickety. In a whisper she told Monty to sit on the bed and wait, and make no noise. He did, and watched with great interest as she dragged aside a strip of old brown carpet that lay on the floor, and went down on her hands and knees on the bare boards.

There was, he saw, a short floorboard, and with a teaspoon she produced from her apron pocket Minnie levered it up and put it to the side, out of the way, to reveal thick joists and the ceiling of the room below. At last he understood how he was to be shown the rogering of Gwendolen Fanshawe, and at once he was off the bed and down on hands and knees beside the maid. She turned her head to grin at him, and moved away a little to let him see that there was a small spy-hole in the plaster of the ceiling below. Directly under it lay Selwyn's bed, virginally made up with sheets and checkered counterpane.

It was to be presumed that Selwyn and his visitor were still having tea in the sitting room. The refreshment did not detain them long – in not more than five minutes from the time that Monty first looked through the ceiling, he became aware of the sound of voices in the bedroom beneath him. Very greatly to his disappointment, there was nothing to be seen, for the occupants of the room were out of range of his limited view. He sat back on his heels to rest, and motioned Minnie to keep watch.

Very soon she tugged at his sleeve and pointed downwards with a grin that told him the curtain had risen on the drama he had come to see. He applied his eye to the hole, and to his delight observed Gwendolen on the bed. She had removed whatever stylish gown she had been wearing that day and lay on her back with her pretty chemise turned up high and her rounded legs spread apart to show her lace-trimmed white drawers.

She was so very beautiful that Monty's heart was in his mouth and he could hardly breath for the emotions that had him by the throat. In his trousers his shaft was almost painfully stiff, and it throbbed to little tremors of sensation. Then Selwyn was kneeling beside his sister on the bed, and he had undressed to his shirt, which he had tucked up round his waist, Gwendolen stretched out a dainty hand to grasp her brother's outstanding shaft, and her eyes seemed to glow with a languishing desire.

For truth to tell, Monty was in honesty compelled to admit to himself, Selwyn Courtney-Stoke's shaft was outstanding indeed. At full stretch, it was a good eight inches long, and thick in proportion. Monty had always regarded himself as pleasantly and well-enough endowed, but he had never been able to muster more than six inches, however provocative his partner, however deft her touch, however enchanting the circumstances of the poke. He was, he had to admit, jealous of Selwyn for yet another reason besides his privilege of rogering Gwendolen.

Monty put his head as close to the joist as he could get, to bring his eye closer to the aperture for a better view. He saw Selwyn open the slit of his sister's drawers to reveal the most charming curly-haired pussy Monty could ever recall seeing in his life – a delight of a pussy that pouted out between smooth-skinned white thighs. Gwendolen raised her head from the pillow to murmur a few words in a low voice to her brother, who leaned over and pressed a kiss on the plump lips of the pussy Monty would have killed for.

'Oh, oh, my dearest Selwyn ,' exclaimed Gwendolen, speaking loudly enough this time for the Peeping Tom in the room above to hear her words. Selwyn was staring intently into her glowing eyes while he ran his hands up the insides of her parted legs, from the tops of her white stockings right up to the delicate skin nearest the bush of dark curls that covered her pussy.

'What's he doing to her?' Minnie whispered in Monty's ear. 'He has a plate of mutton sometimes .'

'Plate of mutton? What do you mean?' Monty asked.

By way of answer Minnie stuck out her tongue and made rapid licking movements with it.

'Oh my Lord!' Monty sighed, smitten by the thought of using his tongue on Gwendolen's pussy mutton to bring her off.

'Oh my darling!' Gwendolen exclaimed loudly below, as Selwyn slid his fingers into her pretty pink slit.

'Oh, my darling boy!' she cried out again, and her body was twitching to the darts of sensation that shot through her.

'How I do love to watch myself feel you like this, dearest,' said Selwyn, staring down at his fingers ravishing his sister's wet pussy, 'even though I am keenly aware that what you and I do together is very wrong and unnatural. Ah, if only I had the will to refrain from submitting to your lusts! This fearful moral weakness is a great source of turmoil and anxiety to me.'

It was obvious to Monty up above that the turmoil within her belly that Gwendolen was experiencing owed nothing to a sense of moral weakness and everything to Selwyn's fingers playing in her. She had begun to sigh without pause and to gasp out words of endearment and encouragement to her brother, whose skilful fingers stroked and fluttered in her open pussy, gliding over her hidden button until she uttered a shriek and writhed in convulsive joy on the bed.

To observe the woman of his choicest dreams come off caused Monty's shaft to jerk hard, so that he felt compelled to take hold of it through the material of his trousers and hold it tightly. He was unaware, rapt as he was in his erotic pleasure, that Minnie was crouching close beside him, her cheek pressed against his cheek, so that she too could look through the spyhole with him and observe what went on below.

Well might she huddle against Monty to catch a glimpse of the enthralling drama that was being enacted on the stage of the bed, for the final act had arrived and the denouement was close at hand. Monty caught his breath when he saw Selwyn beside his sister, supporting himself on one elbow, while she spread her stockinged legs wider still. To prepare the way for his entry, Selwyn pulled her dark-curled pussy open with his inquisitive fingers, so displaying the deliciously moist pink interior.

'Oh, how your pussy throbs to my touch,' Selwyn cried

loudly enough for Monty to hear, 'even though I have just made you come off! I promise you will faint in ecstasy before I have done with you!'

He seemed completely reconciled to his moral weakness as he pushed his sister's legs wider apart with his knee and lay over her belly, guiding with his hand the bare and purple head of his impressive shaft between her thighs, to bring it to her open pussy. For Monty it was as if he were in the room himself, his hand between those creamy thighs to feel the pink lips of Gwendolen's pussy, set in its nest of dark hair. His breathing grew shorter and he was unable to prevent his hand from tightening its grip on One-Eyed Jack and sliding up and down in his yearning.

Truth to tell, he was so very far gone that he had forgotten about Minnie's impudent sense of humour. Whilst he knelt with his head down and his bottom up, she reached under his jacket from behind and, through the tight-stretched material over his bottom, ran her fingers briskly up and down between the cheeks and under his knick-knacks. One-Eyed Jack was pleased by what she was doing and he began vibrating in Monty's trousers like a violin string plucked *pizzicato*.

Down below, Selwyn was up his lovely sister to the hilt and plunging hard and fast, eliciting cries of bliss from her.

'Oh, oh, Selwyn – how quickly I feel myself coming on!' she cried, her legs kicking up in quick jerks off the bed while he poked away at her with the appetite of a man who has not had a woman for a day or two.

Under this urgent stimulus, Gwendolen's body writhed and twisted on the bed, the sensations within her gathering towards a luscious climax. Again and again she seemed almost to swoon from the exquisite thrills that coursed through her, and each time she recovered her force and jolted her belly up at him in time with the thrusts of his darting shaft. Her stockinged legs kicked up off the bed, as high as if stretching up towards the hidden observer above, and her prolonged shrieks of bliss told of the arrival of the supreme moment.

Monty moaned softly and shuddered, and under the stimulus of Minnie's fingers rubbing fast and furious between the cheeks of his backside, One-Eyed Jack leaped like an Australian kangaroo and then discharged his frantic lust in Monty's underdrawers. Monty collapsed forward, pressing his cheek painfully against a hard corner of the joist, whilst he squeezed both his hands against the front of his trousers to control his throbbing shaft, which continued to spit its defiance until it was satisfied. When the outpouring stopped and Monty caught his breath, the absurdly comic aspect of what had happened struck him, and he chuckled – till Minnie clapped a hand over his mouth to silence him.

The sudden emission had calmed his nervous system so fully that he got up from the floor and went to lie on Minnie's bed to rest for a while. His drenched shirt-front and underdrawers were clammy and sticky on his belly, and he considered that he had had a good ten shillings' worth. There was to be a bonus, for he had barely dozed off when Minnie shook his arm.

'Come and have a look at this, Mr Standish,' she whispered urgently, 'you'll never guess what they're up to!'

Monty went back to the spyhole at once, and what he saw drew a long sigh of astonished delight from his lips. Down below on the bed, beautiful Gwendolen was stark naked, having taken off her thin chemise and drawers for a most unusual purpose. She had rolled her chemise into a sort of rope, and with it she had bound Selwyn's hands together above his head, and attached them to the bed head by means of her stockings. With her drawers she was gagging him, even as Monty watched, forcing a rolled-up part of the delicate garment into his open mouth and tying the legs firmly together behind his head.

When she had him helpless and silenced, she sat across his thighs and her fingers played with his limp shaft, her desire to again provoke and satisfy the most powerful and thrilling sensations of lust that the human frame can sustain. She pushed Selwyn's shirt higher, to bare his belly and chest, and flicked with her fingernails at the red-brown buds on his hairless chest.

'I'm going to lick your barley-sugar stick,' Monty heard her say to her brother, who shook his head violently and struggled underneath her, as if his perception of moral weakness had returned to trouble his conscience.

Demur as he might, Gwendolen had him in her power, and she pressed her beautiful face between his thighs and rubbed her nose in the curls about his shaft, and soon his wriggling came to a stop and he lay still on the bed. His legs parted like a pair of scissors and Gwendolen knelt between them while she bent over and took his lengthening shaft into her mouth.

'By Jove!' Monty exclaimed, his fervid imagination insisting that it would be superb beyond all human deserving to enjoy the privilege of Gwendolen's tongue licking over the distended head of his shaft! It seemed that she was expert at this work, for in a short space of time she straightened her back and held Selwyn's shaft in her fist – grown to its full eight-inch size and strength.

With no more ado, she threw a leg over his belly and sat on top of him, her round and pretty titties rolling up and down to her movements. In a moment she had guided Selwyn's length into her open and slippery pussy. There was no objection now from Selwyn – he was content to lie under his sister and let her do as she pleased with him. For a quarter of an hour Monty watched her delicious ride on Selwyn's belly, before she let him come off in violent upheavals, which brought on her own climactic satisfaction at once.

In Monty's trousers One-Eyed Jack was hard as a ramrod and raging to have his lusts gratified immediately. Without as much as a by-your-leave Monty seized the girl at his side by her ankles and pulled her knees smartly from under her, so that she collapsed face down on the floorboards. He dragged her clothes halfway up her back and ripped open her drawers to bare the cheeks of her backside, and dabbled with his fingers into her wet pussy, for she too had been greatly affected by what she had watched.

'Put it up me,' Minnie gasped, wriggling her bottom about. Monty jerked open his trouser buttons and pulled his shirt up to his chest and flung himself upon her. Her thin thighs were wide apart when he passed his hands under them, to pry open her wet slit and finger her button.

'Do me,' she gasped, 'do me quick!' and she lifted her loins up from the floor until the velvet purple head of Monty's shaft found the entry to her pussy and he rammed in with fast jerks. Ecstatic sensations flooded through him, whilst the thrusts of his shaft inside her and the rub of his fingers on her button roused Minnie to an intensity of pleasure that made her gasp in time with his strokes. She was writhing under him, the cushions of her bare cheeks against his belly serving to intensify his pleasure to a veritable delirium.

'Oh Minnie, you lovely little slut!' Monty gasped out as he approached his zenith. 'Your pussy's drenching wet!

'Do me hard!' she moaned. 'Fill me full!'

'I'm fetching off, Minnie!' he cried, and his belly thumped against the cheeks of her behind, whilst his plunging shaft gushed hot essence into her. She shuddered beneath him, heaving her backside up to meet his furious strokes and she came off so intensely that she collapsed senseless. Monty lay tranquil on her hot and limp body whilst he recovered from his delightful exertions, feeling his last creamy drops dribble into her.

CHAPTER 3
An Exchange of Confidences

Selwyn Courtney-Stoke had only been a few months in London with his position at the Board of Education and had not yet made any friends of note. He was therefore flattered to be invited to lunch at a decent restaurant by Monty, in furtherance of the plan the latter young gentleman had formed to bring Gwendolen Fanshawe's personal charms within his grasp.

To achieve, without waste of time, the degree of cordiality needed for his purposes, Monty plied his guest with food and drink – most especially drink. The meal started with a meaty beef soup, and continued with goujons of turbot cooked in white wine. Then came the main course – thick slices from a baron of beef, with roasted potatoes, parsnips and sprouts. Afterwards they tucked into cabinet pudding with cream, and finished with generous portions of Stilton. To wash down all this deal of food they drank between them four bottles of claret and two of Sauternes, and then turned to a fine crusty old port with their cheese.

Selwyn ate everything set before him but, as Monty guessed, he was not accustomed to drinking on this heroic scale and was soon in a most receptive state of mind. He listened with great interest when Monty told him how well he had been acquainted with Mr Naunton Cox, the previous occupant of the rooms Selwyn now had, and he asked Monty many questions about him.

'You may find my curiosity in regard to Mr Cox somewhat odd,' said Selwyn, speaking carefully to disguise his intoxication, 'but there is a particular reason for my interest. What it is, I cannot possibly, as a gentleman, reveal, but you may take my word that it is quite extraordinary.'

'Everything to do with dear old Naunton was extraordinary,' Monty replied with a knowing smile. 'His secrets are safe with me – you may tell me your reason.'

Selwyn dropped his voice and leaned across the table top to whisper that, on moving into the rooms vacated by Naunton Cox, he had to his amazement discovered in the bottom of the bedroom wardrobe a pair of female drawers. What did Monty make of that? he enquired.

'Why, only that some lady friend of his went home with a bare backside,' said Monty, with a laugh. 'He entertained ladies in his rooms very frequently and, beyond a shadow of doubt, they all removed their drawers for him.'

'Lord above – he was a ladies' man!' Selwyn exclaimed.

'I am sure that you are a gentleman who may be entrusted with another gentleman's confidences,' said Monty, as he topped up Selwyn's half-full glass. 'I was never present when Naunton's lady friends visited him, but I shall confide to you the secret particulars of a most enthralling outing he took me on – not long before he was compelled to quit London in a devilish hurry and install himself in Paris for the next twelvemonth or so – or until all has blown over and is forgotten.'

'Great Scot!' Selwyn cried 'How on earth did his misfortune come about?'

'That's another story altogether,' said Monty, 'and one which I do not yet feel able to entrust to you. Let me continue with the account of my call with him to the home of Mrs Gladys Lee in Margaret Street, which as I am sure you are aware, runs off Regent Street at the top end, joining it to Cavendish Square.'

'Mrs Lee?' said Selwyn, wrinkling his forehead in thought, 'I am sure I have heard the lady's name mentioned. Is she well-known in society?'

'Only in a certain kind of society,' Monty informed him. 'She is a well-known whoremonger, catering to the gentry. Naunton had the pleasure of her acquaintance for some time past, making use of the facilities of her private establishment whenever the mood came upon him. We lunched together at Romano's one day and sat talking over the brandy until past three in the afternoon, when of a sudden Naunton declared that he had a hard letch for a fresh young girl's commodity. I was in a like condition, for the liquor had brought me on stiff, and when he proposed a call on Mrs Lee and at his expense – I was delighted.'

'It was decent of him to pay,' said Selwyn, 'I can see that you were good friends, indeed. But how fresh can a girl be in a house like that? Surely the incessant pounding of lustful men takes off the bloom of youth?'

'Naunton said something of the same to Mrs Lee when we sat in her parlour and shared a bottle of port wine with her. "That may be," said she, "but I have a charming young girl in the house who is not a day over seventeen and has all the appearance of the dew of tender youth and virginity still upon her. You may make the fullest use of her for three guineas apiece."

"Five guineas the pair of us and we'll have her together," was Naunton's rejoinder, and Mrs Lee winked at us and said, *Done*! She led us upstairs and tapped on a bedroom door, advising us that Miss Emmy was resting in preparation for a most important visitor that evening, for the Earl of Atherton was expected to call after dinner and regale himself with her youthful charms.'

'Good Heavens,' said Selwyn, 'she mentioned his name to you? But he is a most respectable gentleman, and the newspaper never fails to report in their fullness the stern warnings he utters in the House of Lords – how decent family life is in threat of decay when thoughtless and pleasure-seeking men squander their substance on the pursuit of immorality.'

'Yes, I've read his Lordship on the subject a time or two,' said Monty, a broad grin across his face. 'Yet nevertheless it seems that he is well-known at Mrs Lee's. To resume though, for I have scant interest in the lewd fumblings of ageing noblemen, Mrs Lee left Naunton and me to go on into Miss Emmy's room. Ah, what a beauty she is, that dearest girl! Seventeen, as the old bawd had told us, and with fine golden hair and a skin like cream. She lay on the bed in her chemise and stockings – no stays or drawers, and my heart was pounding at the sight!'

'She wore no drawers?' Selwyn whispered, his pale blue eyes shining. 'Could you see her thighs, Monty?'

'Her thighs,' Monty repeated slowly, 'her soft, lovely bare thighs – yes, I could see them. And much more besides. Her eyes were closed, her shoes off and her stockinged legs spread apart, the knees drawn up. There in full view lay that choicest flower of female beauty, that delicious plaything that nestled between her creamy-white thighs! Oh, the heart-stopping beauty of what I saw then

– her curly bush of nut-brown hair and the soft pink lips of her pussy. Her dainty hand lay across her belly and between her legs, her long slender fingers moving slowly to pleasure herself.'

'You mean she was stroking her pussy to fetch herself off?' Selwyn asked breathlessly. 'I can't believe it – never have I seen a girl do that to herself! I don't believe they do.'

Monty noted away in his memory the declaration of disbelief, promising himself to take advantage of Selwyn's innocence when the moment was right, by showing him a woman pleasuring herself with her fingers.

'On hearing our entry into the room,' he continued, smiling to see how tight a hold he had on Selwyn's imagination, 'Miss Emmy's blue eyes opened to gaze at us, and a fond smile spread over her pretty face. Her fingers lingered in her pussy as she bid us bolt the door and come to her. She spread her legs a little more as we approached and my greedy eyes devoured her pussy. The sight of it drew me irresistibly to her, just as if it were a strong magnet and the hard shaft in my trousers a bar of iron to feel its attraction. I could see that Naunton felt the same keen lust, more so perhaps even than I, for he undid his trousers and was rubbing his shaft in his hand as we sat on the bed-edge, on either side of the lovely girl.'

'But . . . was this not embarrassing for you – and for him – to have another man present and observe you in so excited a state of mind and body?' asked Selwyn, his cheeks pale from emotion.

'Why, no,' Monty answered with a laugh, 'a stranger perhaps might be inconvenient, but a friend – neither he nor I gave the other a thought, we were too intent on Miss Emmy's bare pussy. She spoke to us then, and her words sent thrills of delight up my spine.'

'What did she say?' Selwyn whispered. 'Tell me, Monty.'

'She drew open her pussy a little to show us the pink inner lips and her proud little nub standing above the entrance to her depths and she said, *This is what you've come to see, isn't it*? I could hardly speak for the intensity of my emotions, but succeeded in saying that it was very beautiful indeed, and to think that so tender a morsel could give such rapture to a man. Naunton was quite as strongly affected as I was, if not more so, but he retained sufficient control of his voice to request, *May I kiss it, Miss Emmy*?'

From Selwyn there issued a soft moan that brought a smile to Monty's lips.

'She gave him permission in an affectionate murmur,' he went on, 'and Naunton knelt on the bed between her parted legs and put his lips to the soft and yielding pink blossom that was the centre and heart of her female nature. I half-heard the softest of sounds then, between a sigh and a moan, and for the life of me I knew not which of them had uttered it – Naunton or Miss Emmy. I saw his tongue flickering up and down between delicious parted pink lips in the nut-brown little nest and this time it was clearly she who made the sweet sounds of delight I heard.'

Selwyn's face was becoming an ever darker red and his eyes had closed almost completely, as the account continued. Monty noted the signs and congratulated himself that it would not be overly difficult to separate him from Gwendolen, so that he might the better enjoy her himself.

'By now I too had my trousers open and my stiff shaft in my hand,' he said, 'stroking myself a little whilst I watched the pleasuring of Miss Emmy. She was gasping breathless words of instructions to Naunton the whole time – *lick slow, lick fast, slow down, put the tip of your tongue to the left, now over to the right* . . . and all this he most dutifully and carefully obeyed, ravaging her with sensations so divine that she was rolling her backside on the bed and her titties were rising and falling vigorously in her chemise, to her heavy breathing.

'I could see there was only one way of it. Her hips moved in a rapid motion and she shook convulsively from head to foot. A shriek escaped her lips and she came off, rubbing her wet and open pussy against Naunton's fiery red face, I could bear no more – with an exclamation of impatience I pushed him aside and threw myself on Miss Emmy. One hard push took me deep into her hot belly, right to the very hilt, until my curls were entwined with hers.'

'Oh my dear Lord!' Selwyn gasped, his slender body shaking with the force of the emotions that Monty's description aroused in him. 'Oh Monty – I would give anything to have been with you then – anything!'

'There is better yet,' said Monty. 'She was still coming off from Naunton's stimulation, and whilst I plunged hard and fast into her pussy, she continued coming off and coming off. She cried out without stop and tore at me with her fingers, pulled at my hair and bit at my lips and cheeks in the very fury of her passion. It could not last – no human frame was capable of withstanding sensations so immensely overpowering! I felt the fast surge of my sap up One-Eyed Jack, and in great spasms I flooded her pulsating pussy . . .'

'Heavens above!' Selwyn gasped, his eyes staring wildly and his weakly handsome face crimson with emotion at the high point of Monty's story.

'Hardly had I squirted my last drop into her than

Naunton gripped me by the shoulders and dragged me from her. I rolled over on the bed, my wet shaft still jerking spasmodically in the aftermath of spending in her, and lay still in a delightful lethargy to watch Naunton use her pussy for his pleasure. She lay twitching and murmuring, her chemise up to her belly button and her body limp and unresisting. Naunton was on his knees between her open thighs – he seized her under the knees and hoisted her legs up in the air, parted them and hung them over his shoulders, in such a way to raise her backside right off the bed. His fingers were dabbling at her wet pussy, and in an instant I saw him bring his stiff affair up to the mark and drive it into her with a powerful push.'

'But she didn't come off a third time?' Selwyn asked in a gasping whisper, so that Monty wondered if his new friend had perhaps fetched off in his trousers by accident.

'Patience, and all will be revealed,' said Monty with a grin, 'Miss Emmy moaned and shook to his thrusts, and he moaned too, in time with her. Her bare backside swayed and squirmed against Naunton's thighs, and on a whim I pulled her chemise up to her chin, to observe how her bare titties wobbled like jelly to his thrusting. *Suck them*! she moaned, her eyes darting a look of pleading at me. I rolled close to her and set my mouth to the nearest of her pleasure domes, and sucked at its red-brown tip. My new position on the bed put my back toward Naunton, but I heard the rasping of his breath and felt the force of his jabs through Miss Emmy's soft body.

'How he held out so long I cannot tell, but when at last he spent, it was as if a mighty earthquake tore its way through Miss Emmy's belly. She screeched and shook to the spasms of his fetching off, as she had to mine, and then gave a soft sigh and fainted clean away through the intensity of her ecstasy.'

'Monty,' Selwyn whispered in an expiring voice, 'give me your word that you will take me to Mrs Lee's house so that we may share Miss Emmy together, for I shall never be capable of sleep again until I have experienced for myself the ecstasy you have described. Do this for me, and I am in your debt forever!'

'Nothing easier, my dear old fellow,' said Monty, pleased to see that his angling had landed the fish he was after, 'but let us finish the bottle first. I'm glad you accepted my invitation of lunch today – as you can imagine, since poor Naunton fled I've missed having a good chum to roust about with.'

'After what you've told me about him, I can well understand,' said Selwyn, emptying his glass quickly. 'What terrible chain of circumstances brought about his downfall? Do you feel able to confide in me?'

'Well, if I have your word of honour never to repeat what I tell you,' said Monty.

'I swear it, on my honour!' Selwyn exclaimed.

'The Church of England was his undoing,' said Monty. 'He had been to visit an old uncle near Effingham – an uncle from whom he had important expectations, there being no other relatives with any claim on the old fellow's fortune when he finally pops off. All went well, according to Naunton, and after lunch he bade his uncle goodbye and took the next train back to town. It was the middle of the afternoon and a stopping train, with very few on board, and he found him himself travelling with a lady to whom he had been introduced and knew slightly.

'This was the wife of the vicar of the church attended by Naunton's uncle, and the vicar and his wife had been guests at uncle's house for lunch on a couple of occasions when Naunton had been there. Mrs . . . I will not reveal the lady's surname, for that would be the despicable act of a cad and a rotter, but I will refer to her as Louise.

'You must understand, Selwyn, that I have never met Louise and have only Naunton's word for it that, though near on forty, she is still an attractive woman. Fair-haired, he said, with a porcelain complexion and an hour-glass figure. Since you have not met Naunton, you cannot have any inkling of how personable he is and how attractive he can make himself to members of the opposite sex, when he has a mind to avail himself of their dear little facilities. Not even a respectable married woman going on forty, the mother of grown children – and moreover – the wife of a vicar of the Church of England, could long withstand his blandishments.

'As to why he wanted Louise – even he himself was not wholly sure, when I questioned him after disaster had struck. He said that he was bored by the visit to Uncle Harriman, that he was bored by the slow train journey, that he had lunched very well and given uncle's best port wine a thrashing, that nobody else was in the compartment and it seemed a dreadful waste not to take advantage of that – in brief, he had a letch for a woman, and the only one to hand was Louise. He set himself to winning her affections, and such is his charm of person that before long she made no objection when he undid the buttons down her jacket and had a feel of her titties through her blouse.

'They were, said he to me afterwards, nicely swelling titties and when Louise had become accustomed to his hands upon her, he undid her blouse and felt down inside her chemise, above her stays, to get his hands on these bounties of nature in their bare state. She made some little complaint but he closed her mouth with a kiss to spare himself an intended reproach.

'Her silence secured, and she almost swooning from the excess of her conflicting emotions, Naunton treated himself to a good and generous feel of her big soft domes, talking to her all the while in a soothing and comforting manner. When he thought her ready for it, he leaned over and plunged his face between those plump titties, and with both hands pressed her soft flesh to his cheeks.'

'Oh, the bliss of it!' murmured Selwyn, putting the palms of his hands to his cheeks. 'Lord, Monty – this friend of yours is a sheer delight to hear about! I wish I could meet him!'

'No problem there,' Monty replied at once, 'we can pop across to Paris at any time and see what the rogue is up to. I warrant he'll have us rogering a troupe of mademoiselles before we've had time to unpack. Ask for a few days off from the Board of Education and we'll slip across the Channel by the weekend.'

'The weekend,' said Selwyn, suddenly crestfallen, 'no, that won't do, Monty – I have given my word to stay with my sister and her family this weekend next.'

'A pity,' said Monty, eyeing him thoughtfully, 'let me know when you can.'

It was clear to him that Selwyn's sister had the ascendancy of her brother to the point where he could take no independent action of his own, but deferred to her wishes in all. He could not go to Paris to roger a Frenchie or two because Gwendolen wanted him at the weekend to satisfy her – that was about the size of it.

'Well then, to get back to Naunton and Louise on the train to town,' said Monty with a grin. 'We left our hero in process of plunging his face between her bare titties. Louise allowed him to enjoy that pleasure for some time before she announced that matters had gone as far as they were going and commanded him to desist. Far from releasing her, now that she had shown herself to be prepared to submit to him in this – and therefore would submit further, according to all his previous experience with women, Naunton had it in mind to hoist up her skirts and stroke her muff a little.

'Whether Louise could be aroused within the duration of the train journey to so delightful a condition that she would lie along the compartment seat for Naunton to put his shaft up her was not yet clear to him – which was as good a reason as any to make the attempt. So make it he did – he put his hand under her skirt and petticoats and up between her legs. When he got as high as her knees, he told me, her eyes opened so widely that they seemed round in shape, and her obvious surprise caused him to wonder if the vicar had never put his hand up her clothes during the hours of daylight.

'Be that as it may, her knees moved apart and his hand passed on between her thighs and into her drawers, to touch her hairy pussy. He played with it for some time, by his account, teasing it to become slippery with the moisture of excitement, soothing Louise, and raising up her expectations of what further delight might follow. Before anything could ensue, the train slowed and came to a stands till in a station.'

'How very vexing,' Selwyn exclaimed, his fingers drumming on the white tablecloth in his agitation, 'to be interrupted at so precious a moment!'

Monty nodded his agreement and continued his narrative.

'Needless to say, Naunton had the strongest determination to prevent any busybody passenger from entering the compartment and spoiling his game with

Louise – and to this end he let down the window and rose to stand with his head out of it. He spied two or three waiting on the platform, and thought it prudent to stand there with a stern expression on his face to drive away any inconsiderate traveller. At last the train pulled out of station, he closed the window and turned to face Louise again, hot with the letch for her.

'During the halt she had done up her blouse and her jacket, and her fleshy charms were concealed from him. She told him to stay away from her and remain where he was, standing with his back to the window, and make no further attempt on her honour. None but her reverend husband had ever touched her person before today, she informed him, and although Naunton had taken caddish advantage of a moment of weakness on her part, that was the end of it.

'Well, of course, Naunton knew better than to believe a word of this pious rigmarole. Louise needed to be coaxed a little, that was all. She was staring at the bulge in his trousers, for One-Eyed Jack was at full stand and vibrating merrily. He flicked his buttons open and let it leap out like a Jack-in-the-Box, at the level of her face, she sitting and he standing. *But it's so big!* cried she in surprise, from which he deduced that the Reverend was not so generously endowed. *And strong too*, said Naunton, *feel for yourself!*

'Her cheeks fiery red and with incoherent words on her lips, Louise leaned forward to take hold of his monster and feel its strength. He rested his back comfortably on the closed window and stared down to watch her pull out his palpitating item and his hairy accoutrements from his gaping trousers and gaze at all in wonder. In a frenzy of lust his thick shaft stood to its fullest height and shook between her fingers, trying to thrust ever higher and swell itself up to an impossible girth.

'Louise's eyes rolled up to meet his, and he claims that they were shining with admiration and curiosity, and she was visibly impressed by the size and promise of his apparatus. Her hand slid up and down its length, sending continuous little ripples of bliss along Naunton's nerves. Not that his sensations stopped him from wondering how a vicar's wife had learned to pleasure a man's part so expertly that she was fast bringing him to the point of spending.

'*You'll make me fetch off in a minute, Louise*, he gasped and reached down to rip open her jacket and blouse and plunge both hands down her chemise to grasp her titties and squeeze them. She, too, had become highly aroused in handling his parts, and both she and he were so entirely engrossed in sensual delights that neither was aware of the train's rattling pace slackening. Louise bent forward to engulf the purple head of his shaft in her wet mouth, her hand slipping rapidly up and down all the while, and an instant later he cried out and she jerked her head away from him as he came off in joyful spasms.'

'Oh, my Lord,' Selwyn was murmuring, his hands out of sight in his lap beneath the tablecloth.

'There was Naunton, doubled over, One-Eyed Jack spurting in Louise's hand, and her face streaked with the creamy trickles of his spending – and the train had stopped in the station at Clapham Junction. Even then not all was lost, you might think, for Naunton's back was to the window and nobody could get in past him. But horror of horrors – the platform was now on the other side of the train – and the door beyond Louise was opened and a middle aged gentleman handed up into the compartment his wife and three half-grown children.

'There was no possibility of Naunton concealing what he and Louise had been at. The wife fled with shrieks of distress and outraged modesty to fetch the nearest railway official, driving the children before her like frightened sheep. For a moment or two, Naunton confessed to me afterwards, it was in his mind to leap out of the door behind him and make his escape over the tracks, abandoning Louise to her fate. But that would have been the act of a complete bounder, to leave a lady in the lurch.

'But apart from that, it was pointless to run, for Naunton and the indignant gentleman happened to be well acquainted with each other, he being the manager of the branch where Naunton banks. There was nothing for it but to tuck away his wilting mascot and put the best face on things he could. But Mr Bramley, for that is the name of the banking gent, refused to be talked round. Louise was allowed to depart, after a long lecture on vice and depravity, Bramley holding the view that Naunton alone was to blame, and had forced his vile attentions on a married lady travelling alone.

'It took Mrs Bramley so very long to find a porter while her husband held Naunton by the arm on the platform, that as soon as Louise was clear of the station, Naunton broke loose from his captor and ran for it. He came back here, and while he threw a few clothes into a bag, he told me what had happened. He asked me to look after the rest of his things and vanished in a cab to catch the boat train and leave these shores before Bramley had time to find his address at the bank and send a constable round to arrest him.'

'Interfering with a vicar's wife on a train!' said Selwyn, his voice faint with wonder at the prospect. 'I see the truth of your claim that Mr Naunton Cox is an extraordinary person in all respects. Oh, to have the courage to undertake so very exciting an act! I would give anything to be so bold!'

'But my dear fellow, you must not underrate yourself,' said Monty, seeing by the high colour of Selwyn's cheeks and the bright shine in his eyes that the moment was right to risk all, 'to my mind, rogering your own sister calls for more sustained bravery than most men possess, or are ever like to.'

Selwyn's mouth fell open and he stared dumbly over the table at Monty, who calmly poured the last of the port wine into their glasses.

'Come, come, Selwyn,' he said easily, 'no need for that look of surprise. We are men of the world, you and I, and we have no difficulty in understanding these things. Mrs Fanshawe is very beautiful, and you are a lucky dog to have the pleasure of her intimate company. How long has she been yours?'

'Since you have guessed so much,' said Selwyn, 'you may as well know all. It will bring me some relief of mind and heart, I do believe, to tell another of my darkest secret. You are a most understanding friend, Monty, and I am more grateful to you than you can know for not condemning my moral weakness.'

'We all have moral weaknesses,' Monty said generously. 'Mine is an inability to leave a pussy untouched, however inopportune the circumstances. Poor Naunton's was much the same, hence his misfortune on a railway train. How did it first come to pass, this unusual connection between you and your charming sister?'

'Years ago,' Selwyn confessed, eager now to unburden himself of his secret. 'We were brought up near Reading, and since my Father's constrained circumstances made it impossible for him to send me to boarding school, I was a day school boy and grew up therefore in close proximity to Gwendolen. She is two years older than I am, and was a pretty child who has since grown to an attractive woman.'

'A beautiful woman,' Monty corrected him.

'Yes, well . . . how it came about I cannot now remember, but at an age when she and I were neither children nor fully grown-up, I fell into the habit of feeling Gwendolen's titties, under the pretence of examining their size, as each day they grew riper. She, loving her brother, made no objection to this solicitude, and one day, whilst I was engaged in this way, unfamiliar and powerful sensations tore through my unsuspecting body. A hot stickiness made itself apparent in my underwear – what it could be, I did not know, for I was as innocent as a babe of fleshly things even then, at sixteen years of age. You will laugh at me perhaps, but I had fetched off for the first time in my life! My exclamation and shudders had captured the keen interest of my dear sister Gwendolen, who wished to be informed of what had taken place. Since I could not explain, she took it upon herself to open my trousers and investigate – and we together saw the wet evidence of my climax of sensation.'

'Without knowing what it was, even then?' asked Monty.

'Exactly so, but with all the enthusiasm of youth, my wilting shaft quickly stood again when Gwendolen fingered it to see how it worked. I asked her to show me hers, and she lay down on the sofa and lifted her skirt. I opened her drawers and saw she had no long thick part as I had – indeed, for the first time in my life I saw a girl's pussy. It seemed to me to be so delicious a thing that I could not forbear kissing it – and from that I progressed to licking the pretty toy. Soon enough,

Gwendolen cried out in surprise and joy, and shook to the spasms of her own first coming off.'

'I say!' Monty exclaimed. 'What a piece of luck for you!'

'I do not see matters in that light,' responded Selwyn, 'for the events of that day undermined my moral nature so profoundly that I have been a victim of my own sensuality from then up to this very day. When Gwendolen was tranquil again, she sat up on the sofa and I stood in front of her, guiding her hand to my shaft, which soon grew stiff again when she felt it. The devil was in me that day – I asked her to take my shaft in her mouth, and she sucked it until I fetched off again.

'You can well imagine that from that day onwards we repeated the pleasure whenever opportunity served us, sometimes bringing each other off two or three times a day, by hand and mouth, and in this wicked course we continued together for three or four weeks. But then came that fateful day when Nature prompted our ignorance to join the organs of our pleasure, Gwendolen's and mine – in short, blind and fumbling Chance taught us how the deed was done, and we committed the fearful crime of incest with each other! I thrust my shaft into Gwendolen's pussy and we came off together, my sticky fluid spurting into her belly!'

CHAPTER 4

A Two-Step with Mrs Massingham

Twice a week it was Monty's pleasant custom to pay a visit to a dear friend of his, Mrs Cecily Massingham. She was a widow of seven-and-twenty, who lived in St John's Wood in a pleasantly secluded villa. Uncharitable persons might incline towards a harsh description of Mrs Massingham's mode of living, but to do so would serve merely to illustrate their unfeeling ignorance of the facts. She was not the kept woman of a wealthy man, as were so many of the pretty ladies of St John's Wood. No, having been once married, she had vowed and declared never again in all her days to entrust her happiness and well-being to any one man, no matter how well-to-do or good natured.

The truth of it was that Mrs Massingham took up subscriptions from five or six gentlemen who were captivated by her personal charms. Each was allotted his afternoons or evenings, and this prevented the inconvenience of two gentlemen finding themselves calling on her at the same time. Each was aware that there were other admirers, but no questions were asked and no details were forthcoming. In this way, all were kept happy, and the expense to each of the admirers was moderate.

It was to Mrs Massingham's villa that Monty conducted Selwyn the day after their lunch together. Selwyn had wanted to visit Mrs Lee in Margaret Street to avail himself of the delights of Miss Emmy, but he was far too fuddled by drink when they left the restaurant, and Monty was compelled to put him in a hansom cab and take him back to their rooms, to sleep it off. With the aid of Minnie he had removed Selwyn's outer clothing and got him into bed, after which Monty went out again to pay a short visit to Mrs Massingham.

It was not his day to call, and he ran a fearful risk of interrupting some other gentleman busy about his own legitimate affairs with the lady, but it was necessary to give her certain information for the following day – information that concerned Selwyn and how he was to be dealt with.

'Bamboozle him for me, my dear Cecily,' Monty instructed her, 'he has never had but one woman in his life, and that his own sister, and may therefore be judged very nearly a virgin. It is my most urgent necessity to take this sister away from him, with your very able assistance. Nor shall you be the worse off by it, Selwyn shall be enrolled amongst the privileged few who share your affections, for he can well afford it.'

In this curious manner and for these more curious reasons, Selwyn found himself carried to St John's Wood in the afternoon of the very next day, and introduced to the charming Mrs Cecily Massingham. She was in her upstairs sitting room when the maid brought them to her, and she was dressed with exceptional and improper informality in a long silk negligee of pale pink. The pretty ribbon-bows down the front served not to keep it closed about her person, but as adornment, and from beneath its dainty hem peeped out the toes of her little slippers of finest white kid-skin.

The introductions were made, and while Selwyn shook her hand, Cecily rendered her apologies in blushing confusion for her very informal attire. She had been suffering from a cold in the head, she said untruthfully, and this had compelled her to keep her bed. She was now fully recovered, but not yet strong enough to venture out of the house, and Monty had surprised her in *déshabille* by calling unexpected.

There was a great deal more of this, all of which Selwyn took seriously and believed. The upshot of it was that he sat down by Monty on the sofa, as suggested, and joined in the small talk with no suspicion that pretty Mrs Massingham was any other than a lady of virtue and reputation, albeit one with eccentric notions of propriety of dress when receiving gentlemen callers. She had seated herself in an armchair opposite the two men, and during their conversation she unobtrusively allowed her pink wrap to fall open below the knee, while her legs surreptitiously moved a little apart, to stretch the thin silk material across her thighs.

Monty winked secretly at her in approval, and looked at her legs with pleasure. He glanced across at Selwyn, sitting beside him with his back straight and his hands clasped in his lap, to make sure that he too had a proper appreciation of what he was being given a glimpse of. Selwyn's face blushed a faint pink to be caught in the act, as he looked up and caught Monty's eye, but Monty gave him a conspiratorial grin. They both stared at Cecily's legs – she all this time pretending not to be aware of their lustful gaze.

Whilst she engaged in stylish small talk, her negligee

fell open a little further yet and the firm flesh of her rounded thighs could be seen – only for a little way, of course – a gleam of creamy flesh to about midway, let us say, to where her legs joined. Naturally, this was in itself sufficient to set male thoughts racing and speculating on the dark-haired mystery that undoubtedly lay hidden between those beautiful thighs.

'I am so glad that you came to visit me today, Monty,' said Cecily, 'for I have been very dull this past day or two with my head cold. And to invite Mr Courtney-Stoke along to meet me was a friendly thought. I am in your debt, my dear friend.'

Until then, her warm feminine secrets had been protected by the overfold of her negligee, though only just. She changed her position on her armchair slightly, as if to make herself more comfortable, and for an instant the sweet mystery was visible! The dark-curled charms between smooth thighs were shown – if only for the space of a heartbeat – to the staring eyes of her two visitors!

There was not even time to gasp in surprise before she rose from her chair and took a turn slowly about the room, her silk negligee decently in place again, concealing all, right down to her slippered feet. She pulled the thin material closely about herself, displaying her hourglass figure to good advantage – the swelling of her bosom, the smallness of her waist and the fullness of her backside. She strolled about the room as if to stretch her legs a little, and the delightful manner in which the generous cheeks of her bottom rolled under the negligee caused Monty and Selwyn to exchange a glance filled with surmise.

Cecily stood for a moment at the window, seeming to gaze out, though screened from the observation of pedestrians below by the full white lace curtains. She turned on her heel to face her visitors, and uttered a little exclamation of dismay – her left slipper had twisted from her foot! Before either of the men could fling himself gallantly on his knees at her feet, to replace it, she raised her leg crossways before her, the knee crooked, and she bent over to replace the errant slipper. In doing so, the bowed posture seemed to cause the front of her negligee to fall open under the weight of her bosom. Her pair of plump white titties rolled out into plain view, making Monty and Selwyn sigh in the same instant.

With a little cry of embarrassment, Cecily stood upright once more again and swiftly lifted her bare titties back into her evidently inadequate negligee, pulling it close to conceal her soft delights. There was the faintest flicker of a smile on her face as she stared at the two men and saw the long bulges that had appeared in their laps. She apologised most sincerely and humbly to them for the embarrassment she had caused and the offence to their sense of propriety, by allowing her person to become exposed in so very awkward and impolite a manner.

Monty grinned and said nothing, leaving it to Selwyn to give his solemn assurance that no offence had been taken – indeed, the accidental uncovering of so beautiful a lady's charms was, as every visitor to the Royal Academy of Art could explain, a source of the truest aesthetic pleasure. The sublimest of oil paintings by our greatest artists, said he, depicted the nude female form in classical poses, and were generally accepted to be inspirational in their grandeur and style.

Furthermore, Selwyn continued, if the choice were left up to him, far from feeling aggrieved in any way by a brief glimpse of Mrs Massingham's uncovered bosom, the exposing of her truly exquisite bodily form would be not be of so brief duration, but prolonged and enduring

– and far more *complete*, if he might so term it, than blind Chance had allowed!

'You are far too kind, Mr Courtney-Stoke,' Cecily murmured in a thrilling voice. 'So meagre a store of female charm as I have been endowed with by a niggardly Providence can scarcely appeal to a man of taste and distinction like yourself. Dear Monty is pleased to flatter me at times by informing me that I am not outright ugly, but I know very well that his protestations rise from friendship, not from a strict regard for the truth, though they are none the less welcome for that.'

'No, no, no,' Selwyn exclaimed, 'I must forbid you to discount your own charms in this excessively modest way! Monty speaks no more than the plain truth – you are a very fine woman, Mrs Massingham, beautiful of face and divine of form!'

Instead of returning to her armchair, Cecily joined the men on the sofa, placing herself right in the centre of it, between the two of them. They exchanged a glance of secret delight, and gazed downwards, and were rewarded by a most thrilling view of Cecily's smooth white thighs, her negligee having fallen open at her lap once more.

'Forgive what may strike you as excessive familiarity, but I am still a trifle feverish from my head cold. Do you really think me beautiful?' she said to Selwyn, her dark brown eyes gazing soulfully into his.

While the young man so addressed struggled to find words adequate to convey to her his deepest feelings, Monty took Cecily's slim hand in his own, raised it to his lips and kissed the palm.

'Cecily – you are a stunner,' he told her, admiration in his voice. 'I might even go so far as to say that you are the most deliciously provocative woman I am acquainted with.'

'Only *might* say?' she exclaimed. 'Fie, sir – what sort of a compliment to a lady is that? What do you say, Mr Courtney-Stoke – is it only *might* with you ,too?'

'Mrs Massingham – you are wholly adorable,' he babbled. 'May I hope for the inestimable privilege of calling you Cecily?'

'You may do so,' she answered softly, 'for your heartfelt and open devotion has surely earned that right. As for you, Monty, you conceal your true feelings – however unconcerned you may try to appear, the strength of your adoration for me is no less than dear Selwyn's – and the proof is prominently visible.'

With those flattering words, she reached out into both their laps and lightly tapped a long bulge with the forefinger of each hand. At the touch, both the men shivered in delight, and Monty responded by tugging open the bow of her belt and parting her thin silk negligee. His hand slid up Cecily's smooth flesh and cupped the big soft bubbie nearest to him.

There followed an astonished expostulation of *I say, really*! from Selwyn, a pause, and then Cecily took his hand and raised it to her other plump bubbie.

'Oh, Cecily,' Selwyn murmured in an expiring voice, 'this is far beyond my wildest imaginings, to experience such bliss as your tender and agreeable nature now affords me!'

'Imaginings?' she responded. 'What can you possibly mean by that, Selwyn? Am I to believe that you have forgotten yourself far enough to have the unmitigated impertinence to imagine that you might indulge in familiarities with me?'

'No!' he exclaimed in horror that he had offended her.

'Then what?' she demanded. 'I insist on being told what your words meant – explain to me at once how far these *imaginings* of yours have been encouraged to go in your overheated mind.'

While Selwyn was suffering agonies of mind, Monty sat with a grin of pure joy on his face, enjoying the opportunity to watch Cecily use her wiles on an innocent. To encourage and stimulate her efforts, he put his other hand behind her and slid his palm down the thin material that covered her smooth back, until he could feel underneath her. He pressed his fingers between the plump cheeks of her backside, until an exploring fingertip found the tight little knot that nestled between them, and he tickled it through the silk.

'Forgive me, Cecily,' Selwyn was gasping, 'forgive me, I beg you – the truth is that your beauty of face and form is so very arousing that I was unable to control my emotions when you were walking about the room – my degenerate imagination began to suggest to me the most shameful things. I confess freely that I suffer from a moral weakness that has been with me since my youth, but in spite of the reprehensible flaw in my character, I do respect you greatly, you must believe me!'

'Respect me indeed!' Cecily exclaimed in a voice trembling to the lively emotions Monty's stimulation of her rearward opening was causing. 'How can you claim to respect me when you imagined yourself performing shameful acts on my naked and defenceless body? Tell me what it was you thought of doing to me – or I shall request you to leave my home at once!'

'I am a beast – unfit for the company of delicately nurtured ladies – I fully confess it!' Selwyn moaned. 'I throw myself on your mercy and beg humbly for your forgiveness.'

'Confess fully – and I shall not be harsh with you,' Cecily replied. 'I have formed a warm regard for you,

Selwyn, I cannot deny it, but I must have your confidence – and therefore I must have a full knowledge of your moral weakness. What did you want to do to me? Tell me now or leave instantly!'

'You give me no choice,' Selwyn said in a shaking voice. 'To be cast out from your adorable presence and barred from seeing you again would be a fate far worse than death. I shall admit all, bitterly ashamed though I am.'

His agitation of mind was so extreme that he seemed to have lost sight of the fact that his cupped hand clasped Cecily's right bubbie and kneaded it, or that on his thigh lay the warm hand of the brunette beauty who tormented him by demanding to be told thoughts he would have preferred to keep to himself. Nevertheless, the mutual touching of sensitive portions of the body was having an effect upon him, turning his cheeks a bright and feverish red, and putting a quaver into his voice when he made his confession to Cecily.

'It was when you were standing by the window,' he said in a voice so subdued that Cecily leaned towards him to hear him the better. 'There was the unbelievably sublime moment when you leaned over to adjust your slipper, and your heavenly bosom was uncovered . . . I know that in politeness I ought to have averted my eyes from your private person, but I lacked the strength to do so. And while I in my uncontained rudeness gazed in rapture at your personal charms, I suddenly and unaccountably imagined – no, I cannot say it aloud!'

This was the man, Monty was thinking, who had been rogering his own sister on a regular basis. Whilst he did that twice a week without a qualm, he had become tongue-tied and bashful in the presence of Cecily – who was a paid woman. There was only one possible explanation he could think of for this reluctance – Selwyn was so taken by Cecily at first sight that he was halfway to being in love with her, a most satisfactory state of affairs for Monty.

'You must say it to me,' she urged Selwyn. 'Say it, my dear, and you will be relieved of this burden of guilt that weighs on you. Tell your friend Cecily what it was that came into your mind to do to her, when she stood at the window.'

'You give me courage,' he replied. 'I shall be in your debt forever, Cecily. You are so understanding that I shall risk my reputation with you by setting out my moral weakness in full. While you stood there at the window, adjusting your negligee to cover your bosom, I experienced a most tremendous urge to fling myself on my knees before you . . . how can I go on? But I must – to kneel at your feet and press my lips in a kiss of reverence to the wonderful treasure that I knew must repose between your divine thighs . . . can you bring yourself to pardon so gross an intrusion on your perfection – imaginary though it was?'

'I see,' said Cecily in a dreamy voice, and she quivered a little to Monty's skilful manipulation of her little knot-hole, 'you are confessing that you wanted to bare my body and lick my pussy! Is that it?'

'Your *pussy*,' said Selwyn in a whisper of hushed reverence, 'ah, my dearest Cecily – how courageous you are to speak out so frankly! Tell me that you are not angry with me!'

'I respect your frank confession,' she replied, 'and to prove to you that I am not angry with you, I shall permit you to kiss my pussy. Your imagining shall come true – I shall stand by the window, for you to kneel at my feet and kiss me.'

Selwyn was trembling so much that Monty feared he might fall off the sofa. Cecily stood up, adjusting her negligee to cover her titties and legs, and walked to the window, and turned to stand with her back to it. Selwyn's face was purple with strong passion, and he stared at her with glazed eyes, much like a rabbit mesmerised by a stoat. When she held out her arms to him in welcome, his breath rasped in his throat, and Monty had to tap him on the shoulder to attract his attention.

'Go on, old fellow,' said Monty, 'Cecily is waiting for you – lucky dog that you are!'

Like a knight of Old throwing himself on his knees in homage before his Sovereign Lady and Queen of his Heart, Selwyn flew across the intervening space and knelt at Cecily's feet, gazing up into her face in blind devotion. She touched his cheek lightly and smiled graciously down at him.

'Dear Selwyn – I truly believe that I have been smitten by a unexpected affection for you that is not far removed from love itself,' she said softly. 'There is no other way I can explain my immodest conduct towards you.'

As if to prove the truth of her words, her hips moved just a little inside her silk negligee, and it fell open just enough to give her admirer a glimpse of the dark-brown curls that grew lightly over her pussy. When she saw his ardent gaze fixed on her most intimate delight, she smiled and accused him of trifling with her affections to bring her to this condition of indecency.

'No, it is I who am infatuated by you,' he murmured.

'Ah, how cruel are the sufferings we poor women endure at the hands of heartless men,' she sighed, making not the least move to close her negligee and hide her brown-haired pussy from his burning eyes, 'if only I could trust you as I trust Monty!'

'You can!' he replied fervently. 'My heart is yours, Cecily, and from this day on, yours alone!'

As if reassured by this declaration, Cecily unfastened her fragile pink silk garment and let it fall open. Selwyn cried in joy as he saw presented to his eager eyes a delicious pair of titties, large, round, and firm, with crimson buds set on milk-white skin. In dumb delight he stared at them, and from the rapt expression of his face it could be seen that he yearned with all his heart for the privilege of kissing those peerless globes. A stern little look crept over Cecily's beautiful face as she prepared to take advantage of his enchanted condition.

'You forget yourself, sir,' she rebuked him, 'you aspire too high already. Lower your eyes at once!'

Mumbling heartfelt apologies, Selwyn dropped his gaze – and found himself looking straight at her uncovered pussy. With a long moan of bliss, he swayed forward on his knees, to press a feverish face between her thighs. Cecily parted her feet on the carpet, opening her legs to let him have a full sight of her fleshy mound and its thatch of dark-brown curls. In a moment his tongue was at the pouting lips of her pussy, seeking out in delight her hidden nub and licking at it. The stimulus had a galvanic effect on her – her body trembled all over and she sighed, *Oh, Selwyn my dear – you will make me come off if you continue! But if it will make you happy to submit me to this shameful ordeal, then I willingly give myself up to the embrace of your mouth . . .*

Through all this bamboozling, Monty sat on the sofa watching the by-play between the two, with all the interest and relish of a theatre-goer in the Drury Lane stalls. Cecily, dear clever Cecily, was smiling at him over the top of Selwyn's head, and when he gave her a wink, she put out her tongue and waggled it at him, as if to convey that she was enjoying the sensations emanating from the rapid up-and-down motion of Selwyn's tongue in her pussy. Monty suddenly felt somewhat excluded from the proceedings, and decided to amuse himself.

He unbuttoned his trousers, pulled up his shirt-front and let his stiff length jut impudently out. Over Selwyn's fair-haired head, Cecily smiled at the sight this old acquaintance of hers now brought out of concealment to be presented to her sight. Her smile grew broader yet to see Monty's clasped hand gripping One-Eyed Jack tightly and jerking him up and down. Freed from the restraint of dark trousers, that ever-eager gentleman began to jump for joy in Monty's friendly clasp and thrust his purple and swollen head boldly upwards.

Monty leaned comfortably back on the sofa, breathing lightly and quickly through his open mouth, his limbs shaking a little to the blissful tremors that rippled through him from head to toe. Cecily was regarding his lascivious actions with much interest, he noted, and a thought came into his head.

'Have I ever recited Mr Southey's verses to you, Cecily?' he asked. 'His ballad of the cruel fair one?'

'Not to my recollection,' she sighed, her eyes half-closed as Selwyn continued his caresses. 'Why do you ask now?'

'They seem appropriate to the present circumstance,' Monty replied with a grin. 'Listen, my dear:

She showed a pair of titties ivory white,
A belly white as snow, a lily hand,
Enrapt, I watched her with my secret stand,
That tented out my trousers hard and tight;
Her taper fingers in another's hair
Held close his head, while he her pussy saw
With ardent gaze for that he must adore,

The soft-lipped treasure she for him laid bare.
Methought the toy he played with was her heart
(Ah, beauteous wretch whose pussy is her pride)
But my keen shaft which steadfast still she eyed
And would not let it pierce like Cupid's dart;
Shall I not then condemn this cruel hussy,
Who lets me see another kiss her pussy?'

'Oh Heavens – I'm coming off!' Cecily gasped. She shook like a slender branch of a young tree in a gale, and kept her balance only by grasping Selwyn's shoulders to hold herself up on her feet. The enraptured expression on her lovely face advised Monty of the depth of her feelings for him, and at once his hand flew up and down One-Eyed Jack in a manner that allowed no further delay.

'Oh, Cecily!' he gasped, feeling that the dammed-up torrent of passion in his belly was about to burst through the barriers that held it back. One-Eyed Jack was straining himself upwards to an impossible size as he prepared to gush his hot flood.

'Oh, you dear lustful beast!' Cecily gasped out breathlessly as she stared transfixed at Monty's throbbing shaft. 'Who gave you permission to excite yourself? But let me see you fetch off, you beast!'

Selwyn, his tongue still busy with her pussy, took her words to apply to himself, and though his shaft was decently confined within his trousers, it was evidently in a condition of highest arousal. He groaned and shook, his shoulders heaved, his back arched – and he spent mightily inside his trousers and drenched his underclothes.

'Selwyn, how could you!' Cecily exclaimed in astonishment.

There was a greater surprise yet to come, for having attained the supreme point of ecstasy, Selwyn moaned and swayed and then fainted completely away. Under the staring eyes of Cecily and Monty, his wet and open mouth slid slowly down her bare thigh and then he fell sideways to the fine Turkey carpet, where he lay limp and still.

With a muttered oath, Monty thrust away his clamouring shaft and did up his trousers quickly, before rushing across the room to where Cecily knelt at Selwyn's side. She chafed his hands between hers and called his name anxiously, but he made no stir in response. Monty got his hands under his senseless friend's armpits, and with Cecily lifting by the ankles, between them the carried him to the sofa.

'This is perfectly absurd,' Monty complained, while Cecily loosened Selwyn's cravat, 'I have watched this fellow roger his sister twice in a row with great energy – yet now he spends at the touch of your pussy under his lips and faints dead away! What do you make of that, Cecily?'

'Why, that he has fallen deeply in love with me and that his nature is so sensitive that his first coming off with me was so profound an experience for him that his nerves proved to be incapable of sustaining the ecstasy,' she answered.

While Monty watched, she unbuttoned Selwyn's waistcoat and trousers and laid him bare, to inspect the long splashes of his creamy white essence that had spurted up a good hands-breadth above his belly button. Monty heard the tiny sigh she uttered when she caught her first sight of Selwyn's dolly-whacker, for though it had collapsed from its full length of eight inches at full stretch, it remained impressive of size.

'How very flattering he should spend so profusely when

he kissed my pussy,' Cecily murmured, her fingers straying lightly over Selwyn's shrinking shaft, as if to prolong its distension for as long as she could, 'I have the greatest affection for him already.'

'Then I shall leave him to recover in your capable hands,' said Monty with a grin. 'Treat him gently when he comes to and he will be your devoted slave for life.'

Leaving Selwyn to come out of his swoon by natural stages, he took Cecily in his arms to bestow a farewell kiss on her lips. She did not ring for her maid, not wanting the girl to see poor Selwyn lying unconscious on his back with his person completely exposed, and so she declared that she would see him downstairs and to the front door herself. But no sooner had he kissed her a second time in acknowledgement of her courtesy, than Monty's interrupted letch for her returned in full force. He quickly pulled Cecily's pink silk wrapper open to bare her body again, and handled her titties freely.

'Come into the bedroom with me, Monty,' she whispered, but he shook his head and said there was no time, for Selwyn would be awakening very soon, and Cecily must be at his side then.

'Then I shall relieve your nervous tension *so*,' she said, and as they stood close together by the sofa on which Selwyn lay in his deep swoon, she flipped open Monty's trouser buttons, and felt inside to pull out his stiffened shaft and massage it.

'No – kneel down for me, dear Cecily,' he said.

Without a moment's hesitation, she was on her knees on the carpet at his feet, her wrapper falling open to display all the treasures of her body. Monty reached down to seize her ample titties, and laid One-Eyed Jack between them.

'Is that what you're after, Monty?' she asked, with a grin, 'To roger my titties? And so you shall!'

He squeezed their fleshy abundance together round his shaft and thrust quickly inside the soft warm pouch they made. Cecily gazed up smiling at his flushed face, and pulled his trousers down his thighs so that she could put her hands under his shirt and grasp the cheeks of his backside.

'Does that feel nice?' she asked. 'Do you like my titties?'

'They're stunners!' he panted, squeezing them together hard to accommodate his long sliding thrusts.

Cecily glanced down at the shiny purple head that emerged and disappeared with regularity between the cleft of her big breasts.

'I do believe that One-Eyed Jack is at the point of having a seizure!' she said. 'How dark is his colour, and how angry his appearance!'

Monty moaned in bliss, his shaft slid hard and fast against Cecily's satin flesh, and his body shuddered to the gushing torrent that he released between her plump titties.

CHAPTER 5
Conjugal Secrets Revealed

Try as he might, Monty was quite unable to get out of his head the question that had enslaved his imagination – whether the rogering of your own sister differed in any way from rogering any other woman? If it was in some measure different, then in what lay this difference and how did it feel? It had been useless to ask Selwyn, for whilst he had experience enough of rogering his dear sister, he had none of any other woman, and therefore he could add nothing to the enquiry. After Cecily had induced him to get astride her a time or two, Selwyn would be able to form a useful opinion on the matter, but that lay in the future.

By ten o'clock that night Selwyn had still not returned from St John's Wood, and it seemed evident to Monty that Cecily was training her new admirer in the ways of love too intensively to let him leave her that night. There would then be no chance of questioning Selwyn before the next evening and this being so, Monty went to bed. He took with him the book that provided interesting insights into the education of young ladies at Lady Bumslapper's academy in Gloucestershire, but it lay unread on the eiderdown while he puzzled over the question of brothers and sisters.

Commonsense and logical deduction informed him of the truth of several pertinent facts. To take the case of a brother and sister parted since earliest childhood – say, orphans brought up separately and ignorant of each other's existence. Suppose them to meet when they are grown up, strangers wholly unaware of the close family bond between them. They are attracted, let us say, to each other, and their kisses lead on to a feel of the girl's titties, and then of her pussy. One thing leads to another, as is the way of life, and the man has her drawers off soon enough and gives her a good rogering. Brother and sister have done the deed together without knowing of their kinship, and so to neither is it in any way special or different.

Or to take another instance, Monty addressed himself in the silent debating chamber of his mind – let us suppose a family in which an unmarried sister of the head of the household lives as a permanent member, and assists her brother's wife to manage the children. On a particular night, for reasons we need not particularise, the wife is away, and in the middle of the night the sister slips into the bed of her sleeping brother. He wakes to find an enticing female hand on his stiff shaft, and forgetting in his newly awakened state that his wife is away from home, he lifts the nightgown of the woman beside him and rogers her.

When he has gone back to sleep she returns to her own bed, and in the morning he finds himself alone and recalls that his wife is elsewhere. A few moment's thought convince him that his midnight poke was only a wet dream, delightful though it was at the time. While he was at it in the dark, nothing was strange to him, for he did not know it was his sister – he was aware only of a soft bare belly under his and a wet pussy holding his dolly-whacker.

Therefore, said Monty to himself, what we may be sure of is that the difference in rogering a sister lies entirely in the mind. It is the knowledge of the close blood relationship that provokes the extra libidinous delight, or else detracts from it, whichever way it may be. This leads on to the inescapable conclusion that if I roger Gwendolen Fanshawe, my emotions can never be the same as Selwyn's, when he rogers her, for she is his sister, not mine. It is possible that I shall be fearfully disappointed when I get One-Eyed Jack into her!

To turn his thoughts away from so dismal a prospect, he took up his book and read a page or two:

'Hear me now, Belinda,' said Her Ladyship, 'you have been entrusted by your papa to my complete charge and I shall demand absolute obedience. Make up your mind to it, you are to mark me well, for I exact the most meticulous submission from the young ladies of this Academy. On your first day under my care I shall teach you this lesson in a way you will not readily forget.'

Belinda's beautiful young face turned pale at the threat and she was scarce able to speak. But propriety demanded that she make her protestations known.

'Lady Bumslapper,' said she faintly, 'I cannot accept that it is correct or decent for me to be summoned from my bed in only my nightclothes at this later hour – to find myself rebuked by you in the presence of a gentleman.'

'The gentleman in question, who is seated upon the divan, is Sir Everard Knightley,' said Her Ladyship.

Sir Everard rose to his feet, a tall thin gentleman

wearing evening clothes, and bowed mockingly to the terrified girl.

'Enough of introductions!' exclaimed Her Ladyship. 'We have a lesson to teach and learn. Bend over the divan, Belinda, and draw your nightgown up to your hips. Hurry, girl – and spread your feet apart on the floor.'

Belinda flushed crimson in shame, but did not dare to disobey the instructions she had been given. She placed herself on the edge of the divan, her face down, and stretched out her legs behind her, her bent toes on the floor. Her hand was trembling mightily as she raised her nightgown level with her thighs.

'What ridiculous modesty!' Lady Bumslapper exclaimed. 'But it will do you no good, for your person is to be fully bare!' While Belinda lay trembling in her refusal to expose herself more completely, Sir Everard laughed lewdly and reached under her nightgown. With a flick of his wrist he jerked the garment up to the small of her back, so that the entire lower portion of her tender young body lay bare.

'Damme! But there's a sight to give a man a hard,' he cried. 'The girl has devilish fine thighs, and a superlative pair of creamy white cheeks to her backside!'

'Then you shall be the first to redden them, Everard,' said Her Ladyship and, stepping up close to the shuddering girl, she put her hands on her back to hold her, and gave her lascivious companion the word to undertake the chastisement.

With a hard hand, Sir Everard smacked Belinda's bare bottom until she wailed and struggled to escape. She could accomplish nothing, for the hands on her back pressed her firmly down on the divan. Belinda kicked out backwards, hoping that her foot might strike Sir Everard on some vulnerable part of his body, but he stood to the side of her, and Lady Bumslapper stood on the other side, where she could not be reached.

The repetition of the kicking motions raised Belinda's legs high in the air and spread them apart, so that without knowing it she was presenting to Sir Everard an opportunity to gaze at her uncovered parts.

'Damnation take me!' he exclaimed gleefully, 'I vow that's the prettiest pussy I've seen for many a day!'

Belinda sobbed with shame to know that a man, Baronet though he might be, was staring into the deep cleft between her thighs where lay her most intimate secret part. She tried at once to close her legs together, to conceal her brown-haired pussy from his lustful eyes, but to her mortification she felt one of Lady Bumslapper's hands inserted between her thighs. A faint shriek of dismay escaped her when pitiless fingers pulled open the soft lips of her pussy and explored within.

'Well done!' Sir Everard cried. 'Give her a good fingering, Hortense my dear, while I tan her backside! We'll see how soon between us we fetch her off!'

Monty closed the book with a sigh of annoyance and dropped it on the night table. His interest lay elsewhere that evening and the dastardly violation of poor Belinda's chaste parts by Sir Everard failed to hold his imagination. Gwendolen Fanshawe was in his thoughts and could not be dislodged by schoolgirl tales of woe. Without closing his eyes he could picture the beautiful Gwendolen as he had observed her secretly through the hole in the ceiling – lying on her back on her brother's bed, her frock off and her chemise turned well up to display her lace-trimmed white drawers.

By this time, acting without thinking of what he was doing, Monty had pulled his nightshirt up to his chest and clasped his hot and hard shaft in his hand. His legs spread themselves wide of their own volition and he jerked One-Eyed Jack briskly up and down, sighing at the pleasurable sensations the simple action provided him. He summoned up in his heated mind the fond memory of the slit of dear Gwendolen's drawers being opened to reveal a joy of a curly haired pussy, pouting between smooth-skinned white thighs.

A strenuous feat of imagination put himself in Selwyn's place on the bed with Gwendolen, so that it was he who bent over her to press a kiss on the plump lips of her charming pussy. His were the hands, not Selwyn's, that slid up the gleaming insides of her parted thighs, right up to the delicate skin nearest her bush of dark curls.

'Gwendolen, I must have you soon!' Monty gasped. 'Unless I may get this hairy monster of mine into your pussy, I shall go mad with longing!'

His hand rubbed up and down his straining shaft, his heart beating faster and stronger as he felt the moment coming closer and closer when his passions would be relieved in hard spasms of delight. A frenzy of sensation seized him then, and his legs kicked wildly as his essence came gushing out in long jets that sprayed the bed sheet above him.

'Gwen, Gwen, my dearest!' he gasped out to each wet throb of his shaft. 'I adore you – this is how I mean to come off in you, again and again!'

For fully fifteen seconds One-Eyed Jack continued to throb and spurt until he was fully satisfied, after which Monty gave a sigh of content and fell asleep, leaving the bedside lamp still burning.

He was already awake in the morning when Minnie brought his morning tea, and One-Eyed Jack was stiff as an iron bar, having been in that condition since before Monty woke. Nevertheless, he did not request Minnie to ease his tension with her hand, as in the past, for he had made up his mind to settle the puzzle that troubled him in the only practical way – by personal trial of what emotions were raised in a man's heart when he rogered his own sister.

Monty had four sisters and three brothers, he himself being the youngest of all of them. The others were all married and had families of their own, with the exception of Gustavus, who was an officer in the Royal Navy and was hardly ever to be seen in England. The sister of whom Monty was most fond was Grace, some four years older than himself, and the wife of a solicitor who lived at Putney. It was therefore to Putney that he went by the train, to present himself in mid-morning at the large house by Putney Heath where the Austins dwelled. Grace was pleased to see her dear brother, and regaled him in the back parlour with a glass of Madeira wine and a slice of seedcake.

Mr Austin was at his business in the High Street, and Grace's small daughter was being given an airing on the Heath by the nursemaid. The housemaid was busy upstairs cleaning, so Monty had a clear run at what he proposed, devilish difficult though it seemed to him to achieve. Sisters do not commonly let their brothers roger them, whatever Minnie claimed was usual in the hovels of the East End. Indeed, Selwyn and Gwendolen were the first pair of siblings Monty had ever known or heard of who pleasured each other in this way. Without doubt, the rarity of the aberration played some large part in Monty's obsession with Gwendolen.

But how to make a start with Grace, that was the question! After a while, Monty told his sister that his head ached, which was an untruth, but it aroused her sympathies. She made him lie on the sofa at full length while she fetched a large bottle of eau de cologne and a fine white linen handkerchief, and bathed his forehead. To accomplish this act of mercy she sat sideways on the sofa by his side, bringing herself into close proximity with him. Monty gazed through half-closed eyes at Grace's bosom hovering above him as she tended his brow, and wished he could see through the grey satin of her frock and through her chemise to her titties.

'Grace, my dear,' said he, 'I have a great secret to tell you and that is why I am here this morning. I have fallen in love with someone you have not yet met – Gwendolen Fanshawe. It is in my mind to propose marriage to her.'

Grace congratulated him warmly and leaned down to kiss him, and for a moment her soft breast rested lightly on the hand he held across his chest. He almost grasped that choice bubbie, but commonsense restrained him, and she sat up again, removing the temptation. She resumed the bathing of his brow with eau de cologne, whilst asking questions about the woman who had captured his heart. Monty was careful not to let it come out that Gwendolen already had a husband, for that would have exploded his plot. After a while he informed Grace that he had a serious question to ask, and begged her not to be offended.

All their other sisters and brothers, with the exception of Gus, were well blessed with children, three, four, five, six, and even seven for Lou, the oldest. In contrast, Grace had been married to Arthur for five years now and had only one child so far. What could be the secret of this freedom from continual pregnancy, Monty asked, surely not permanent abstinence from marital pleasures? Grace blushed and was reluctant to answer him, but he was persistent and eventually came to the truth of it. She and Arthur were followers of the Oneida way of conjugal duties, which brought tranquillity and sweet release from nervous tension without the risk of child-bearing.

'Lord!' Monty exclaimed. 'Do you mean that Arthur pulls out in the nick of time and fetches off over your thighs?'

'No, no!' said Grace, her eyes downcast in modesty at the thought.

'Then what?' he asked, baffled by her disclaimer. 'Are you telling me that you and Arthur satisfy each other by hand, and never join the parts together?'

With a becoming degree of bashfulness, Grace set forth the essentials of Oneida. The husband fondled his wife until he was appropriately stiff, said she, whereupon he mounted himself on her and penetrated her in the natural manner. Then both of the partners lay perfectly still, breathing deeply but in a steady and controlled rhythm. After about an hour of this, said Grace, the nervous tension dispelled of itself, the husband's natural organ lost its stiffness and became limp, and both partners experienced a feeling of gentle content.

Monty found it very difficult indeed to believe this could be true. Never yet had he got One-Eyed Jack into a pussy without fetching off soon after. But he had taken a slight advantage of Grace's bashfulness and averted gaze to slip his hand under her skirts and let it rest lightly just above her knee, only the thin material of her drawers between his fingers and the flesh of her thigh. She seemed not to notice it there, so involved in her explanation was she.

She was willing to explain again, when he insisted that he did not truly understand what she had described, and when she at last overcame her very natural embarrassment in referring to physical matters, she spoke more frankly. Although the male and female organs were joined together, she said, it was completely different from the ordinary common tiresome form of marital intercourse, and far superior to it, for it could be repeated at will, and did not exhaust the participants.

'Then this is what I shall teach my darling Gwendolen,' said Monty, who had no such intention, 'but first you must teach me, dearest Grace, or I shall get it wrong and spoil everything by spending.'

'Teach you? But how?' asked Grace, her fine dark eyebrows rising up her forehead.

'The best method of teaching is surely a demonstration,' said Monty.

She blushed fiery red and refused to contemplate so unnatural a proposal, but Monty used his charm and considerable powers of persuasion to convince her that, in her own words, there was no comparison at all between physical intercourse and the ethereal connection of Oneida. So it came about that while he remained on his back on the sofa, Grace sat over his hips and spread her wide skirts over him, so that nothing was to be seen. Beneath their covering folds, Monty unbuttoned his trousers and let his stiff shaft stand boldly out, then felt between Grace's thighs to pull open the slit of her drawers and feel her pussy.

He saw her cheeks blush crimson at the touch, and she stared fixedly at a painting on the wall of a wicker basket of oranges and apples. In another instant he brought his shaft up to the mark and pushed inside Grace's warm pussy. He was aroused to an extraordinary degree by the feel and the thought of being up his own sister, and it was with a struggle that he controlled his voice when he spoke to her.

'What next, Grace? Enlighten me, my dear.'

'Breathe slowly and deeply,' she said, looking down

at his face at last, 'take your time from me, and remain absolutely still – do not move a muscle, not even an eyelid!'

Easier said than done! Monty suppressed a sigh of delight at the feel of the soft and velvet folds of her pussy enfolding his hot shaft.

'Arthur is no fool,' he said. 'The sensation is very fine – and this you and he enjoy together every night, you say?'

'And twice on Sunday afternoons after church,' said Grace, her eyes sparkling at the pleasant thought. 'Now, Monty dear, I have gone further than is decent between brother and sister, to make you understand how best to manage your relations with your wife after you and Gwendolen are married. You must withdraw now and give me your word you will never mention what we have done to a living soul.'

'You have my word,' said Monty at once, making not the least attempt to withdraw from the warm haven that held One-Eyed Jack so snugly,' but unless I remain where I am lodged for a while, how can I believe that the tension fades away of itself, with no bodily spasm?'

'Very well, then,' said Grace, 'but you must lie very still.'

'Not a flicker will you get out of me,' he promised.

He watched as Grace closed her eyes and seemed to pass into a blissful trance, her face tranquil. He closed his own eyes and gave himself up to the thought of rogering Gwendolen. There was no need for him to stir himself – One-Eyed Jack did all that was required, by throbbing away gently but persistently inside Grace. She evidently was accustomed to a similar throbbing by her husband's shaft in the early stages of this strange marital rite, and she explained it to Monty.

'Do you now understand what I tried to make plain to you?' she asked, her cheeks a faint and becoming pink. 'The bodily sensations increase of themselves at first, to provide a degree of pleasure to the participants, and then they subside slowly until total calm and content is achieved – to the health and wellbeing of male and female alike.'

'Yes, I understand what you mean,' sighed Monty faintly.

After ten minutes inside Grace's pussy, his sensations were not decreasing at all – the reverse was the case, in fact. His shaft grew thicker and longer, and its throbbing became ever stronger. It could not last – Grace stared down in alarm at his flushed face and heard his rapid breathing – and understood that, far from his emotions fading away as she had promised, he was at the very brink of spending! At this supreme moment she jerked herself backwards away from him, and his leaping shaft was dragged willy-nilly out of her pussy, at the very instant his torrent of desire gushed out.

At the touch of his hot elixir soaking through her drawers to wet her belly, Grace's eyes opened wide in a stare of mingled amazement and outrage – and she herself came off silently! She clenched her fists and bit her teeth together, but otherwise her body hardly moved at all, as she fought to exercise control over herself. Then she was still and sagging forward, the expression on her face indecipherable.

'Grace, Grace!' Monty moaned, his belly still shaking with the force of his fetching off. He had partly answered his own question – physical connection with a sister had proved to be powerfully exciting.

Grace was not in a equal state of blissful reminiscence. She would have jumped off Monty and run out of the room, her face hidden in her hands, to lock herself in her bedroom and abandon herself to unnecessary shame and grief, but he took her by the waist and held her tightly, to keep her astride him.

'My dear girl,' he said, truly grateful to her.

'Oh Monty, what have you done, what have you done!' cried she. 'You've committed an unnatural act with your sister and we are both defiled by it! Why did you do it? Why?'

'Hush, Gracie, hush,' he soothed her, 'nothing of significance has happened, merely a trivial accident of nature while I am as yet unaccustomed to the Oneida way. Let me wipe you dry.' He took the handkerchief with which she had bathed his brow, shook out its folds scented with eau de cologne and carried it under her covering skirts, to wipe her belly gently. When she had recovered from her shock and realised that she had not been put at risk in any serious way her tense muscles softened and she sat still while Monty played with her wet pussy under the pretence of drying it for her. Under his fingertips it had a warm and inviting feel, and he longed to look at it, but knew that a request to do so might startle Grace and undo all that he had achieved so far.

His restraint paid him good dividends. Grace smiled when he told her that her pussy was now scented with eau de cologne, and she let herself be soothed to the point at which she felt underneath her spread skirts, where nothing could be seen, to take the handkerchief herself and use it to wipe his sticky shaft. The touch of her hand on One-Eyed Jack was galvanic! From his torpid, half-soft state, he leaped into hard-standing uprightness, with such vigour that Grace gave a little laugh.

'Monty, you are impossible,' she said, 'I am not

accustomed to the male part stiffening again so shortly after coming off. Are you always like this?'

'Always,' he assured her, making Jack twitch between her long fingers, as if in agreement.

'But how then do you resolve it?' she asked, a puzzled look on her face. 'Surely no woman has the stamina required to allow you a second connection with her so soon after the first?'

'Some have, I do assure you,' he answered.

'I am not one of them,' said she. 'Arthur has never made an approach to me in less than a hour after the first, nor would I ever wish him to.'

It was in Monty's mind that his brother-in-law's rogering of Grace did not truly satisfy her, and that the Oneida business was mere foolishness. The mere touch of his own shaft shooting out its essence had been enough to bring her off, without it even being inside her pussy. She had pretended that nothing was happening to her, from modesty maybe, but Monty had seen enough women in their climactic throes to be able to recognise Grace's condition at the moment of his spending.

What was also in his mind was that she felt all the better for having come off in the proper way for once. Her eyes were sparkling and there was a healthy touch of pink in her cheeks. Her hand was gliding up and down his stiff shaft in a way that gave rise to sensations of an extremely satisfactory nature, and he took her pleasuring of him as a sign of her gratitude.

'Naughty, naughty Monty,' she said, 'to want to do it again so soon. You must make do with the handkerchief as recipient of your second fetching off.'

'Dear sister!' he sighed blissfully.

CHAPTER 6
A Lesson in Self-Control

On the next day after his introduction to Mrs Cecily Massingham Selwyn returned from his employment at the Board of Education to his digs in Seymour Place a little after his usual time. He looked pale and fatigued when Monty, who had been waiting with his door open to the stairs for the past hour, dragged him into his sitting room and sat him in the best armchair.

'My dear chap,' said Monty, with a grin, 'you look well done up – though content. Let me pour you a stiff brandy to restore you while you give me a faithful account of what passed between you and Cecily yesterday.'

'Even now I can hardly bring myself to speak of that sublime experience,' said Selwyn, his voice shaking with emotion. 'You will recall that dearest Cecily was so understanding and tender of my fearful moral weakness that she permitted me to kneel at her feet and kiss in humble reverence between her legs.'

'You are a lucky dog,' said Monty, to encourage him into more confidences. 'This I saw, and told myself that you are one man in a million, to be allowed that familiarity.'

'She spoke to me,' Selwyn said dreamily, taking a long

sip of the brandy Monty had handed him,' she uttered words I never thought to hear from a beautiful woman, words that sent thrills of delight coursing right through me – *that she submitted to this shameful act if it made me happy*! Happy! The word is too puny to describe what I felt then. My emotions became so intense that I fainted away with joy. When I came to myself again, I was lying on the sofa and you were gone.'

'I thought it best,' said Monty. 'Cecily feared you might be agitated when you came to your senses again, and the fewer you found about you, the better. I'm sure that she took good care of you.'

'Yes,' Selwyn whispered, his pretty face flushing pink, 'she was an Angel of Mercy to me, though this I did not understand at first. You see, when I returned to a proper consciousness of my surroundings, I found that my buttons had been undone and my parts and belly lay bare, and were splashed with the cream of my spending. Cecily sat beside me, chafing my hand, and when I looked up at her in some embarrassment, she chided me. She told me that she now understood the cause of my moral weakness, and that if she and I were to remain good friends, I must let her help me to overcome it.'

'How noble a woman she is!' Monty exclaimed. 'So very kind and considerate towards those who have her affection! I really must offer you my congratulations, Selwyn, on your good fortune in finding a place in her heart in so short a time!'

'I am the happiest and the luckiest of men,' Selwyn agreed. 'Cecily has pledged her unswerving support in overcoming my moral weakness, now that she knows in what it consists. This I confessed in full to her, for she had mistaken it for a more common weakness at first.'

'To have a friend like Cecily!' said Monty. 'You and

I are amongst the blessed of this world. What do you mean?'

'Since we share her affections, you and I, I am emboldened to tell you all that passed between us,' said Selwyn. 'She took in her lily-white hand my limp and sticky part and spoke frankly to me. She said she believed that to have come off so easily in my trousers, and swooning away at the sensation, must indicate that I was a slave to the habit of self-abuse. I assured her it was not so, that never in my life had I brought myself off by the use of my hand, but she did not believe me. She insisted I must be taught a lesson in self-control, and ordered me to roll over and lie face down on the sofa.'

'Self-control!' exclaimed Monty. 'What a fearful thought! I give way instantly to every sexual temptation presented to me – and thereby derive a great deal of pleasure. Take my word for it, Selwyn, a pleasure put off is a pleasure lost. Although my affection for Cecily is by no means diminished by what you have said, I trust that she will fail in this disagreeable venture to teach you self-control.'

'No, no!' said Selwyn, his face pale with dismay at Monty's words. 'Cecily is right – because of my moral weakness my life has gone askew. If she can teach me to control my passions, it will be much better, I am convinced.'

'As you wish,' said Monty. 'What took place when you were on your belly on the sofa?'

'Cecily took down my trousers,' Selwyn replied. 'She had them down round my knees, and my underthings, to lay my posterior bare. A moment later she brought her slipper down across the cheeks, and the fierce pain made my body jerk as I cried out. *Bite your lip and be silent, sir*, she said, *I mean to teach you to keep your hands away from your shaft*. She leathered me ten or twelve times, and to my utter amazement my shaft grew to a tremendous size and stiffness. It was tightly pressed between my belly and the sofa cushions, and it throbbed so hotly to the blows of Cecily's slipper that I feared I would fetch off.'

'My word!' Monty interjected. 'I've never tried whipping – is it really so arousing?'

'I found it to be astonishingly so,' said Selwyn, red-faced with emotion. 'By great good fortune I was spared the further shame of fetching off on the cushions only because Cecily tired herself in chastising me. One more stroke would have finished me, but it was not delivered – she dropped into an armchair, declaring that she had exhausted herself for my moral benefit. *You are forbidden to play with your shaft from henceforth*, she said, *no one is to handle it when it is stiff but I – mark me well, or your backside will be beaten red-raw*!

'To show my gratitude for her efforts on my behalf, I crawled across the carpet to kneel at her bare feet and kiss them in adoration. It was if I was in Heaven itself when I glanced up – Cecily's wrap had become untied while she was so vigorously chastising me and it lay open, presenting the sight of the most delicious titties ever yet seen in the world. The skin was white as milk, tipped by full scarlet berries.

'I stared at those matchless delights of hers speechless with emotion, and she saw how my heart yearned for her. A smile of pure affection crossed her beautiful face and she rubbed the sole of her bare little foot against my rampant shaft. She said it was the biggest and strongest she had ever seen, and I very nearly spent over her foot.'

His words reminded Monty of an occasion when Cecily had held his shaft between the soft soles of her feet and rubbed slowly until she brought him off and splashed herself up to her knees. This was no time to tell that to Selwyn, who seemed almost to have undergone a religious experience with Cecily.

'The moment came,' Selwyn continued, 'when my nervous system could tolerate no more! I flung myself forward between dearest Cecily's thighs, forcing them to open widely! With a shriek of surprise, she fell back in her armchair, and in an instant I thrust my tongue between the pouting lips of her pussy! The touch caused her to cry, *Oh, Selwyn, you will make me come off, my dearest one*! My tongue licked at her pleasure bud, and in another minute her feet were waving in the air as she attained the supreme point of ecstasy and fainted away, just as I had myself earlier.'

'This is bamboozlement of the highest order,' thought Monty, for never yet had he known Cecily to faint when she came off, no matter how often the pleasure was repeated on the trot. He mentally raised his hat to her, for the skill with which she had played Selwyn.

'That is astonishing!' he said. 'Let me refill your glass to help you bear up while you continue. I see that when *you* roger a woman, evidently she feels the effect of it, my dear fellow! I commend your prowess!'

'What occurred next makes me ashamed of myself,' said Selwyn mournfully. 'I am a beast, and not fit to be the friend of such a noble and good-natured lady as Cecily. I needed then all the self-control she promised to instil in me but alas, I gave way to temptation. While she lay helpless in a swoon, I lifted her legs over my shoulders and plunged my raging shaft into her. At the shock, her senses revived, and she stared at me and sighed, *No more, no more! You will kill me with coming off, Selwyn*! But I was deaf to good sense and seized her lovely titties in my hands and violated her – I thrust furiously into her pussy, whether she would or not. The warm throbbing of that adorable pussy on my swollen shaft aroused me so fiercely that I gushed a stream of hot sap into her.'

'Well done!' exclaimed Monty, unable easily to reconcile the account of Selwyn rogering Cecily in a rage of lust with his opinion of him as an ineffective weakling.

'No, it was not well done!' Selwyn contradicted him. 'It was rape, not to put too fine a point on it. I used Cecily's body for my despicable pleasure without her consent. No sooner had my tallow been spilled than I pulled out and hid my blushing face against her belly in an agony of shame.'

'Did she rebuke you for making use of her so freely?' Monty enquired in surprise.

'She asked me to explain myself, and I could do no other than tell her of my abject weakness and how I had undermined my own moral nature in my youth. As you may imagine, she was shocked to hear of my depraved habit of feeling Gwendolen's titties day after day. I hung my head in shame and told her of my advance into wickedness, and Gwendolen with me, till we regularly undid buttons and raised skirts, to bare each other's privities and feel them.'

'And more than that as I recall you told me,' said Monty. 'You soon found how to bring each other off.'

'It's true – I cannot deny it,' said Selwyn in a low voice. 'You may imagine my humiliation when I related this precocious delinquency to Cecily. When I reached the point of telling her how a day came at last when I thrust my shaft up Gwendolen's pussy and fetched off in her belly, my shame was so great that I could hardly speak.'

'You are fortunate in that Cecily is a most

understanding and good-hearted person,' said Monty, who knew full well that there was no manifestation of human desire, be it never so curious or unlawful, that would surprise or dismay Mrs Massingham.

'She is an angel!' Selwyn declared again. 'She held my head on her soft belly and stroked my hair while she calmed me. The she gave me her solemn word that she would use all her power to break me of this habit of rogering Gwendolen. I was so glad to hear her words that I pressed kisses of gratitude to her belly, and then her thighs, which had parted, and soon I found myself kissing her pussy – wet still with the essence I had spent in it when she was helpless.'

The thought of Cecily permitting herself to be at the mercy of Selwyn – or any other man – seemed laughable to Monty, whose acquaintance of the lady was extensive. Nevertheless, he kept his face straight and nodded sympathetically.

'My confounded moral weakness gripped me again,' said Selwyn in a mournful tone of voice. 'From chaste kisses on that divine pussy I had violated in beastly fashion, I soon found myself pushing my tongue between the soft lips – and I had no strength to prevent myself licking her darling little bud yet again!

'*Ah take care, Selwyn*, she cried – *you may pay your resects with your tongue, but with no other part of your person*. In my gratitude for her kindness and forbearance, I continued to pay homage to that Heavenly part of her person, until she reached the very acme of delight. Judge my condition – I was on fire to plunge my shaft into her, but she pushed me away and spoke very calmly, informing me that this was the beginning of my lessons in self-control.'

'Good Lord!' said Monty. 'I don't believe I could bear

it if I had been kneeling between Cecily's legs then – I'd have had no choice but to push One-Eyed Jack right up her and roger her to a standstill! But what of you, Selwyn – were you able to contain your emotions at so exquisite a moment?'

'I thought I would have fainted with the effort,' said he, a pallor on his cheeks that told of his ordeal. 'My bared shaft was jerking up and down, and I would have seized upon it, but Cecily ordered me to put my hands behind my back and fix my gaze between her thighs. She parted them to the limit, the lips of her darling pussy were pulled open by the position, to show the pinkness of the inside, and the wetness of her excitement! I begged her to let me look away, for this was torture of the cruellest kind, in my aroused condition. But she reproved me sternly, saying that no lesson worth while was ever yet learned without suffering.'

'Heavens above – this is agony so refined that it surpasses imagining!' said Monty. 'I'm on tenterhooks!'

'You cannot form the least idea of my torment then,' Selwyn told him. 'My shaft was standing longer and thicker than ever before, and waving up and down furiously. *Stop that at once* was Cecily's command and when I confessed that I had no power to do so, she put her dainty bare foot against it and held it still against my belly. *Control yourself, sir!* said she, *keep gazing between my thighs and learn that feelings of lust are not to be indulged in at will, only when permitted*. The touch of her foot on my shaft was sending waves of delicious sensation, rushed up my spine. I stared into her wet and open pussy, and in another moment I would have fetched off over her foot!'

'Delicious thought!' said Monty, his shaft trembling within the prison of his trousers. 'I once was permitted that honour – and I treasure the memory of seeing myself gushing between the delicate little soles of Cecily's feet!'

'She denied me that pleasure,' Selwyn confessed, red-faced and hot-eyed at the memory. 'She removed her darling foot from me, closed her legs, and instructed me to breathe deeply and slowly, until I became calmer. You cannot conceive of my mental and physical torment – every fibre of my being was yearning to come off – while Cecily held my gaze with hers and said again and again, *Control yourself, Selwyn*!'

Secretly, Monty could find no words of praise sufficient for Cecily's female skill in getting the upper hand over Selwyn. It was evidence, he thought, of her true devotion to himself, that she had performed with such diligence his request to attach Selwyn to herself. Aloud he enquired, in a manner appropriately sympathetic, what had ensued when Selwyn gained self-control.

'She caused me to lie on the sofa,' said Selwyn, 'and she sat beside me, speaking most kindly now that with her help I had at last gained a victory over my moral weakness. My trousers were still unbuttoned and open, and she held my shaft in her little hand and rolled back the skin to allow full view of the purple dome while she spoke. *Give me your solemn word*, she said, *that this monstrous proud and ill-disciplined fleshy implement of yours will never fetch off again, never, never, never, neither in my pussy, nor any other woman's pussy, nor in any woman's hand, mine or another's, nor in your own and, however fierce may be your lust, without you first seek my express permission. Swear it now!*'

'Gracious – I hope you refused!' Monty exclaimed, tongue in cheek, but Selwyn shook his head.

'How could I refuse my dearest Cecily anything?' he said, his eyes alight with the fire of devotion. 'I have no desire to roger any other woman now that I have found her – I gave her my word at once!'

'But what about Gwendolen?' asked Monty. 'When she visits you next, she will expect your loving attentions – what will you do?'

'I must disappoint her,' Selwyn told him. 'I have pledged myself. No drop of sap shall ever escape my shaft from this day forth except when I am with Cecily and have her consent to come off, either in or about her divine person!'

'A little more brandy,' said Monty, tipping the bottle, 'I am lost in admiration for your strength of purpose, and Cecily was surely touched to the heart by the warmth of your affection and allowed you a spasm or two of delight as your reward?'

'She spoke to me in the most loving manner,' Selwyn breathed, as if describing a momentous event in history, 'and while she told me how glad she was that we had become close friends in so short a time, she slowly fondled my shaft, until it stood like a flagpole. *O that is delicious, Cecily*, I cried, *but you will ruin my self-control and make me fetch off if you continue so*! She replied that I had her complete permission and rubbed at a brisker pace. My heart sang with joy to hear her words, whilst my shaft thrust and heaved in her dainty white fingers. A mere heartbeat before I came off mightily in her hand, she ceased her massage, and applied the most forcible pressure at the base of my shaft – and stopped me dead in my tracks!'

'By Jove!' Monty exclaimed. 'Had it been me to whom she did that, I fear I would have undergone a seizure on the spot! Did she then resume her stimulation?'

'When she saw by the shocked expression on my face that I was in no danger of fetching off, she recommenced her titillation – first a soft fondling, then a firm rubbing, until she again had me trembling on the brink of ecstasy. And again she balked me of the crisis at the last moment!'

'But the Spanish Inquisition could have inflicted no worse torture on a helpless victim!' said Monty. 'This is an aspect of Cecily's character of which I have been hitherto ignorant.'

'It was delicious, what she did to me,' murmured Selwyn, his face bright and his eyes aglow, 'ten times she used her hand on my quivering shaft to lead me up to within a breath of felicity – and each time she dashed my hope with a calculated pressure! I truly thought her purpose was to precipitate a heart attack and so put an end to me – and I was happy to die with my shaft in her hand. Then the eleventh time, when she had weakened me almost to swooning with her forcible lessons in self-control, she smiled sweetly on me as her fingers glided up and down my shaft, and said, *You may come off now, Selwyn*. At once my emission burst forth in hot gushes, wetting her hand, and soaking my shirt as high as my chest!'

'Capital!' said Monty, his mind elsewhere, as he carried out a feat of calculation. 'But to reckon from when I left you, and allowing your swoon to endure for somewhat longer than is usual, and your sweet torment at Cecily's hand to have lasted a half-hour, it would by then be five o'clock in the afternoon. But you had not returned here by the time I retired to bed. How were the several intervening hours passed, Selwyn?'

'Cecily had her maid bring up food and drink to refresh me – her kindness knows no limits! I, in the meantime, had adjusted my clothing to be decent again, and we sat together, Cecily and I, and ate and drank and talked merrily. After that pleasure, I was granted the greatest privilege of my life.'

'Namely?' Monty enquired, pouring more brandy.

'Darling Cecily invited me into her bedroom! O the joy of that shared moment! I thought I would die of purest bliss when she threw off her wrap and permitted me to see her in her naked beauty! Then she assisted me to remove my clothes, down to my shirt, and she asked me to lie on her bed! *Now, Selwyn*, said she, *you had me when I was helpless and at your mercy – I mean now to have you – what have you to say to that, sir?*

'Only that I adore you as no woman was ever adored before, I replied. *I mean to ride a St George on you*, she said, *but you are not to come off until I give you permission – otherwise I shall be angry with you – do you understand me?* I had scarce time to assure her I would obey her, before she was astride me. She squeezed my shaft in her hand and brought its head up to the mark, uttered a tuneful little laugh, and with a sharp jerk of her loins, thrust me deep into her warm pussy.

'I nearly came off at once, to feel soft flesh throbbing and gripping my enslaved shaft, but I compelled myself to remain still, and as calm as was possible. Cecily rode me slowly, and paused every few minutes, to draw out her own pleasure and to imprint on my whole being another lesson in self-control. Half an hour at least passed with my beloved in the saddle, before her sensations caused her to sigh and to shudder, and then she gasped in delight *O Selwyn – I cannot prevent myself coming off any longer! I must have you now, my dear!* So saying, she plunged very fast up and down my shaft, moaning as she fetched off and I moaned in joy beyond compare to feel the gushes of my essence pouring into her.'

'By Heaven – my shaft is as stiff as a broom handle!' said Monty. 'I must find an accommodating woman at once, or I shall expire of thwarted lust! It's me for Mrs Lee's house!'

'No need for that,' Selwyn assured him, 'Cecily expects both of us to call on her at nine this evening.'

Monty was surprised to be invited to St John's Wood at short notice, but Selwyn reported that Cecily's only appointment that evening was a stock-broking gentleman who dropped in for an hour on his way home from his place of business. By seven she would be at liberty, and by nine rested and refreshed. That being so, Monty took Selwyn to a chophouse in Welbeck Street, and they ate well, to build up their strength. At nine o'clock sharp, a hansom cab deposited the two of them outside Cecily's villa.

The maid took their hats, coats and sticks and said they were expected. She added that Mrs Massingham had been taken by a fit of the vapours earlier in the evening, and had retired to her bed to rest. If the gentlemen did not object to being received informally, they were to go up. Needless to say, neither Monty nor Selwyn had the least objection to being received in their dear Cecily's bedchamber, and the maid led them upstairs and announced them.

Cecily was propped up in bed against large soft pillows, her hair unpinned and loose about her white neck. She wore a little bed jacket of quilted pink satin, edged with white fur. Monty and Selwyn advanced to the bed, and took a seat on either side of it, each taking one of the hands Cecily held out to them. As they chatted, commiserating with her on her indisposition, she gently allowed her bed jacket to fall open, revealing that her breasts were only half-contained in her flimsy silk nightgown.

Monty took full advantage of her almost naked condition right away, by slipping a hand into the lace-trimmed front of her garment for a good feel of her titties. From there, he slid his hand down under the bedclothes, gliding down Cecily's warm and smooth belly, with only thin silk between his fingers and her flesh. The nightgown was drawn up about her thighs, he found, not stretched down to her ankles. He fumbled under it until he had a hand between her legs, and happily felt her hairy pussy.

His long middle finger slipped without fuss between the warm and moist lips and he tickled her button with delicate little movements that brought a charming flush to her cheeks and sent tremors of sensation through her belly. She parted her thighs a little wider in the bed, to afford his skilful finger an easier access to her person.

Monty saw that with her right hand she had undone the buttons of Selwyn's trousers and she was rubbing his shaft. In the same way, her other hand had found its way into his own trousers and was performing the same agreeable office for him. When both had reached a degree of stiffness that pleased her, she pulled them out of their gaping trousers, and Monty was slightly abashed. From his secret observation through the ceiling, he knew that Selwyn at full stretch had the advantage of him, being blessed with a good eight inches, but Cecily had the courtesy to make no comparisons, saying only that to bring her out of her vapours, she needed a sound rogering.

'By all means,' said Monty with a laugh of delight. 'Which of us will you have first, my dear?'

'You and Selwyn are both so hard-on that there is nothing to choose between you,' was her tactful reply.

'I shall have both shafts up me together – the two of you shall roger me at the same time.'

She threw aside the bedclothes to show her bare legs and her dark-curled pussy, Monty having pulled her nightgown up round her waist while he was fingering her. She parted her legs wide and stroked herself between them with both hands, smiling the while at the two men. Selwyn was at a loss – the thought that two friends might share a woman together had never entered his head. He glanced from Cecily's pussy up to Monty for guidance on what should be done next, and Monty laughed and dipped into his fob pocket for a golden sovereign.

'Call,' he said, flicking the coin high into the air with a jerk of his wrist.

'Heads,' said Selwyn, waiting until the last moment.

Monty caught the spinning coin on the back of his left hand and clapped his right over it.

'Heads, you say?' he cried. 'We shall see who has the first choice!'

He exposed the sovereign, to show the tails side uppermost, before slipping it back into his pocket safe out of sight. It was not a genuine sovereign at all, if the truth were told, but a trick double-sided coin he had purchased years ago. He had found it useful on many an occasion, for the majority of those asked to call would choose heads without thinking.

While Selwyn was recovering from the disappointment of losing the call, Monty had his clothes off and lay down on the bed on his back. Cecily sat up and slipped off her bed jacket and silk nightgown, and then, naked as Venus, she sat herself astride Monty's legs. He sighed to feel her take hold of his straining shaft and direct it into her slippery pussy. Her delicious wet warmth engulfed his stiff flesh, and she forced it up into her.

As soon as he was well accommodated, Cecily glanced over her bare white shoulder where Selwyn still held his place on the bed in open-mouthed contemplation of the coupling below him. To enlighten him as to what was required, she reached behind her and spread open the soft white cheeks of her backside with her slender hands.

'Selwyn!' she said. 'Why do you delay? I want to feel you up me too – come here and put it in!'

He obeyed her at once, removing his clothes quickly, before kneeling on the bed behind her. Although unfamiliar with this mode of congress, his sensual nature taught him by instinct how to go about it. He put his hands on the cheeks of Cecily's bottom and pulled them wide, pressed her little knot open with his thumbs and brought the tip of his stiff shaft up to it. A hard push, a cry from Cecily, and he had penetrated right into the tight passage!

'Deeper!' she moaned. 'Push deeper, Selwyn!'

On this occasion she did not ride a St George. She held still and let the men do the work – Monty underneath her was poking strongly upwards, and Selwyn behind her was matching Monty's rhythmic strokes with his own – and she throbbed in ecstatic sensation between them.

'Oh my Lord!' she gurgled, her tender body shaken violently by the double thrust of their desire. 'Do me hard! O my God, I can't stand it! I've come off twice already!'

Monty felt the floodgates burst open in his belly and he gave a throaty gasp as he flooded Cecily's clinging pussy. She too cried out in a soprano wail, instructing Selwyn to come off at once! Her hot and naked body convulsed in another climactic release, this time brought on by Monty's furious discharge into her. The squirming of her body undid Selwyn – he brought his hands up from her hips to clasp her bare titties, and he gave voice to a long-drawn moan as, in half a dozen quick spasms, he emptied his passion into her rearward opening.

'Oh Cecily, Cecily my dearest, I love you,' he gasped.

Monty grinned in satisfaction that his scheme was working out so well. In future Cecily would keep Selwyn too busy for him to have time to roger his sister. Monty had plans of his own for darling Gwendolen.

CHAPTER 7
Monty Reaches an Understanding with a Lady

Monty's plans for beautiful dark-haired Gwendolen were put into operation on the occasion of her next visit to London. By then he had talked very seriously to Selwyn, reminding him of his sworn oath to Cecily never to allow himself to fetch off with another woman but her, and offering to relieve him of the heavy burden of Gwendolen's carnal passions. At first, Selwyn could scarcely believe the offer was genuine, but when he was at last convinced that it was, he expressed his gratitude to Monty with words of everlasting respect and friendship.

For beautiful and desirable though Gwendolen was, Selwyn told Monty that he regarded himself as her hapless victim, shackled unwillingly to her by his own moral weakness – a destruction of character he had unwittingly brought about himself when he had first been tempted to feel her young titties. He had hoped, he said, that he would be free of her desires when she married Mr Elliot Fanshawe of Reading, a well-to-do gentleman of a kindly disposition.

Alas, this was not to be. A month after the wedding,

hardly a week after she had returned from honeymoon in the Highlands of Scotland, Gwendolen commenced her twice-weekly expeditions to London to visit the shops, she told her husband, but in actuality to engage in rogering her brother Selwyn. Worse yet was to follow, for after only a week or two she declared herself to be fatigued by the travelling and asked Selwyn to give up his digs and move to Reading to live with her and Mr Fanshawe. This he had steadfastly refused to do, being afraid that if he lived in the same house, Gwendolen would soon become careless and her husband would find out the truth.

Over a bottle of Madeira an arrangement was reached between Monty and Selwyn to the satisfaction of them both. Selwyn was to become a subscriber to Mrs Cecily Massingham's services and call upon her regularly to be taught how to overcome his moral weakness and learn self-control. Gwendolen's affections were to be transferred, without her prior knowledge, to Monty.

So it came about that when Gwendolen arrived for tea with her brother in his digs in Seymour Place, she discovered Monty with him, partaking of tea and cake and conversing as a friend. She several times glared at Selwyn behind Monty's back, willing him to get rid of this inconvenient visitor, so that nothing would impede their removal to the bedroom and a fine rogering on the bed before she left to catch her train. Selwyn pretended not to see, or to understand, her signals, and Monty continued to make cheerful conversation. Finally, at a wink from Monty, Selwyn stood up, consulted his pocket watch and announced that he had an urgent appointment.

He was well gone before Gwendolen had time to recover from her open-mouthed astonishment. Monty smiled at her in his most encouraging manner and told her that her brother had confessed, in agony of mind, his moral weakness, and that he, Monty, had agreed to help him overcome it. While Gwendolen was digesting that unwelcome news, Monty said that it was obvious to him that she had a deeply passionate nature that craved to be loved – he understood this very well, for he had a like nature himself.

Gwendolen stared at him icily, as if he had taken leave of his senses. Undaunted, he continued by telling her that he was here to offer himself humbly, an admirer only from a distance hitherto, who would deem it a proud honour if the beautiful Mrs Fanshawe could find it in her heart to look to him to assuage her needs.

'How dare you speak to me in this way!' she cried. 'I shall report this to my husband, who will thrash you in the street like a dog!'

With that, she leaped to her feet, clutching her gloves and reticule, to hasten away from an interview that was highly distressing to her refined nature. As she turned towards the sitting-room door, Monty threw himself violently to his knees on the carpet, and reached out to seize her. Gwendolen gasped aloud in horror to feel his hands on her hips, preventing her escape from his presence. She gasped even louder when he seized the hem of her skirt and raised it high behind, to uncover her legs in white stockings, and her lovely rounded thighs in white percale drawers with blue ribbons below the knees.

'Unhand me at once!' she cried, her face flushed scarlet as she glared back over her shoulder and down at him.

Monty was quite impervious to the demands of either reason or decency at that moment. His mouth hung open in panting delight whilst he observed how the fine material of her drawers clung into the deep and luscious crease between the cheeks of her backside. His shaft bounded rock-hard inside his trousers, and without hesitation, he parted the rearward slit of Gwendolen's pretty drawers and pressed his lips in an ardent kiss to the bare flesh of her right cheek. It was with keen gratification that he heard her long indrawn gasp of disbelief.

'Stop this unspeakable indecency!' she exclaimed hotly, and grasped at his hair to drag his mouth away from her exposed person. By then Monty had his head up under her skirts and both arms around her, and was stroking her soft belly. She struggled in his grasp to put an end to the vile and audacious advantage he was taking of her, but in the grip of his passion he had the strength of ten men. Gwendolen writhed and exclaimed to no real purpose, but he had her drawers wide open behind and was running his wet tongue up and down the cleft between the soft rounded cheeks he had so brutally uncovered.

'I shall scream and alert the neighbourhood to your infamy!' Gwendolen threatened.

It was too late for such warnings. Monty's stiff shaft leaped so wildly in his trousers that he ripped open his buttons and let it stick out nakedly. His clasping hand held it tightly, as he tried to still its uncontrolled jerking, but matters had already gone too far to draw back. He pulled Gwendolen to her knees on the carpet before him and, panting with lewd desire, thrust One-Eyed Jack bare-headed into the rearward slit of Gwendolen's drawers. She shrieked at the touch against her bare bottom and with five passes of his hand Monty came off and sent a raging flood up the crease between the fleshy cheeks of her rump.

At the sudden warm and wet emission, she uttered a long cry of dismay and fell forward, half-fainting in her ordeal, to lie with her upper body on the seat of an armchair. Her sadly abused body was twitching in spasms of horror, whilst Monty's manly elixir foamed against her soft flesh.

'You have defiled me, you cur!' she moaned, as Monty's last squirt pulsed up between her cheeks. 'My clothing is soaked all through and my person has been molested!'

'I adore you beyond reason,' Monty sighed in his delight. 'My dearest Gwendolen, you have no idea of how often I have woken up in the night to find myself ensnared in sweet dreams of you, and my nightshirt wet and sticky against my belly! I simply must have you, my dear, or it will be the end of me!'

She was most conveniently placed where she had fallen in her swoon, her bosom supported by the chair seat and her bottom toward Monty. Without waiting for a reply to his declaration of love, for such it was, he raised her skirts and petticoats over her rear and with a trembling hand pulled open her drawers to view the cheeks of her bottom, firm-fleshed and round. He stared in loving wonder at her hairy pussy, and was completely unable to resist the urge to finger it.

The warm essence he had spilled was trickling down from her bottom – he dabbled his fingertips in it and wet the lips of her pussy, before burrowing a couple of fingers inside it to stroke her nub gently. So intense was his desire for Gwendolen that his shaft remained long and hard, displaying not the least abatement from its full size, despite its having fetched off in her drawers.

'Forgive me, my dearest girl,' Monty sighed, his fingers well into her pussy, 'but the temptations of your naked person lies far beyond my enervated power of resistance, even if I wished to resist. Accept your Fate – I am going to roger you!'

'You are a cad, to treat a defenceless woman so!' she

cried. 'If you must, then be quick, the sooner to release me from this hideous ordeal!'

Monty brought his throbbing shaft up to her pussy and pushed, and sank in deep. The backs of her thighs pressed against his belly and he rogered away with a firm yet unhurried stroke, not wishing to dissipate the unforgettable pleasure of this moment too hastily. Gwendolen groaned, to feel her beautiful body used against her will for a man's delight.

'This is indecent beyond words,' she moaned. 'To be violated on hands and knees – like a female dog in the street! O, you shall pay for this, Monty Standish! My brother will horsewhip you on the steps of your Club – if there is any organisation so indiscriminating to accept you for a member! And my husband will have you thrown into prison and serving hard labour for the term of your natural life!'

'What nonsense,' Monty sighed, his engorged shaft gliding in and out of her wet pussy to his extraordinary delight. 'Selwyn knew when he left us alone together that it was my intention to poke you – he condones it completely, it being his opinion that you have forced him to roger you too often against his better judgment. Nor will you dare to say anything to Mr Fanshawe, for fear I shall inform him that you have been letting your brother roger you for years!'

'All is known! I am lost!' shrieked Gwendolen.

'Not at all,' Monty murmured, 'for I declare I adore you to distraction, dearest Gwendolen – my heart was given to you the first moment I laid eyes on you. I shall love you and cherish you and roger you forever! You may forget about Selwyn and the husband you deceive – here am I, your new lover!'

'No, never!' she cried.

'As to your other question,' Monty breathed, sensations of purest pleasure volleying through him to the slide of his shaft in her, 'why from behind? To roger a beautiful woman from in front and kiss her soft mouth and feel her heaving breasts all the while, is surely amongst the sweetest delights to which the human race may aspire. But by enjoying her from the rear, he brings her breasts and belly within reach of his roving hands – and the additional gratification of feeling her plump, warm bottom against his belly . . .'

He would have said more of the delights of rearward coition, but the spasms of joy coursing through his body grew too strong to permit further coherent speech, and he fell to sighing and panting as he thrust into her. Nor was Gwendolen unmoved by his words – she was a woman of strong sensual appetites and it was not long before her feelings overcame her outrage.

'Monty, you wicked, wicked man!' she cried. 'You are imposing your lustful will upon me – on a helpless female whose brother has taken advantage of her without respite, almost since childhood, and now the wife of an uncaring man who demeans her daily with his unwelcome lusts! Ah me, am I never to escape the vicious and cruel desires of men!'

During the whole of her mournful complaint, she was jibbing her bottom at Monty, to meet his strokes.

'Ah me . . .' he sighed in echo of her words, 'I love you . . .'

'Finish it, I beg you!' Gwendolen cried.

Monty was so fully possessed by his frantic desire to have her that he hardly knew what he was about. His steady thrusts became rapid jabs, then became a strong pounding against her, and finally a furious ramming into her. Ultimately, with a cry of triumph he reached the pinnacle of sensation and shot his hot sap into her pussy. She groaned and sobbed and shook under his weight, and whether with dismay or delight, he could not certainly tell, but the wet grasp of her pussy gave him reason to hope that she, too, had come off.

When their breathing had returned to its normal pace, he set her on the sofa and himself close to her, his softened shaft out of sight in his trousers. He held both her hands in his own while he spoke to her of his fond admiration for her, and his hopes that she would accept him as her dearest friend. She was at first most unwilling to speak of what had transpired, or to take heed of his expressions of deep affection. She no longer threatened him with reprisals for the violation of her person, and soon he came to understand why, when she asked him outright what Selwyn had told him of their frolicking together. For all her bluster when he had assaulted her person, she knew her Fate to lie in his hands, and wished to acquire his friendship.

'Selwyn had told me everything,' Monty replied, 'from when a keen interest in your titties led him to feel them, to when he first got his shaft into your belly. Though of that he was sparing in the details.'

'Then to show you that I trust you to keep my shameful secret I shall relate how that came about,' said Gwendolen, her face a pretty shade of pale pink.

'You may trust me with your life, as I trust you with mine,' Monty assured her, kissing her hands as he spoke.

'It happened like this,' said Gwendolen, giving him a forlorn smile, 'my brother Selwyn was confined to bed for a day or two with a sprained ankle from a fall, and I went to his room to keep him company for an hour one afternoon. I sat on the bed next to him and we exchanged words, but about what I have now no recollection, for my emotions became so stirred that nothing else made a lasting impression.

'While we were talking, I saw that his nightshirt was pulled up round his chest and I jumped to the conclusion that he had been seeking to pass the time by playing with himself. To find out whether or not he had fetched off, I slid my hand under the sheet and stroked his bare thigh. You must remember that by this stage in our familiarity we had been bringing each other off by hand for a month or more, several times a day, and I was thoroughly acquainted with the capabilities of his body.

'At my touch, Selwyn smiled at me and put his hands under his head on the pillow, and I put my finger to my lips to warn him to be quiet, for the servants were below. I tiptoed to the door and locked it, and went back to the bed, where I stood with my frock lifted and my drawers open at the front, to show Selwyn my pussy. The hair was growing well on it – thick and dark and shiny, and I was proud of it.

'Selwyn put his hand there and started to feel me, as he had many a time before, and I became aroused, I thought he would bring me off with his fingers, and I pulled back the sheets to see his shaft. He was naked below the chest, and his long shaft stood up hard – whereupon a new thought came into my head! He had a shaft between his legs and I had a opening between mine – what if the one were put into the other?'

'No sooner said than done! I held my skirts well up and sat astride him. Greatly daring, I sank down upon him, to push his shaft into me – with scarcely any discomfort at all when he burst into my maiden pussy! O Monty, I cannot describe to you the sensation of it as I started to roger him . . . I knew it was wrong to do this with a brother, and that made it all the more exciting.

'I began to have fantasies of what was going to happen when my brother fetched off inside me! My own dear brother Selwyn – fetching off in my pussy! The thought of it sent me wild with sensation and I came off myself – and two seconds later I felt the squirt of his hot sap. That was the first unlawful love we shared, he and I, but we have never ceased doing it to each other since that day – nor ever wanted to relinquish the sweet shame. There, I have told you everything now, Monty, all my darkest secrets. I am in your hands.'

'Yes,' Monty agreed simply.

He unbuttoned her long lilac jacket from throat to waist and ran his hand over her bosom through her blouse. In another moment he had the bow at her throat untied and the blouse open on her white chemise. He thrust his hands down the top of it to feel her bare titties.

'Consider this, Gwendolen my darling,' said he, 'there are no better hands for you to fall into. I shall love you and protect you and cosset you as no other man ever has, or ever will. You are mine, my dearest!'

'Oh Monty, can I truly believe your words?' she asked, her eyes misty with unshed tears of emotion.

She let her head fall against the high sofa-back, her lovely eyes half-closed. Monty knelt in silent homage at her feet and lifted her breasts right out of her chemise, baring those big white-skinned titties for his hands and lips to ravish. As his mouth flew from soft globe to globe, he sighed in bliss, whilst his tongue licked each in turn to the tip, where his lips took possession of each little rosebud and sucked at it.

Meanwhile, his hand was between Gwendolen's soft thighs, to force them apart and roam boldly over the smooth flesh till his fingers touched her silky haired pussy. He raised his head to kiss her mouth, whilst his fingers invaded her warm slit – and the feeling was evidently so delicious to her that she opened her thighs wider. He knew that he must have her again, for One-eyed Jack was more than half-hard, and twitching in fast little spasms at the sweet taste of Gwendolen's titties.

Indeed, so hard did One-Eyed Jack bound that he gained his liberty from the unbuttoned front of Monty's trousers and was sticking lewdly out towards dearest Gwendolen! This fierceness had been brought on by Monty's sudden memory that, not fifteen minutes ago, he had fetched off in Gwendolen's drawers, soaking them through, when she was on hands and knees on the carpet, and his shaft had rubbed bare-headed on the smooth skin of her bottom, until he had drenched it with his foaming flood.

With a shaking hand, Monty raised Gwendolen's skirt in front until he had a full view of her legs, encased in white silk stockings, and her rounded thighs in her white drawers. Through the forward slit he touched her handsome dark bush, then took her by the ankles to draw her feet wide apart. In mounting desire, he untied the string of her drawers and laid bare her curved belly and its delicious button. He pressed his mouth to it in hot and passionate kisses, then licked slowly down from her belly button to her dark curls.

He gazed in fascination at her uncovered pussy, fingering the soft fleshy lips, and hugged himself in secret congratulation at the recollection that he had already once plunged his shaft into this treasure and gushed his sap. An ecstatic proceeding he proposed to repeat in a very short time! He introduced two joined fingers gently into the delicious slit before him, found Gwendolen's sensual little button and tickled it. At once she sighed luxuriously, and the tempo of her breathing quickened.

Monty continued to play with her and soon her belly began to rise and fall, while her uncovered titties heaved and rolled in the agitation of her breathing. Her pussy had become very wet, and as the climax of sensation came ever nearer, she opened her beautiful dark eyes to look at Monty in loving affection, while her bottom slid forward along the sofa cushions, to bring her pussy closer to him.

Seeing his hard-on shaft jutting from his trousers, Gwendolen took a firm hold of it and brought it to the moist lips of her slit. In one more second she had the shiny unhooded head inside her and with a determined thrust, Monty slid into her right up to his hairy pompoms. He seized Gwendolen's bare breasts where they hung out from her chemise and rogered her furiously. She returned push for push, urging him on at his pleasant task.

'Dear Monty – what bliss!' she sighed. 'Push in deeper yet, I beg you! Push all of it inside me!'

'Oh Gwendolen!' he gasped. 'We are one – accept the tribute of my love, my dearest – I'm fetching off in your pussy!'

Gwendolen's round bottom heaved and squirmed on the sofa and she uttered exclamations of delight whilst she received the hot gush of his admiration, and she came off delicately and lay in Monty's arms, trembling and spent.

When they had recovered their tranquillity, Monty led her by her hand into Selwyn's bedroom, where she had been rogered more than once. In a daze of pleasurable emotion, he helped her out of her clothes, until she lay on the bed in only her chemise. He threw off all his own garments and lay stark naked beside her, kissing and feeling her. The chemise scarcely impeded him at all –

he reached under it to give his darling girl's bottom a thorough feel, then her belly and breasts, until he had made their buds firm and prominent again.

He rolled her on her side and slipped behind her, to lay his hard-on shaft in the cleft between her soft cheeks and slide it against the delicate skin there, while his restless hands were playing feverishly over her titties.

'Oh, my dear one, if only I had the words to tell you how much I love you!' he exclaimed, but Gwendolen's response was not what he expected – she jerked her body away from him!

'You are not to do that!' she exclaimed nervously. 'Be so kind as to keep your manly shaft away from my bottom. You may do anything else to me – even use my mouth – but I will not let you poke my bottom!'

'Heavens!' said Monty, startled by her vehemence. 'What can you be thinking of, my angel? I had no such thought in mind!'

In truth he had rogered Cecily Massingham's bottom enough times to be aware of what it was like, and Cecily seemed to find enjoyment in the proceeding.

'I am pleased to hear it,' said Gwendolen, calmer now for his assurance. 'The shameful truth is that my husband is addicted to that practice – three times a week he asks me to lift up my nightgown at the back and lie face down, while he makes use of my rearward entry. I find it aggravating that he ignores my womanly pussy and spends his strength elsewhere! It holds no pleasure for me, I give you my word, and I resent his lack of interest in satisfying me properly.'

Monty turned her round in his arms and kissed her face and felt her pussy until she was tranquil again.

'Mr Fanshawe is an inconsiderate husband,' he declared, 'but do not tremble, my dearest girl, my adoration will compensate for all the unsatisfactory state of his conjugal attentions.'

'Dear Monty – I believe you!' she replied tenderly.

'When were you first made aware of this tendency in your husband's nature?' he enquired, his hand between her legs to soothe her fears.

'On my honeymoon, before we had been man and wife for three days,' she said. 'The first night we were in Glen Pitlochry he displayed a man's normal desires – in short, he had me on my back with my nightgown round my waist and rogered me. I was no virgin, as you know, having surrendered my maidenhead to dear Selwyn years before but Elliot was not to know that. I made myself appear bashful and inexperienced, and he believed that his was the first male part to enter me.'

'He thinks so still?' Monty asked.

'He has never suspected otherwise. Nevertheless, on the next night he unmasked his true interest. Whilst I lay on my back in bed and awaited his entry into my pussy, he laughed and rolled me over face down and spread himself on my back. You can well imagine that I had no idea at all of what he intended to do to me. But I was not left in ignorance for long – I felt his hard shaft at my rear entrance and before I had time to complain of this unnatural conduct he pushed it right up me! He took his pleasure, kissed me goodnight, and went to sleep!'

'Lord!' Monty exclaimed. 'What a brute to treat a young girl like that! If that is his pleasure, he ought to have taken care to bring you to it by slow steps, and put himself out to ensure that you too were gratified to the point of coming off.'

'He cares nothing for me,' said Gwendolen, her musical voice trembling. 'My husband cares only for his own selfish pleasure. I have never asked why he prefers to use me in this unseemly way, and as a dutiful wife I submit to his desires, unnatural and unsatisfactory though they are!'

'My dearest Gwendolen, let me wipe away from your memory all such thoughts and fill your heart with happiness,' Monty said, his fingers wet with the moisture of her desire.

Without another word she spread her legs wide on the bed, and he sat up to lean over her and gaze in admiration at her pussy while he played with it. The curls that adorned the plump mound between her legs were wet, as were the lips. Monty's heart beat fiercely in his breast at the thought that he would in another instant be lodged inside his beloved.

He raised her chemise to her throat, baring her white belly and titties, and placed his belly on hers. With a hand between his legs he brought One-Eyed Jack up to the mark and pushed in, feeling Gwendolen tremble with passion as she accepted the full length and thickness. She threw her arms about him to hold him close to her bosom, kissed him hotly and squirmed underneath him to make him start poking her.

'Such heavenly bliss!' she cried in her joy, her belly all the time pushing upwards to meet his thrusts. 'Twice a week will never satisfy me, Monty – you must roger me more often, my dearest boy! Tell me that you are virile enough to sustain my desire! If only you could have me every day!'

Monty's fast-beating heart soared with love and desire when he heard these words from Gwendolen's sweet lips. But before he could give her the assurance she wanted, One-Eyed Jack bounded inside her wet pussy and spouted jets of thick essence, shaking Monty with rapture. He grasped her soft titties fiercely and held her tight while he spent inside her, and she moaned and dissolved into ecstasy.

It was only after his last drop had been delivered into her warm belly that he remembered the peephole in the ceiling! He wondered if Minnie was lying on the floor above with a hand up her clothes to finger herself while she spied on him rogering Selwyn's sister. The thought amused him, and also excited him, for One-Eyed Jack was still long and stiff. He decided to give Minnie a run for her money if she was watching, and rolled over on his back to let his wet shaft stand upright.

'You see for yourself that I am able to satisfy your desires, dearest Gwendolen,' he said, his fingers busy between her legs. 'I am eager to have you again now – if you are ready for me.'

'Then have me! Or shall you rest while I do you?'

He nodded, pleased that she had thought of what he was about to suggest himself. Gwendolen stripped off her chemise and sat naked astride his belly, her white titties dangling above him. He put up his hands to feel them and whilst he rolled them in his palms, Gwendolen reached between her thighs to hold his shaft upright and push it up inside her.

'How shall we arrange it so that we may enjoy each other day after day?' he murmured. 'If I take the train to Reading twice a week, is there somewhere we may meet in private?'

'I shall find somewhere,' she said softly, 'somewhere secret where you can roger me as often as you wish.'

She rose and fell on him, the silken folds of her pussy round his shaft sliding delightfully. He would very soon have fetched off, and she with him, but for her artful precautions in rogering him languorously and pausing every few minutes, to prevent too impatient a response by his pulsating shaft.

After ten or fifteen minutes of this rapture, Gwendolen was unable to tolerate any more sensation and was compelled to seek a climactic finish to the delight. Almost swooning, she jolted up and down on him so fast that his emission gushed up into her and she sobbed for joy to feel it. Monty's wide-staring eyes were fixed on the ceiling, where he knew the peephole to be, close to the gaslight fixture. He hoped that Minnie was there, bringing herself off with her hand while she gazed down at his fine manly body and hard-on shaft, and spent on her fingers when she saw him fetch off in beautiful Gwendolen's belly.

CHAPTER 8
New and Interesting Discoveries at Putney

Now he knew what it was like to have Gwendolen, Monty was more than ever interested to learn how that superb experience could be compared with having his own sister, so that he would be in the same position of vantage as Selwyn. Sad to recall, although Grace had shown herself to be not without all sympathy for his incestuous advances, he had not really rogered her when he went to call at her house in Putney He had almost succeeded – his shaft had been deep in her pussy, but she had pulled away when she guessed he was about to fetch off, and he had splashed his hot sap over her drawers.

Afterwards, when he had at last calmed her anxiety and fear, she had allowed herself to be persuaded to hold his new-risen shaft in her hand and play with it. It seemed that her interest in the fleshy advantage he had to offer had been heightened by the so-called accident of his emission in her drawers, for she had willingly manipulated it until she caused him to come off again, into the scented folds of a handkerchief. For Monty the enjoyment had been keen – so much so that he veritably believed that to roger a sister must be a greater pleasure than a poke with another woman.

It might almost therefore be said that Monty set off by train for Putney in a spirit of scientific enquiry to try his luck once more with Grace. The short journey passed most pleasantly in reminiscences of rogering Gwendolen and feeling Grace – and his disappointment was great, as may well be imagined, when the housemaid who opened the door to him informed him that Mrs Austin was not at home. His further enquiry elicited the useful information that she was walking the baby on Putney Heath, the day being so warm and sunny, and he set off in pursuit.

Ten minutes stroll on the Heath were sufficient to find Grace pushing the high-wheeled perambulator. She was pleased to see her brother, and they strolled on together until they came to a convenient wooden bench set in an obscure corner under a tree. There they sat down to talk, and Monty made quite certain that the perambulator with its happily gurgling little passenger was placed as a screen in front of them.

The idea had become firmly fixed in Monty's mind that the way in which his brother-in-law rogered Grace without coming off or letting her do so, did not truly satisfy her, and that the so-called Oneida method was mere foolishness. By her account it took an hour of lying still under her husband with his shaft in her before her desire faded – probably from sheer boredom, in Monty's opinion. In contrast, it had taken no more than a touch or two of his own shaft to bring Grace off.

At the supreme moment, she had clenched her muscles tightly and pretended that nothing was happening to her – it seemed her modesty required her to deny that her brother had brought her off! But Monty had seen enough women in their climactic throes not to be deceived by Grace's display of stoicism, He had felt the wetness of her pussy and felt her tremors against him – and easily recognised her lapse into ecstasy.

Grace was in an excellent humour this fine morning. Her eyes were sparkling and there was a healthy touch of colour in her cheeks. Observing this, Monty put an arm round her waist kissed her until she was breathless, and enquired the reason for her satisfaction. She blushed slightly and then confessed that she had persuaded her husband to roger her hard and fast the night before – not just lie passively on her belly.

They had together both come off most satisfactorily – or a least Grace had found it so. Whether her husband was equally pleased, she did not ask, but it seemed logical to suppose that coming off was enjoyable for him. She would have liked a second bout before they slept but Arthur declined, insisting that to do it twice would be to surrender their worthier and higher instincts to animal sensuality. Nevertheless, it was obvious to Monty that his sister felt all the better for being rogered in the proper way for once, and he said so.

'It is a great source of satisfaction to me to hear that your dear Arthur has been persuaded to do his duty by you and give you that divine pleasure which is the right of every wife,' he said. 'Now, to show that we're the best of friends again, dear sister, and that there remain no uncharitable feelings between us for whatever trivial accident may have occurred when I saw you last time – I mean during our discussion of the method of marital relations you and Arthur employed until you were able to convince him that the old ways are still the best and most worth pursuing with enthusiasm – allow me to give your satisfied pussy a brotherly and affectionate squeeze . . .'

Without waiting for her answer, he bent down to slip his hand under her skirts and up between her legs, high above her knees, and between her thighs – and so at last into her thin drawers. She sat quietly while he stroked her and he, too preserved a joyful silence in his voluptuous amusement, fingering the warm and hairy lips between her legs.

'O Monty,' said she at last, 'it is wrong of me to allow you to do what you are doing, I know that all too well. Modesty and chastity – and duty – insist that my person is the property of my husband, and he alone. Yet I ask myself where lies the harm in so pleasant a caress from the hand of a cherished brother?'

'Not the slightest harm, dear Grace,' said he, 'which I shall prove by letting you fondle my shaft, if you wish to do so.'

'No, no – that would be going too far!' she breathed in her modesty, seemingly forgetting that she had brought him off when last he was in Putney. 'There is only one male part I may lawfully hold in my hand, as you well know – my husband's.'

'That selfsame shaft of his which last night was plunged into your pussy and poked you to ecstasy,' said Monty, fingering her delicately beneath her clothes. 'How sad that you were only once raised up to the summit of bliss!'

'If I'd had my way, it would have been half a dozen times at least,' said Grace, 'but Arthur restricted it to once, assuring me that any excess of sensual gratification was known to be injurious to the physical organism, not to mention the risk of enslaving the mind and soul to the habit, which he informed me would be pernicious. So once it was, and once only.'

'Dear me!' Monty said mildly. 'Were you able to sleep,

dear Grace, when your body still cried out for satisfaction?'

'Not for a long time,' she confessed. 'Arthur lay fast asleep beside me, but I was restless and unable to settle.'

'This insomnia brought on by undischarged desire is a fearful threat to the health,' Monty explained judiciously. 'Sensible people relieve themselves of it in a very simple way.'

'Surely you are not suggesting that I would ever satisfy my urges by hand!' Grace exclaimed in apparent indignation. 'That would be a most unladylike thing to do!'

'Of course you do,' said he, 'everybody does. The question is not *whether* you fingered yourself off last night when Arthur left you high and dry, but *how many times* you did it before you sank into a satisfied and refreshing sleep?'

Grace blushed scarlet and refused to answer his impertinent question. Nor did she avail herself of his kind offer to feel his shaft which was, it is needless to remark, in a condition of quivering stiffness. Nevertheless, his words affected her, and she sighed open-mouthed, and rested her bonneted head on his shoulder. She justified this to him – and to herself – by saying that she was somewhat fatigued from what Arthur had done to her the previous night. In this loving posture on the wooden bench, she was admirably well positioned for what Monty was doing to her under her full skirts.

'Rest, dear Grace,' he said softly, 'close your eyes and sink into a light slumber – I will watch over you.'

A glance about him revealed that there was no one in sight on the Heath and emboldened him to continue. No sooner were dear Grace's eyes shut than he raised her skirts up to the level of her waist, revealing white drawers with pale blue ribbons. He opened them and bared her pussy. This was his first glimpse of her female treasure – on his previous visit all had been covered by her voluminous skirts, so that even when he attained to the intimacy of being inside her, he was afforded no sight of her person, not even when he came off on her belly.

He feasted his eyes on Grace's pussy greedily – light brown curls grew not too thickly over her pale mound and the pink soft lips of her pussy. He parted the short curls and fingered Grace's warm lips in glee, till they opened as if by themselves and let his middle finger enter. He heard her sigh when he touched her tiny slippery button and rubbed it gently. Grace kept her eyes tight closed, though she was trembling all over before long.

'You must stop this now, Monty,' she murmured, 'or you will make me come off.'

'Dear Grace – how hot a nature must be yours if you fear to come off so quickly! I have scarcely touched you, and already your pussy is slippery wet and throbbing! I do not wonder that you are unsatisfied when Arthur abandons you after only once rogering you to a crisis of delight!'

He was not speaking the truth, for his hand had been up her clothes and his fingers stimulating her for five minutes.

'It is true,' Grace confessed, 'I am excessively hot-blooded and never content. On the first night of our honeymoon Arthur did me three times, and not even that was enough for me – I would have had him do me again, if his strength had not been exhausted. He has never risen to those heights since, alas.'

'You are and I are two of a kind,' said Monty, soothing her with his fingers on her secret nub. 'We need to come off again and again before we can rest easily. I have rogered a female friend of mine six times in an evening before my shaft would lie down and stay soft.'

'Six times!' Grace cried. 'How wonderful be to be poked six times! Monty – I do believe I'm coming off!' and she rubbed her wet pussy hard against his fingers.

'That's very nice, Grace,' he said, while she shuddered and moaned, 'your belly's quaking like jelly on a plate.'

When she'd finished and calmed down again, she was pleased to unbutton Monty's trousers and slip her ungloved little hand inside, under his shirt.

'Turn and turn about,' said she, giving him a shy smile. 'Who is the female friend you did six times, Monty – surely not the young lady you hope to marry?'

'Darling Gwendolen? No, I have not had the enjoyment of her beautiful body yet,' he lied. 'I was speaking of a young widow with whom I am acquainted in North London.'

During the conversation, Grace's hand was playing along the swollen length of Monty's shaft, exciting it to grow longer and harder still. Monty sighed in delight, telling himself that few more interesting ways of passing a Thursday morning had been devised than for a man to sit in the sunshine on Putney Heath while a pretty woman felt his shaft – and when the woman was no other than his own sister, then the experience was lascivious to the point of incredibility.

'You have a long and thick shaft,' Grace commented, her hand occupied out of sight in his trousers. 'Do you believe it has grown so because of the excessive use to which you put it? A man's muscles grow stronger and bigger with regular exercise – is this also true of his sexual organ?'

'I have always believed so,' Monty sighed, breathing faster and more irregularly as his passions were raised towards their zenith. He felt that at any moment now he was going to fetch off in an explosive manner.

'Monty, my dear – you are jerking so wildly!' said Grace, the swift movement of her fingers sending passionate thrills through him, 'are you about to come off?'

Monty cried out in a delirium of sensation, too far gone to give an answer to her question. His legs kicked spasmodically, his loins jerked, and the thick essence of virile love gushed in long jets up his belly inside his shirt. Grace uttered a gasp to feel the warm wetness flood over her fingers, and kept up the speed of her strokes until the emission was completed.

When Monty had recovered from his climax of delight and Grace had fastened his trouser buttons over his wet shirt and belly, she replaced her glove, got up from the bench and insisted that they return to her home, lest they be discovered by some casual passer-by. Reluctantly he agreed, and strolled beside her while she pushed the perambulator. Five minutes brought them to her home, where the baby was handed over to the nursemaid, tea was ordered from the housemaid, and Grace went upstairs. She said it was to take off her hat, but Monty was certain her purpose was to wash her hands and her person – for he guessed her to be nervous of having his sap on her skin.

After ten minutes absence she came to the parlour, where she found the tea had been served. Monty was drinking a cup of best Darjeeling, stretched out on the sofa, his trousers undone and gaping wide to let his stiff shaft stick out.

'This won't do, Monty,' said Grace with a slight frown, 'you must put it away, my dear, and let us have no more impropriety. I cannot think what came over me on the

Heath to permit you the familiarities not even my husband may claim in a public place.'

'But in all honesty, you cannot deny that you very thoroughly enjoyed it, Grace my dear,' said he.

'Then I am ashamed of myself,' she said, 'put it away, I beg you, or I shall feel compelled to leave the room.'

At that Monty tucked his rampant shaft under his sticky shirt and did up his buttons. Thus appeased, Grace sat beside him on the sofa and poured a cup of tea for herself.

'Your remark about a husband's claim on your person is true,' said Monty. 'The rights of a husband consist in raising up your nightgown in bed at night and having you on your back. This he may do every night if he wishes, and several times a night if his strength runs to it. Moreover, he has the right to take you upstairs on Sunday afternoons for an hour's lie-down, when only the outer garments are removed and the pair of you rest on top of the bedclothes, whereupon he gives you a good feel through the slit of your drawers and pulls up his shirt to lie on your belly and give you a good poking.'

'And what then?' Grace asked. 'What point is it you make?'

'Why, this point,' cried Monty, 'the rights of a woman's dear and loving brother are in all respects different from those of her husband. For him there is no marital bed to share with his sister, but in compensation for that, his is the right to take every opportunity that serves, indoors and outdoors, to stroke her titties and feel her pussy, as a sign and a token of his fraternal love for her.'

'What a fib!' Grace exclaimed, seeing where his words were leading. 'You shall not touch me again!'

'It is your duty to yourself and your nature – the hot

nature you share with me – to let yourself be satisfied as often as I am able to oblige you. How your eyes lit up when I mentioned I had rogered a female friend six times in an evening! Your own words lay bare your heart – you wished that you could be poked six times – deny it if you dare!'

'It's true,' she whispered, her eyes downcast and her cheeks a pretty pink in her confusion. 'I cannot deny it, Monty.'

'Then let me feel you again,' he said, taking her hand.

'But are you sure that a brother has this right?' she asked, 'and why, if I may be allowed to ask, why is your interest so strong in me, Monty, when you have female friends in London to accommodate your lustful desires?'

'Why you, my dearest girl? I hardly know that myself,' he admitted, 'but I have found it wisest all my life to listen to the urges of my nature and obey them. That way lies happiness, in my experience. Feel here, and you will know how strongly my nature impels me towards you.'

So saying, he thrust her hand down the top of his trousers, until she touched his virile shaft, stiff as a broom handle. At the touch of it, Grace laughed and said he was talking nonsense – but in spite of this objection, she seemed to be interested in One-Eyed Jack. She undid Monty's buttons with her free hand so that she could raise his sticky shirt-front and pull out his shaft. She held it between thumb and finger and stared at it.

'I fear you are a sensualist, Monty my dear,' said she. 'You allow yourself to be in this reprehensible condition all too often. Arthur has made it plain to me many a time that the proper state for the male organ is a modest slackness and smallness, not this feverish and demanding engorgement.'

'Not if a fellow is in bed with a pretty girl,' said Monty.

'Only husbands and wives have a right to be in bed together,' she reprimanded him.

'Very well then, if your wish is to be so loyal a helpmate to Arthur. But as you have confessed to me – when you and he lie in bed together, his shaft rarely stands up hard. Mine, as you have reason to know, is like a ramrod for the best part of the day and much of the night.'

'Arthur's way is to lie close to me, belly to belly, with our nightclothes raised and his organ clasped between my thighs,' said Grace. 'Together we experience a divine harmony many hold to be superior to the coarse act of coition.'

This seemed to Monty to be rather less than she had formerly told him took place between her and her husband.

'Whoever believes that anything is superior to poking is an idiot,' said Monty. 'Shafts were made to fit into pussies, and pussies were made to take shafts – the whole scheme of creation testifies to that.'

'The animal creation,' Grace agreed, 'but we are humans and not to be likened to beasts, nor follow their ways.'

'I've never heard that argued before,' said Monty, changing tack to come at the harbour another way, 'lie here by me while you explain it in more detail.'

He changed position to lie along the sofa, and pulled Grace to lie facing him. While she held forth on the moral nature of Mankind, he pulled up her skirts between them, to uncover her drawers to her waist, so that her pussy was close to his shaft in her hand. He felt between her legs for her hairy pussy, and soon had his fingers in her to titillate her slippery nub.

'In the Oneida method, which Arthur has studied,' said

Grace, her voice a trifle shaky, 'it is forbidden to approach with a hand the spouse's private parts.'

'Really?' Monty said. 'Why is that? How else are the parts to be joined together easily but with the guidance of hands?'

'The handling of the parts is conducive to lust,' said she, 'and it is for that reason that boys and girls are forbidden to touch their own private parts, as you very well know.'

'I seem to recall you admitted to me on the Heath that only last night after Arthur had fallen asleep you played with your own pussy until you came off a time or two,' Monty accused her.

'No . . . no . . . I said no such thing . . .' she breathed faintly.

Her distress of mind did not cause her to cease stroking his shaft, or require her to ask him to take his hand from between her thighs, and so they lay lewdly handling each other. As he expected, Grace's body was responding strongly to his handling, and a sensual experience longer and more intense in enjoyment, was well under way.

He made it last a good twenty minutes, for there was no need to hurry – his ambition was to subjugate her entirely to his will. She lay with her thighs wide apart, the slow teasing of his fingers in her pussy causing her to savour to the full the somnolent voluptuousness she had never known before. His shaft stood full size in her hand, jerking to its own rhythm of lust, while Grace held it fast and stroked it in a slow rhythm.

'You are to come off now, Grace,' Monty said at last, when he judged her ready for it. 'Squeeze your pussy on my fingers and let it happen.'

'Not yet,' she sighed, 'don't end this ecstasy yet!'

'Very well,' he murmured, 'a sister has rights over her

dear brother too – including the right to be raised up to heavenly sensation whenever she wishes it.'

He continued his slow manipulation, feeling her shaking and sighing against him, Eventually there came a time when her body could tolerate no more of the intense sensations he was giving her. She exclaimed, *Monty*! sharply, and thrust her belly hard against him. Her back arched and her nervous system collapsed in frantic delight – while One-Eyed Jack jumped furiously and spat hot essence into her clasping hand.

When they had recovered themselves a little, Monty gave her his handkerchief to dry her hands, and tucked away his dwindled shaft. Since both found it most comfortable to lie on the sofa instead of sitting up in a decent and respectable manner, they remained lying while they continued their discourse about human sensuality, and whether it should be sternly repressed, as her husband claimed, or continuously indulged, as Monty professed.

Needless to relate, no conclusion was reached between them, nor was any intended, and when at last Monty became bored with the conversation, he ended it by telling his sister that she was an extremely pretty woman. That was most gratifying to her natural female vanity, and she made not the least objection when his hands found their way up inside her clothes to feel her bare titties. Indeed, she responded to praise of her person by unbuttoning his trousers again and taking hold of his shaft – which lengthened fast the longer he played with her loose and soft titties. Their hands titillated each other, whilst they lay silent with voluptuous thoughts and sensations.

'Let me bring you off again,' said Monty.

'I can't, so soon!' she said, but he shifted his position on the sofa to bring his face over her thighs and bent to kiss her through the slit of her drawers, and bury his nose in the curls of her pussy.

'Oh Monty!' she exclaimed. 'I've never been kissed there!'

'Then you have no possible thought of what you have missed.'

He was certain now that he had found the key to his sister's lubricity. He licked with the tip of his tongue along her wet slit and her thighs opened wide, even though she at first cried out that he must stop doing that to her. Then she submitted and he put the end of his tongue on the wet little button that stood exposed in her open pussy and licked gently. This soon aroused a tremulous motion of her belly and thighs, which grew stronger and stronger still.

She sighed and moaned and cried out, she rubbed furiously at his shaft, strained her thighs wider apart yet and cried out to be brought off! Now she was Monty's to take! He had her on her back in a trice and his belly flat on hers – and with a shaft as stiff as a rod of iron, he pushed in between the loose wet lips of her pussy, until he was right up her.

Grace was almost delirious with pleasure, and the inside of her pussy was slippery, smooth, clinging and very warm. Monty rogered her slowly and delicately, intent on savouring the strange emotions that arose within his breast from this act of forbidden intercourse. He wished to know once and for all if to have his sister was at all different from having another woman, such as his dearest Gwendolen.

He was constrained to admit to himself that he was enjoying the experience very greatly, but he could not determine whether this was because he was wild with desire for Grace herself, or whether it was because the pleasurable act he was performing was prohibited on pain of penalty by Church and State. Hoping to clear up this question, he took care to control himself, and make the poke a long and delicious one.

Only by slow and measured stages did he let his sensations rise towards the peak, all the while taking every advantage he could of Grace's body – feeling her titties under her chemise and rubbing his belly on her warm belly. He felt her wet pussy grip him tightly and she moaned, 'You shouldn't be rogering me, Monty . . . you know you mustn't . . . stop it, you beast . . . make me come off, please!'

He paid little attention to her gasping words, but continued his rhythmic poking until he felt an exquisite convulsion inside his belly and knew the crucial moment had come at last.

'Oh Grace, my dearest girl,' he murmured as his desire raced up his shaft, 'I'm fetching off in you!

He shot his sticky essence up her in hard spurts, and she at once cried out and writhed under him, until her spasms of bliss had exhausted her and she lay quaking and twitching. When he was able to arrange his thoughts, he concluded that the sensations of rogering a sister were heavenly in the extreme – even more delicious than doing it to Gwendolen – or any other woman he had poked.

This seemed to him strange, for though he had all his life been fond of Grace, in beauty of face and figure she could not be compared with lovely Gwendolen, moreover, for ingenuity and sheer delicious lustfulness, neither woman could be compared to Cecily Massingham. And even Cecily could not quite touch the depths of lewdness with which Minnie the skivvy could make his shaft stand hard in an instant. It was all most confusing, this question of how much of ecstasy was in the shaft and how much in the mind.

To the Devil with that, said Monty to himself, what need here is there of elaborate reasoning and speculation? The plain fact of the matter is that to roger dear Grace delights me far beyond mere words. She, too, feels something of the same, for she almost swooned in pleasure when she came off now. Therefore the sensible thing to do is to roger her again as soon as she comes to herself. And then again. After all, she has never been done six times in a row before, and I did promise her!

CHAPTER 9
The Diversions of a Rainy Evening

On the day after his visit to Putney to settle the question of how pleasurable it is to roger a sister, Monty found himself in the unusual plight of being on his own and at home all evening. Selwyn, now a regular subscriber to Mrs Massingham's intimate circle of friends, had gone to St John's Wood to receive at her hands another lesson in overcoming his moral weakness. Monty's next time to call upon her was not until Sunday afternoon, and he gave consideration to strolling round to Mrs Lee's to see if lovely seventeen-year old Emmy was available for an hour or so – assuming that no noble Lord had got there first!

Against that must be laid the objection that the end of the quarter was close and Monty's purse would remain thin until the next regular payment came to him from his banker. This made him reluctant to lay out a couple of gold sovereigns for the use of the girl's commodity, no matter how pretty it was. Furthermore, it had come on to rain, which always put hansom cabs in great demand, and he had no intention of walking through the rain to Margaret Street and back afterwards.

He decided to pass a quiet evening at home, and read

another chapter of the book on educational methods for young ladies he had bought in Soho. He donned his crimson smoking-jacket with the frogged front, and made himself comfortable in his armchair with a cheroot clenched between his teeth. The account of Lady Bumslapper's Academy soon gripped his attention, and he read on for an hour before he felt the need for refreshment. He rang to have hot water brought up, to make a glass or two of toddy with a bottle of old Jamaica he had in the sideboard.

Minnie brought him a jug of hot water from the kitchen and stood grinning at him.

'Well, minx?' said he. 'What has amused you?'

'Something I saw not ten minutes ago,' she said.

'And what, pray, was that?'

'I was going down the stairs from my room and I heard a sort of gasping noise,' she said.'

'What sort of gasping do you mean?'

'Well,' said Minnie, grinning again, 'I was outside your door when I heard it. It was quite loud – it made me wonder if you were all right. I nearly knocked on your door to ask, but then I thought to myself – what if he's got a young lady in there and is poking her on the sofa? He won't thank me to interrupt him if that's what he's at. So to be safe, I had a quick look through the keyhole, just to make sure you were all right.'

'Well, well,' Monty said, grinning back at her from where he sat in the armchair. 'I begin to catch your drift, Minnie. Tell me what you saw – I won't mind.'

'I saw you sitting in your armchair, like you are now,' she told him, 'only you were in a great state of agitation. You had a book in your hand, and your trousers were unbuttoned all the way down. Your dolly-whacker was sticking out, hard and stiff as a broom handle, and you were rubbing it for dear life. Your face was flushed red, and your eyes were starting from your head, the way you stared at the page of your book. I could see your lips were moving, as if you were reading in a whisper to yourself.'

'You saw all this in one quick look?' asked Monty in a tone of sarcasm that was lost on the girl.

'That's right,' she agreed, 'I only looked for a second, not wanting to disturb you.'

'Then you saw no more?'

'Oh yes,' she said, 'I saw your hand increasing the speed of its rubbing, and a creamy white spend spurted out of your shaft with such force that it landed on the carpet a yard or more in front of your feet. You lay back in you chair listless, with your eyes closed, and the book fell from your hand. So I knew you were all right and went away.'

'You're a wicked girl to watch a gentleman amusing himself in the privacy of his own rooms,' said Monty with a grin. 'Suppose I were to report you to Mrs Gifford for eavesdropping?'

'And let her know what you get up to on your own?' Minnie retorted, 'apart from poking me, that is.'

'Naturally, I deny it,' said he, grinning wider still, 'it is a figment of your salacious imagination, Minnie.'

'But you leave traces,' she replied, returning his grin, and she pointed down at the carpet. Monty glanced in the direction of her finger and saw the dark stain where he had spattered it.

'I was reading some very provocative scenes of disciplining a young lady in a boarding school,' he said, 'and I allowed the feverish excitement it aroused to carry me away, to the result that you observed.'

'What a lecherous gentleman you are, Mr Standish,' Minnie said, taking two steps nearer to him. 'Your backside ought to be properly tanned for reading books like that!'

'I might enjoy that, to judge by what I read,' he retorted. 'Listen to this, Minnie.'

She stood with folded arms while he read aloud to her the passage that had affected him so strongly:

. . . trembling with terror, Cynthia tapped at the door, and when she heard Lady Bumslapper's voice, she went into the room where Her Ladyship awaited her. Her face was so stern, and her cold blue eyes shone with such severity, that Cynthia threw herself to her knees and, with sobs and cries, entreated her to spare her youth and inexperience.

'Enough of your complaining,' said Her Ladyship briskly, 'you understand perfectly well that your misconduct has been so very abominable that Miss Harriet felt unable to deal adequately with it, and has sent you to me for chastisement. This happens too often, my girl – I have been too lenient and forbearing.'

'But I have been punished already,' Cynthia sighed miserably, 'Miss Harriet has beaten me so hard that I cannot sit down.'

'Former smackings have achieved nothing in improving your behaviour,' Her Ladyship replied. 'I know full well you've had your skirts up round your waist to have your backside beaten to a blazing red often enough – this time you are to be taught how I deal with young ladies who offend against the school rules.'

So saying, she seized the girl's wrists and tied them with a long sash to a ring fitted to the wall. Then with another sash she blindfolded her hapless victim, whose flowing tears soaked quickly through the soft muslin over her eyes. Poor Cynthia was helpless, her back pressed to the wall and her arms lifted high above her head.

'I never gag the mouths of the young ladies sent to me to be chastised,' Her Ladyship explained, 'I prefer to hear all their shrieks of mortification.'

With remorseless hands she removed the veils of modesty that protected Cynthia's young body. She opened the girl's blouse, and pulled down her chemise to bare her tender titties – and, as if inspired by the sight, she pulled up her skirts and pinned them about her slender waist. Not satisfied by even that act of indecency, she proceeded to untie the tape of poor Cynthia's drawers, and let them fall down her legs to her feet.

The outraged girl emitted a forlorn shriek, to feel the other woman's lustful hands roaming freely over her bare titties – and then the suck of a hot mouth at their youthful tips of pale pink! Nor was this to be the full extent of the molestation – for with flushed face and panting breath, Her Ladyship sank to her knees and pressed hot kisses to Cynthia's quaking belly . . .

'Lord! Is that what goes on in posh schools?' exclaimed the skivvy, her plain face a bright pink.

'So this book assures us,' he answered, and put his free hand under the hem of Minnie's frock and up between her legs, until his fingers were in her drawers and on her warm pussy.

'What do you think of a young lady's titties being handled by another woman?' he enquired.

'I doubt if there's that much difference to the girl, whether it's a man or another woman who feels her,' was Minnie's reply – to Monty's great surprise, 'that's enough of your hanky-panky, Mr Standish – I've got my work to do and no time for this.'

'Ah, but there's always time for a nice feel,' said he in a most winning way. 'Think of this, dear Minnie – in fifteen or twenty years no one will want to feel you, or me. So take all that life offers while you may and never turn away a friend's helping hand.'

'The things you say!' she exclaimed. 'It's no secret what you'd be doing to yourself if I weren't here – your trousers would be gaping open again, I'll be bound, and you'd be playing with your dolly-whacker.'

Monty's breathing grew shorter and with a trembling hand, he opened his smoking-jacket and unbuttoned his trousers. Minnie moved to stand between his parted knees and leaned forward to pull up his shirt-front until she had bared his belly. The attitude of her body brought her titties close to his face, and only a layer or two of thin clothing shielded those soft young danglers from his eager mouth. In her hand his uncovered shaft gave a vigorous bound.

'Lord, how it jumps!' she exclaimed. 'You've gone and put yourself in a worse state than before when I saw you through the keyhole. It'll cost you two shillings for a helping hand!'

At his nod she massaged One-Eyed Jack with cunning, unaware that Monty's ambitions were ranging further than her offer. He raised her clothes in front and tucked them up round her waist, held in her apron strings. Through the slit of her drawers his fingers sought her pussy and teased shrewdly at her wet button, stirring her emotions to outpace his own. She began to gasp and sigh and press her cheek close to his, the passes of her hand on him quickening in proportion as her sensations grew – but she was no match for Monty in this game.

'I'm coming off!' she cried. 'I can't help myself!'

As her spasms began and her parted legs shook under her, Monty seized her with his free hand, and pulled her down to sit bow-legged across his thighs. His hand was down between their bodies, to take One-Eyed Jack from her hot grasp and guide him in through her drawers and into her pussy, for he was not very far from fetching off himself.

As events proved, Minnie had provoked his emotions much too strongly for his stratagem to be successful – at the moment he insinuated his throbbing shaft into her drawers, the familiar sensations started in his belly. The time to go further was not at his disposal – he gave a long sigh and his hand raced along his shaft as he came off on the girl's thin belly in a raging flood, his hot essence spurting over her pussy, not into it. She wriggled and heaved and kicked, but he held her firmly down across his lap until he had finished completely.

'You beast!' she cried when he released her and she at last rose to her feet. 'You've wet my drawers! Look at that!'

'Then you shall have two shillings and sixpence,' said Monty, pleased that he could have much the same entertainment in his digs as at Mrs Lee's, and at a fraction of the cost.

'That's all right, then,' said Minnie, smiling again, 'you're a gentleman, Mr Standish.'

'And you're a lickerish little minx,' he answered, determined to get his money's worth. 'I'll swear to it that you play with your pussy every night before you go to sleep – am I right?'

'What I do at night in my bed is no concern at all of yours, if you're not there,' she retorted.

'Then I may make it my concern,' he said, 'I shall creep up the attic stairs when the house is dark and everyone asleep, to get into your bed and roger you through the night. What do you say to that, miss?'

'I'm only a poor servant-girl and I can't be giving anything away for nothing to randy gentlemen,' said she. 'And besides, there are creaky boards in the attic stairs – Mr Courtney-Stoke would be sure to hear you and make a report to the landlady. I'd lose my position if she knew what I let you do to me.'

'I don't expect to have the use of your pussy for nothing,' said Monty. 'Haven't I always paid fair and square?'

'That you have,' she acknowledged.

'And as for Mr Courtney-Stoke, you need have no anxiety on that score, Minnie. He and I have become friends and he would never say a word to Mrs Gifford if he heard me on the stairs.'

'I saw you poking his sister,' Minnie said slyly. 'First you had her on her back and then she had you on your back. Where was Mr Courtney-Stoke while that was going on?'

'He'd gone out to keep an appointment, but he gave me the use of his bedroom,' said Monty.

'And the use of his sister,' Minnie added with a grin. 'Is he still doing her himself? Are you both having her now?'

'Mrs Fanshawe is mine now,' Monty explained. 'Her brother has made a new female acquaintance in North London.'

During this conversational exchange, Minnie had kept her seat across Monty's thighs, her clothes hitched up to show her white drawers and stockings. His trousers still gaped wide and his limp shaft lay in full view. He parted the slit of her drawers again to look at her brown-haired pussy and run his fingertips along the lips.

'Look at this plaything,' he said with a broad grin. 'You've the lewdest-looking pussy I've ever seen, Minnie – have I told you that before?'

'It's the same as every other,' she replied, not following his meaning at all. 'I know a rhyme about it – do you want me to say it?'

'Yes, do!' he cried, slipping two fingers into her wet slit.

Minnie paused to collect her thoughts and then recited:

'Pussy's a greedy unsatisfied glutton,
Girls are all ready to offer their mutton,
Finger them, roger them, do as you please,
Make them come off till you put them at ease;
Lick her and suck her and poke her galore,
A pussy's so greedy she'll soon pout for more.'

Monty laughed aloud while he fingered Minnie's most intimate portion and explained what he meant.

'Yours is by no means the same as every other,' he told her, 'nor are any two ever alike, take it from me, and I've seen a few, believe me. Some pussies have a maidenly look about them, even if they're been poked to a standstill not five minutes before.'

In this he was thinking of Miss Emmy at Mrs Lee's house, whose exquisite flower of female beauty he and Naunton Cox had rogered lavishly. Wet with the dew of Miss Emmy's desire, and brimming over with the creamy spend of the two men, the soft pink lips framed in nut-brown curls that nestled between white thighs had still preserved an unspoilt virginal appearance.

'Others have a plump and comfortable look about them,' Monty went on, his thoughts straying to his dearest sister Grace at Putney, 'and this may belie the truth, for sometimes a matronly aspect conceals the most sublime pleasure when a chap gets his shaft in.'

Whilst he held forth thus on the individual merits of female parts, Monty was watching his moist fingers sliding in and out of Minnie, to tease the sensitive little nub at the apex of the fleshy lips.

'Yours is a particularly interesting specimen,' said he, 'for as I said before, it has this astonishingly lewd look about it – how I cannot say, but no man could gaze on it without at once growing stiff and wanting to get into it.'

'Oh my!' Minnie sighed in delight under his touch, the cheeks of her bottom squirming on his lap. Faster and faster he rubbed and the girl's breath came in short gasps.

'Oh yes – make me come off . . . Oh my saints, yes!'

'Not so fast, hoyden,' Monty cried. 'You shall come off when I do myself!'

He gripped her waist between both hands and lifted her from his thighs, then set her down again a few inches closer to his belly – and in her aroused condition Minnie knew at once what was required of her. She grasped his stiff shaft as he set her down and steered its head into her wet pussy, and her descent to his lap pushed it home in her to the limit.

'Good girl!' said Monty. 'Now you may come off!'

With her hands on his shoulders, Minnie jerked and shuddered in a flurry of wriggling hips and quivering thighs, seeming to lose control of her limbs. Monty kept his hold on her waist to stop her from sliding off his shaft in her spasms of ecstasy. A moment or two later her writhings brought him off, too, and he sighed joyfully at the sensations of his essence shooting up in her pussy.

When she had quietened down, she grinned at him, her face red from her pleasurable efforts, and perspiration on her brow.

'Lord, Mr Standish,' she said, 'what with Mrs Gifford having me every night and you having me all day, I shall be a rag and fit for nothing before long!'

'What?' Monty exclaimed. 'Mrs Gifford has you at night? Is this true?'

'That slipped out as shouldn't,' said Minnie. 'Promise me you'll never repeat it to a living soul!'

'You may trust me completely,' said Monty. 'Your

secret is as safe with me as mine is with you – poking Mrs Fanshawe, I mean. But tell me the whole affair, Minnie – I find it not easy to believe that our respectable landlady has a taste for girls.'

The tale that Minnie related to him was astounding. The idea that women made love to women was familiar enough to him, this pleasant diversion being a theme in many of the books he bought in Greek Street. Nor was his acquaintance confined merely to literature, for he had actually seen it done a time or two in a house in Kings Cross he had gone to with Naunton Cox. Here it was a speciality of the house for the girls to bring each other off by hand, to provoke the men watching into taking them upstairs for a poke. But that Mrs Gifford, the quiet-mannered landlady of Seymour Place, should play the fingering game with her skivvy – that was the astonishing thing.

Minnie explained that her instructions were to take a cup of hot cocoa to Mrs Gifford at ten every night, when she had gone to bed. Minnie would wait at the bedside while her employer drank the cocoa, so that she could return the cup to the kitchen and wash it. The same routine was followed each night – Mrs Gifford would put down the empty cup and saucer and throw aside the bedclothes, to reveal herself with her nightgown up round her neck, and everything on show.

'She has a full bosom,' said Monty thoughtfully, as he tried to picture the scene to himself.

'Yes, she's got big titties,' agreed Minnie, 'but they flop about when her stays are off and they're bare.'

What took place next, she told Monty, was that Minnie would get down on her knees by the bed and suck Mrs Gifford's titties, sometimes for the longest time. When the landlady had had her fill of that, she pushed Minnie's head down her belly towards her thighs.

'What sort of pussy has she?' Monty asked.

'Big and fat,' said Minnie, 'and very hairy.'

'My word!' Monty exclaimed, and his shaft twitched as if it would grow long and stiff again.

Minnie would lick Mrs Gifford a few times, and then slide her fingers into her moist groove. Mrs Gifford's belly would quiver to the darts of sensation through it, and she would urge Minnie to 'do her like that, there's a good girl!' Minnie was clever at finger play, having practised this form of enjoyment since she was a child, alone and with others. She was soon able to bring the landlady to seventh heaven by her attentions.

'She comes off very noisy,' said Minnie. 'I wonder you don't hear her upstairs!'

'I am rarely in by ten o'clock,' Monty pointed out. 'But as I am this evening, I shall listen out for the cry. You cover her and leave her to sleep then, do you, after she has come off?'

'Bless you, no!' said Minnie. 'That's only the beginning. As soon as she's got her breath back she wants to have a go at me. She makes me take my drawers down and lie on the bed with my legs open while she plays with my pussy. Oh, she's a Devil when she starts – she tickles and touches and teases till she has me wriggling all over the bed on my back. Once won't do for her – she fetches me off never less than five times in a row before she's ready to be done herself again.'

'Still waters run deep!' said Monty. 'Who would ever have thought it of our respectable Mrs Gifford!'

By now his shaft was fully hard-on again and pressing itself against Minnie's belly, inside her open drawers. He stroked her thighs softly, urging her to continue her fascinating tale, and she told him how she was made to lie on the bed, face down, between Mrs Gifford's spread legs. She would open the wet pussy before her and touch her tongue to the slippery button within.

'How her pussy jerks up to meet my tongue!' she told Monty, 'and how she pushes her thighs wider apart yet! I give her a slow tonguing, the way she likes it, and I keep her waiting for her coming off till she squeals and rolls about and pulls her pussy wide open for me to lick. When I bring her off at last, she heaves her backside right up off the bed and sets up an almighty squealing – if you're listening tonight you'll hear it for sure! After that she tells me to kiss her goodnight and go to bed – and not forget to wash up the cup and saucer first!'

'By George!' Monty gasped. 'You've given me a hard-on stand with your tale that there's only one cure for!'

He pushed Minnie from his lap, leapt up and dragged her by the hand into his bedroom.

'Off with your clothes!' he cried, flinging aside his jacket and shirt and fumbling to remove his trousers. Minnie, her eyes shining lewdly, untied her apron strings and heaved her frock and her chemise over her head. Off came her drawers in a trice and she flung herself backward on Monty's bed clad only in her coarse black stockings.

Monty placed her on her back, with her bottom protruding over the edge of the bed, her thighs stretched wide open, and her legs resting on his shoulders. Seen close to and naked, Minnie could not be said to be a well-favoured girl. Her arms and legs were thin from insufficient to eat all her life, and although she was not yet eighteen, her titties already hung slackly from over-much handling. There was a slackness about the wet lips of her pussy that also spoke of constant usage, and the tufts of light brown hair under her arms exactly matched the hair with which her slit was sparsely furnished.

However, a man with a hard-on standing shaft has no

time to consider niceties of appearance, and Monty was indifferent to whether Minnie was plain or not – the important consideration was her willingness to lie on her back for him and let him make urgent use of her female commodity. She grinned up at him red-faced, and he drove his stiff shaft in between the hairy lips of her pussy.

From the position he had chosen for poking, standing and leaning over her, Monty had given himself a full view of their joined parts.

'Minnie!' he gasped, 'I'm going to watch myself roger you! What do you think of that?'

'My, it feels nice, your big fat dolly-whacker up me!' she sighed. 'I hope you don't think you're getting all this for half a crown, Mr Standish!'

'A first-class poke and you shall have five shillings!' said he, swinging his hips to drive his shaft in and out of her. The sight of his shining wet flesh slipping between the clinging lips affected him strongly, and very soon he was near the end of his course.

'What a magnificent sight, a hard shaft up a pussy!' Monty murmured, his legs shaking under him. 'I'm in you to the hilt, Minnie, and it won't be long now! Are you ready to come off?'

"'Anytime!' she cried. 'Anytime at all!'

She moaned and sighed and bounced herself upward to meet his fierce thrusts and Monty heaved backward and forward with all his might, leaning right forward over her to drive deeper into her lean belly.

'It's all up inside me!' she cried, her eyes bulging at the sight. 'You'll burst me wide open!'

Monty grinned and fetched off copiously, filling her pussy to brimming with his hot flood.

CHAPTER 10
A Husband Deceived

When Selwyn informed Monty that he planned to pass the weekend with his sister and her husband at Reading and invited him to accompany him, Monty was delighted. They made an arrangement to meet on Friday at five o'clock at Paddington station. Selwyn proceeded there directly from his place of employment, while Monty took a cab from Seymour Place, bearing a hand-grip with a change or two of clothes, and Selwyn's luggage in addition.

The journey was passed pleasantly in talk and reminiscence of Cecily and Gwendolen, and from Reading station it was a twenty minute drive by hansom cab to the Fanshawe residence. It was a large house set in gardens of its own, the home of a man of substance, in Monty's estimation. He was eager to lay eyes on Gwendolen's husband, to learn something of the man whom he was cuckolding and so increase his own satisfaction in making good use of the man's wife.

Mr Fanshawe proved to be a man approaching forty, older than Monty had expected, a short and somewhat portly person whose brown hair was fast thinning. His manner was cordial and his welcome to Selwyn's friend seemed genuine enough. Over a lavish dinner they chatted inconsequentially and afterwards adjourned to the billiard room for a game or two. Selwyn appeared to be quite eager to play and, seizing an unlooked-for opportunity, Monty professed himself ignorant of the game. Instead of taking him on at once for a cash bet, as he had expected, Fanshawe dismissed him with a faintly insulting smile.

Seeing her husband and brother settling down to a session of billiards, Gwendolen proposed taking Monty to the conservatory for a game of two-handed whist and to this Mr Fanshawe gave ready assent. The conservatory adjoined the rear of the house with a view over lawns and a rose garden. It was lit by lamps, the gaslight not having been carried through from the house, and a golden glow suffused the many potted plants and shrubs. In these Monty had no interest and as soon as the door closed behind him he turned and took Gwendolen in his arms.

'My dearest, I must kiss you!' he murmured. 'All day long I have been yearning for an opportunity to hold you close to me and feel the trembling of your graceful body against mine!'

'And I, too, have been sick with longing for you,' she replied, her hands on his waist and her face up-turned to be kissed.

Monty's hands slid down her back until he was clasping the cheeks of her bottom through her clothes and pressing her belly hard against him. Her beautiful face coloured faintly when she became fully aware of the strength of his hard-on shaft trapped between them.

'Oh Monty!' she sighed, almost swooning from the intensity of her emotions, her eyes half-closed in bliss while he got his hand under her skirts at the back and raised them, to get into her drawers and treat himself to a good feel of her soft round cheeks. 'Oh, if only we dared!'

'With you, my dearest girl, I dare all!' he declared, his fingers probing between her legs from behind to touch the lips of her pussy.

Inside his trousers his shaft was throbbing furiously to call attention to its urgent needs. Gwendolen sighed to feel the motion against her belly, muffled though it was by layers of clothing, and Monty took her hand and pressed it lovingly against his trousers. At once she ripped open his buttons and delved deep inside, her fingers closing eagerly round his six inches of hard and jerking flesh.

'Monty – it is madness to think of doing anything here!' she said, with a short sigh. 'Suppose we are seen!'

'I am too deeply in love with you to behave prudently,' Monty answered, 'I've got to have you, Gwendolen or I shall come off in your hand!'

'Then so you shall, dearest!' she cried, her hand skimming up and down One-Eyed Jack in her anxiety to please, 'I shall stroke your darling shaft until it pours out its hot tribute for me!'

There was a new note in her voice, for Monty's hands had moved round under her clothes to feel her from the front, and already a knowing finger was in her moist pussy to tickle her button.

'Oh yes, yes!' she sighed, thrown into delight by this touch on her most sensitive portion. 'Bring me off, too!'

'I'm going to have you!' he sighed. 'Nothing less will ease the tension of my nerves.'

'No, that's out of the question!' she replied quickly. 'Not here and now, Monty, I beg you. Be satisfied with my hand until bedtime – I will come to your room as soon as Elliot is asleep, I promise you!'

'Yes, come to my room tonight,' he said, not believing such a meeting was possible, 'come as soon as you are able, and I will roger you to glory all the night!'

'I will be with you by eleven and stay for as long as you want me,' she murmured, her hand busy at his shaft to relieve him of his desire quickly.

In this intention she had mistaken her man – Monty was not at all persuaded to accept the pleasures of her dainty hand and trust that she could get away from her husband later to bestow upon him the supreme joy. The old saying advises that *A bird in the hand is worth two in the bush*, and although Monty's cock robin was in her hand, he wanted it in her bush. He thrust a hand into his trousers to remove his shaft from Gwendolen's manipulating hand, brought it out into the open, and guided it up between her legs.

Her pussy was open and ready for him, but with two fingers he stretched it wider still before pressing his swollen-headed and quivering shaft in to the quick. Gwendolen gasped at the sensation and threw her arms about him, resigning herself to being poked against the glass door of the conservatory.

'You are taking advantage of my loving nature to put me at risk if someone should come looking for us,' she whispered.

'I have the right!' he said, and to impress her he adapted the words he had used to cajole his sister Grace, or as near as he could recall them when he wanted to sample the pleasures of incest with her.

'It is the right of a lover to seize every opportunity that serves him, both indoors and outdoors, to stroke his darling's titties and feel her pussy, as a token of his undying love, and to roger her in whatever attitude is convenient, by day and by night. And it is the bounden duty of a beloved mistress to let her lover satisfy her, and himself, as often as the letch takes him. Surely you understand that, my angel-girl?'

'Oh yes, I understand fully!' Gwendolen murmured, and by then she no longer cared whether her husband found her being poked in the conservatory. Monty was pumping in and out strongly, and he had slipped his hands behind her to steady her by grasping the cheeks of her bottom. Gwendolen raised her mouth to his in a lasting kiss, and pushed against him to meet his thrusts.

'Oh bliss!' she sighed into his open mouth, and he echoed her words back into hers. Each time he jerked forward he felt his hardness slide into her, and each time he pulled back he felt the slither of her wet pussy along his throbbing shaft. He gasped in the delight of sharing the fierce palpitations of pleasure that surged through Gwendolen's body, giving rise to regular contractions of the velvet channel that held him in its loving grip.

She moaned into his mouth and begged him to bring her off – she who three minutes earlier had been fearful to let him sink his shaft into her in case they were discovered! Monty panted and poked harder, until she shook like a leaf in his grasp. A tiny scream escaped her lips and a long spasm shook her at the instant his triumphant desire gushed into her in thick jets. He held her tight while he flooded her darling pussy, she clinging to his shoulders with her fingernails in her excess of delight until she was spent and sank against him with a deep sigh of satisfaction.

They returned in due course to the billiard room, to find the game still in progress, Selwyn being as fanatic a player as his brother-in-law. At ten o'clock Mr Fanshawe drew the proceedings to a close and the party adjourned to the sitting room to partake of a light supper

– cold meat sandwiches with cocoa or tea. Goodnights were said and at ten-thirty all were in their rooms for the night. While Monty undressed for bed he wondered if Mr Fanshawe had brought the evening to a close early because he had a desire to poke his wife. 'At least he uses a different entrance to the one that received me in the conservatory,' our incorrigible hero thought.

He had brought with him in his luggage the book that had on more than one occasion affected him strongly by the very frank report it gave of stirring events at Lady Bumslapper's Boarding School for Young Ladies. Lying in bed with his night shirt tucked up to his middle and a hand on his twitching shaft, he read on:

. . . while Millicent was thus recounting with sighs and sobs to her dear friend Evangeline her sufferings and the outrage of her modesty at the hands of Miss Harriet, a hand was creeping furtively in between the sheets from the side of the bed. When Millicent least expected it, Evangeline's shameless little hand slipped under her chaste nightgown, and between her legs!

Before she could give utterance to the protest that rose at once within her bosom, the hand had hold of her pussy! Nor was that the total extent of these unwarranted depredations – for Evangeline inserted a skilful finger into the sensitive spot at the top of Millicent's hairy little slit!

Millicent trembled mightily and would have moaned, but her treacherous friend threw herself on her, and closed her mouth with a passionate kiss! The busy finger in her pussy tickled her hidden nub into an unwanted moistness of arousal, and tears coursed down Millicent's cheeks. How she had been abused and misused by Her Ladyship! And by Miss Harriet! And now by one she had trusted!

Try as she might to keep her thighs together, she felt them slide apart of their own will, as if inviting Evangeline to do whatever she chose to the maidenly body of her helpless victim. Spasms of shameful pleasure throbbed through Millicent's belly to the manipulation of Evangeline's finger, and in her heart was the humiliating knowledge that in another moment or two she would be brought off by the interfering hand between her legs!

It was too much for a gently bred and tenderly nurtured girl to bear! In the course of a single day she had been made to come off no less than eighteen times, by Miss Harriet and by Her Ladyship, singly and jointly! And now she must bear this undreamed-of renewal of the ravishment of her person by someone she had believed to be a true friend!

Evangeline had so aroused her that Millicent no longer knew what she did. Her groping little hands shook as if in a fever, as they found their way up under Evangeline's loose nightgown, to grasp at her unreliable friend's titties and feel them.

'Millicent, give them a good squeeze while I bring you off a time or two,' Evangeline murmured. 'Then you shall do me!'

So it was not to be once only! Evangeline was of a mind to repeat this shameful practice several times before leaving her alone! At the realisation of what lay in store for her at the hands of the other girl, Millicent felt her back rise from the bed beneath her, to push her belly and her wet pussy up hard to Evangeline's ministering hand. The overwhelming sensations of coming off throbbed through her, and although she squirmed and gasped in the throes of ecstasy, she cried out to her friend:

'Evangeline – traitress! You have undone me – I shall never speak to you again!'

Monty's shaft was throbbing mightily in his hand when, to his astonishment the door of his room opened silently and Gwendolen entered. She was wearing a long dressing gown, close round the throat and descending to her feet, its thin silk outlining the glorious fullness of her figure. With a finger to her lips to enjoin silence, she glided across the room and seated herself on the side of his bed. By then Monty had hurriedly concealed his book between the pillows. He would have taken Gwendolen in his arms and embraced her fondly, but she prevented him while she gave an account of her presence that amazed him.

After first warning him that they must speak very softly, she explained to him that her husband was a martyr to neuralgia. He had broken off the billiards game when he felt some twinges of his old complaint, for which it had for years been his habit to take tincture of laudanum, to still the pain. Tonight Gwendolen had made up an extra-strong dose for him, she said, that would keep him asleep until morning. Thus released from her conjugal obligations, she had hurried to be with the man she loved!

Whilst Gwendolen was explaining all this to him, it seemed to Monty that the scene from his book was being enacted for him, with himself as a principal player. For, as Gwendolen gave him an assurance that her husband would not miss her from his side in the marriage bed that night, her hand crept in between the sheets. Monty lay on his back in speechless delight while the hand slipped between his uncovered legs. In another instant it had hold of his engorged dolly-whacker and was sliding along the shaft in a slow and delicious manipulation.

'What's this?' said Gwendolen. 'So hard and big! And scarce two hours have passed since you raised my skirts and did me in the conservatory! How your darling shaft quivers in my hand – as if bidding me welcome to your bed! Oh Monty – what pleasure shall be ours this night!'

'My dearest girl!' Monty murmured, hardly able to speak.

'But why is your nightshirt round your waist?' Gwendolen enquired, her soft hand exploring further in the bed. 'Why were you lying here with your hard-on shaft uncovered? What were you doing, Monty? I insist on being told!'

'I was thinking of you, my dear one,' he said, 'and all the pleasure we had together in the conservatory! At that memory of delight, my shaft bounded and stood up! That is the effect your beauty has on me!'

'The dear sweet thing!' Gwendolen cooed, massaging it with affection. 'How I love to feel it jumping in my hand.! But what made you so stiff, lying here alone?'

'You had promised to be with me tonight and I knew you would keep your promise. I was resting quietly and waiting patiently for your arrival, so that I might roger you to glory and back.'

Gwendolen moved closer and let him put his arms about her and press hot kisses to her lips and cheeks. His wandering hands confirmed that her long silk dressing gown was her only garment – beneath it there was no nightgown, no chemise, no drawers, no stockings – nothing but her warm soft perfumed flesh. With a sigh of bliss, he pulled the darling girl down to lie beside him while he gave her bottom a good feel through the silk. Then, opening her frail night-attire, he gave her breasts a very thorough feel indeed, until their buds were firm.

'Oh, my dear one, if only I had the words to tell you how much I love you!' he exclaimed, rubbing his shaft against her bare thigh while his hands played feverishly over her titties.

'And I you!' she replied in a soft and tender voice, and took his leaping shaft in her hand to soothe it while he played with the plump and pouting pussy between her open legs. Soon the touch of his fingers told him that its fleece of curls was as wet as the lips of her slit and his heart beat furiously at the thought that he would be inside his beloved in an instant.

He pulled his nightshirt over his head and threw it to the floor, to be as naked as she. She sighed blissfully when he lay on her belly, and with a careful hand she brought his trembling shaft to the mark and held it while he pushed in. He felt her shiver in delight as she accepted the full length and girth and, before he could begin to roger her, she clasped her hands round his waist to hold him still on her while she asked him a question.

'Monty, my dearest – if you were my husband, how often would you do this to me?'

'Very often,' he replied at once, letting his shaft rest quietly in the warm clasp of her pussy, 'why do you ask?'

'It is impossible for me to know the truth of what goes on between husbands and wives,' she said. 'Mr Fanshawe must be considered an eccentric, and his three times a week may not be in any way representative of other husbands. Until that divine day I met you it was my custom to visit London twice weekly to let Selwyn assuage my unsatisfied desires. Before I was married to Mr Fanshawe, and Selwyn and I lived with our parents, we did it every day, two or three times. You will see from this that I am confused over a simple matter.'

'It will be a great privilege for me to enlighten you,' Monty sighed, his hands playing with her titties while he rogered her very slowly and lightly. 'From the ardent urges of your nature you cannot be unaware that healthy young persons revel in the delights of love very frequently. If you and I were married, my dearest Gwendolen, we would do it together twice every night, and another twice during the day.'

'Oh how delightful that sounds to me!' she cried, lifting her loins to push back at him to meet his strengthening thrusts. 'With all my heart I wish it could be so! Twice a night, and in the afternoon sitting astride your lap in an armchair, and lying on the sofa for you after dinner with my legs apart! With all that bliss, my dearest, could you find the strength to poke me in bed in the mornings before we rise, after the tea has been brought in?'

'A time of day I love for a quick poke,' said he, smiling at her most flattering enthusiasm, while his heart overflowed with love and lust. His boisterous shaft leapt joyfully inside its warm lodging and spouted jets of thick essence, shaking Monty with rapture. Gwendolen gasped and shuddered beneath him, and told him no man had ever been so adored as he was!

She stayed with him until past three in the morning, and in that time he had her on her back and rogered her no fewer than five times. It was as well, for all day Saturday passed without the slightest chance for him to be alone with her for a moment. He lived in hope that Mr Fanshawe would take another draught of his medicine at bedtime and sleep soundly enough for Gwendolen to slip away from her marriage bed and join him for a frolic – but, alas, midnight passed and there was no sign of her.

Monty was sure the worst had befallen his darling girl – her husband was claiming his conjugal rights! Surely nothing else would have kept her from her lover's side! Into Monty's mind came a frightful vision of Gwendolen made to lie face down on her bed, her nightgown up round her waist and her exquisitely round bottom bared, whilst her pot-bellied husband stood behind her, his nightshirt hitched up, to push his unwanted shaft up the dear creature's knot-hole!

To banish this atrocious vision, Monty dragged his own nightshirt up to his chest and clasped his stiff shaft in his hand. He jerked One-Eyed Jack up and down angrily, willing Fanshawe to desist, but the picture in his head would not go away and cease to trouble him. In his mind's eye he could see Fanshawe holding Gwendolen by the hips as he thrust in and out, she biting her lips, it seemed to Monty, in her humiliation.

Strangely, the vision in his heated mind served only to make Monty even more aroused than before and his shaft bounded in his clasping hand. *Fanshawe, you cad – I order you to cease and desist this instant*, Monty gasped out loud, hardly knowing what he did or said. *Stop it, you beast – I forbid you to come off in my dearest Gwendolen's bottom!* But his angry words were to no purpose, for they could have no influence on Mr Fanshawe's acts of conjugal connection, whatever they were that night.

In order to drive away with the power of his imagination the scene that haunted his heated brain, Monty pretended to himself that he was bodily in the room where Fanshawe was abusing his wife. He saw himself take hold of his hated rival to drag him off that smooth round bottom he was so cruelly misusing but, to his surprise, Fanshawe was the stronger and kept his position. By main force Monty rolled Gwendolen over on her side and flung himself on the bed beside her. In another instant, to her shrieks of joy, his shaft was deep in her welcoming pussy and he was rogering her with might and main. So, too, was Fanshawe, who had not been dislodged by this manoeuvre and the two men rogered her strongly, fore and aft, matching stroke for stroke. *Leave her, you bounder.* Monty said furiously over her shoulder to Fanshawe, but the latter grinned a vile grin and continued. In the heat of the moment Monty was unaware that his hand was racing up and down his shaft, until without a tremor of warning, One-Eyed Jack spurted his hot and sticky essence over Monty's belly.

On Sunday morning they all went to church together, Mr and Mrs Fanshawe, Selwyn and Monty. Gwendolen looked fetching in a new bonnet and a frock of darkest blue, and Monty felt that his temperature was rising by the hour in his frustration. Selwyn and he were due to catch the five-thirty train back to town, and there seemed no hope left that he could be alone with his beloved in the short time available. Monty's staff stood hot and throbbing in his trousers all through luncheon and tormented him with unsatisfied desire and secret thoughts of sliding through the slit of Gwendolen's drawers and into her dark-haired pussy.

Despair was in Monty's heart, but in all this he had reckoned without Gwendolen's equally hot desire for him. She, the dear charming creature, hot-natured and inventive as she was, found a way to slake his lust. In the front parlour Mr Fanshawe held forth to the assembled company on the criminal folly of taxing honest citizens to teach reading and writing to the children of the labouring classes and so giving them thoughts above their station in life. As a loyal employee of the Board of Education Selwyn argued strongly in favour of universal schooling, and the argument between the two of them swung back and forth while Monty and Gwendolen exchanged longing glances across the room.

By three o'clock, replete with a heavy lunch, Mr Fanshawe was dozing in his armchair but Selwyn was still in good voice and continued to press his case, whether he was heard or not. A nod of Gwendolen's head invited Monty to join her by the window, he nothing loth to quit Selwyn's vehement and radical nonsense and Mr Fanshawe's ignorantly dismissive half-snoring. At the open window Gwendolen and he stood side by side, close together, to gaze out into the well-kept garden. Moving cautiously so as not to disturb Selwyn or Mr Fanshawe, Monty caught Gwendolen's hand and pressed it lightly to the long hard bulge in his trousers. She smiled and glanced over her shoulder at her somnolent husband and her brother on the other of the room and then, greatly daring, she slowly undid every one of Monty's trouser buttons and pulled up his shirt and took out his hot and hard shaft. He sighed softly to feel the delicious sensations set stirring in him by the gentle rubbing of her hand.

'Gwendolen, my dearest, I adore you beyond life itself!' he whispered to her, gazing in admiration and delight at her face, so calm and so beautiful as she stared down to see the effect of her ministrations on One-Eyed Jack.

'And I adore you, my dearest boy,' she whispered back, her head close to his head, and the beat of her hand on his swollen shaft firmer and faster, 'I shall come to London on Tuesday – be ready for me by eleven in the morning and I wish to stay in bed with you all day long. How many times will you do me – five or six. More perhaps? It can never be enough, however often you do it to me!'

At these loving words, the turbulent desire that had hold of Monty tightened with an irresistible force. The muscles of his belly clenched and he swayed on shaking legs, almost falling, as the hot elixir of his passion gushed out in a raging flood. So furious was the strength of his fetching off that his cream flew out through the open window and fell down into the flower bed below, bedewing the red roses.

Perhaps without knowing it he gasped at this supreme moment for, when he recovered himself, Gwendolen whispered to him and he turned to look over his shoulder. Mr Fanshawe was asleep in his chair, his mouth open and his hands clasped over his pot belly, but Selwyn was staring at them. Monty winked at him, and Selwyn made a gesture with his head to indicate the two of them should leave the room for somewhere more secure. Monty tucked his shrinking shaft in his trousers and buttoned up, and went with Gwendolen to the dining room next door, tiptoeing silently past her sleeping husband.

In the dining room Monty took his darling girl in his arms to shower kisses on her beautiful face. Then with a gentle touch, he laid her backwards on the well-polished mahogany table top and pulled up her clothes until he had a superb view of her shapely legs in their black stockings. With her own fair hands she parted the slit of her drawers for him and he stared enraptured at the lusciously pouting lips of her pussy, rose-pink and gaping open slightly between her profusion of dark curls.

She parted her legs wider and he was down on his knees at once, to press his lips to her treasure. He kissed it hotly and licked at it feverishly, to the great delight of Gwendolen who sighed and squirmed with pleasure. Soon Monty could no longer contain his bursting desire and, getting up on his feet, he brought his hot shaft to the charge. Without a pause, he thrust it right in the gaping pussy and laid forward over her belly.

'My darling boy!' Gwendolen sighed, heaving up her bottom as if she would roger him from below! Monty responded to her with a strong poking, whereupon they commenced upon a most exciting struggle, his manly shaft working in and out fiercely.

'You are the most delightful dish ever served up to me at a dining table!' he cried, feeling how the wet lips of her pussy seemed to cling to his shaft each time of withdrawal, as if afraid to lose so delightful a friend.

'And I have never been so well satisfied at table!' his dear girl exclaimed, greatly daring in her passions. 'Feed me, Monty – feed me with rich cream, to sustain me until Tuesday!'

Their furious sensations could not endure long, for a limit has been set by Divine Providence to the degree of stimulation the human organism can tolerate. Their movements became faster and faster, shaft and pussy meeting in a embrace that brought on a wild and convulsive release. Gwendolen half-fainted away in her beloved's arms, and Monty was in no better condition than she, sobbing with love and gratification until his passion was spent. He lay still for a while on Gwendolen's belly, feeling the trickle of creamy moisture that escaped from her pussy and wondered if there was time to do her again before Fanshawe woke up.

CHAPTER 11
Mrs Gifford is Taken by Surprise

After Gwendolen had been to London on Tuesday to share Monty's bed from eleven o'clock in the morning until five o'clock that same day, during which length of six hours she was poked nine times and brought off by hand thrice more, it was a day before Monty's natural vitality restored itself and he was ready for a renewed frolicking. The account Minnie had given him of her nightly exercises with the landlady had remained vivid in his thoughts, and he decided to take a part in Mrs Gifford's revels.

Minnie was at first reluctant to assist him in this, fearing that she might be dismissed from her position. Monty gave her a feel and half-a-crown and explained to her that he would see that no action was taken against her whatever happened, and this assurance settled her doubts. Between them they arranged how it was to be done that evening – she would tip him the wink when she was ready to take in Mrs Gifford's cup of cocoa and he was to let five or six minutes pass before following her.

The remainder of the day passed slowly after that, and Monty went out to dinner to occupy the evening hours until the time was right for the adventure. He dined and drank extremely well, and was in a dare-anything mood when he returned to Seymour Place just before ten o'clock. In the privacy of his bedroom he undressed and put on a clean nightshirt, then his slippers and dressing gown and sat down to wait patiently on the sofa in his sitting room, until he should be summoned.

He had not long to wait. A tap sounded at his door, and then Minnie put her head round it and winked at him. He nodded and set his pocket watch on the sofa-arm to count off the minutes. The house was silent and dark as he crept cautiously down the stairs. In the hallway he paused to listen, but no sound came to his ear from the landlady's quarters. He put his hand on the door knob of her sitting room and turned, then pushed the door open a crack. With relief he saw that the light was turned out and she had gone to bed.

He crossed the room carefully, not wishing to announce his presence by bumping into furniture in the dark. The door of the bedroom was ajar, for Minnie had left it so for him, and from beyond there fell enough light to guide him safely through the dangers. He stood close to the doorjamb and peeped in, to see what Mrs Gifford and the skivvy were about.

Little Minnie was fully clothed still, though she had removed her long apron. She was assisting the landlady to undress, and playing the part of a lady's maid very acceptably. She removed Mrs Gifford's green bombazine frock, underskirt and petticoat, and shortly had her stripped to her chemise. Then Mrs Gifford seated herself on the bedside and drew up her chemise to her lap, displaying white drawers with frills round the legs. While Minnie went down on her knees to roll down the stockings and hang them over the brass bedpost, Mrs Gifford undid the knot of her hair and let it hang loose, shining and dark, over her shoulders.

Monty could see Minnie's hands were under the chemise, inside Mrs Gifford's drawers, and he guessed that the landlady's pussy was being treated to a good feel. In a short time Mrs Gifford's face began to flush, whereupon she stood up and allowed Minnie to remove her chemise and assist her into her long white nightgown. In the interval between the chemise being taken off and the nightgown being put on, the landlady stood revealed in the gaslight in no more than her drawers, her body bare down to the waist.

She was a buxom woman of about five and thirty, blessed with a fine pair of titties, somewhat slackened by the years, but luscious enough still to cause Monty's shaft to stiffen to the full and twitch impatiently. He observed Minnie kneel again and feel up underneath the long nightgown, to take down Mrs Gifford's drawers. It would have been the work of a second or two, but Minnie remained in that posture, as if in prayer, with her hands raised, for far longer than was needed to untie the bow of a pair of drawers and pull them down. By the sighs that escaped Mrs Gifford's lips and the manner in which she swayed on her feet it was evident that her pussy was being thoroughly felt once more.

When her drawers were finally removed she lay on her bed and drew her nightgown up to her belly button. Minnie was soon kneeling on the bed, fully dressed, her lean bottom in the air, her head between the wide-gaping legs of her mistress. For the benefit of Monty whom she knew to be watching, Minnie paused to gaze for some little time at Mrs Gifford's throbbing pussy and its bush of dark hair, so that he might take advantage of the situation to get a good look at it. Then she set her hand to it and plunged two fingers deep inside, causing the landlady to utter a little shriek of surprise and delight. She urged her servant to delay no longer, but to bring her off at once.

Minnie obediently bent her neck and brought her tongue to bear on the pussy she had titillated to a lustful impatience by the use of her fingers. Monty was in great agitation whilst he watched Mrs Gifford being licked so voluptuously. The sight was intensely arousing – Minnie's head down between the landlady's thighs and her wet tongue flickering at the exposed pussy! In a fever of impatience, Monty threw off his dressing gown to be ready when his moment came.

One-Eyed Jack was so big and hard that he was holding out the front of his nightshirt. Monty had no choice but to raise that to his waist, so that he could take hold of his quivering shaft to hold it still. He heard Mrs Gifford's gasping at the force of the fierce sensations she was enjoying beneath the darting caresses of Minnie's tongue. Her smooth bare legs kicked on the bed, announcing the supreme moment would speedily arrive.

Monty could hardly breath for his excitement. His body was ablaze with passion, and to cool himself he drew off his nightshirt and cast it to the floor. Delicious spasms racked him from top to toe, his clasped hand sliding up and down his shaft so gratifyingly that he knew he could not hold out much longer. Then Mrs Gifford gave a loud shriek and fell back on the bed, her belly heaving and her legs shaking to the throbbing of her climactic pleasure.

'I've come off, Minnie!' she gasped. 'It was lovely – do me again!'

That was a signal for Monty to charge into action before he spent against the door. He held his jerking shaft in his hand while he sped to the bedside and pushed Minnie aside. She gave him a conspirator's grin, and yielded her place on the bed to him without demur. Monty, completely naked, his shaft as thick and hard as a rolling pin, leaned over the landlady's belly, staring down at her wet pussy with wolfish glee.

At this sudden and unexpected appearance, Mrs Gifford started upright in her bed. Her eyes were staring wildly and her mouth hung wide open in amazement and dismay to be caught out red-handed – and red-tongued! – in so intimate an embrace with the skivvy. Before there was any time for her to cry out in alarm, Monty took hold of her nightgown and hoisted it up over her slack titties. Mrs Gifford's body jerked, and it seemed as if her titties rolled towards his hands of their own accord.

She stared at Monty, struck speechless by the invasion of the privacy of her bed, whilst he handled the bulky softness of her titties with delight. He noted with pleasure that, although Minnie had brought her off not two minutes ago, the dark tip of each tittie stood up long and firm from its reddish-brown halo.

'Mr Standish – what can you be thinking of?' the landlady gasped, recovering the use of her voice at last. 'Do you mean to violate me in my own bed? Are you drunk?'

'Sober as a judge,' he assured her, with a singular lack of truth, 'and after what I've just seen done to you by Minnie my shaft's like an iron bar and I intend to roger you thoroughly.'

'What!' she cried. 'Do you think that you can burst into my private room and make casual use of my body? This is a foul outrage!'

Monty was fondling her with both hands, greedy for the feel of her soft warm flesh. He bent his neck and licked her buds one after the other and before she had time to renew her protests, he smiled up at her in his most winning way and made clear his point of view:

'Call it what you will, Hannah – I mean to have you!'

Whilst he had been occupied with Hannah Gifford's titties, Minnie had taken a seat on a padded chair in the corner of the bedroom. She was observing the proceedings on the bed with her customary irreverent amusement.

'Shall I run and get a policeman, Mrs Gifford?' she asked.

There was a pause while the landlady gave her consideration to the suggestion. At last she made up her mind.

'No! The shame of it would kill me, if it were known that I had been abused in my person by a man!' she said. 'Sit quiet, Minnie, and be ready to render aid when my fearful ordeal comes to an end!'

'Yes, Mrs Gifford,' said Minnie. 'Will he do you more than once, do you reckon?'

'Ah, Heaven protect me!' the landlady moaned, her plump legs wide open on either side of Monty, as he fondled her titties.

'You asked me what I was thinking of, Hannah my dear, to use you in this way,' said he. 'I shall tell you plainly – I am of the opinion that you are a hot-natured woman, who loves to be fetched off. Having no man to do it to you, who else can you employ for your gratification but Minnie? But if this became known amongst your neighbours here in Seymour Place, or by the parson and congregation of the church you attend so devoutly each Sunday, then you would never be able to hold up your head again for the infamy that would descend upon you. It is most fortunate that your secret has fallen into my hands and not those of a cad or a rotter, who might extort money from you for his silence.'

Hannah, blushing in the gaslight made no attempt to deny the truth of his words and only raised a note of pleading:

'Mr Standish – I am utterly at your mercy!' she exclaimed.

'You must call me Monty in bed,' said he jauntily. 'I mean to fill a void in your life, Hannah – the aching loneliness of an unmarried woman. And this I propose to do by filling the void between your legs.'

'Then you are a gentleman,' she said, 'and I trust myself to you without reserve.'

Monty set his mouth to her titties to tease them, whilst his hands felt up her legs, until he stroked her plump thighs.

'You seem to know your way about the female body,' said she, 'I've had my suspicions about you for a long time – I'd lay a pound to a penny that you've been taking advantage of Minnie. Speak the truth now!'

While she challenged him, her eyes were downcast, but it was not for reasons of modesty. She was staring at the stiff shaft that jutted boldly towards her, its unhooded head shiny purple in the gaslight. Monty thought the moment opportune to make a start with her and pushed her flat on the bed, dragging up her nightgown up over her head to bare all. She murmured a short protest at first, but her murmur turned to one of appreciation when he ran his hands over her plump belly, and her strong legs moved well apart to allow him free access.

'Mr Standish is a gentleman,' Minnie piped up from her chair in the corner, 'he wouldn't take advantage of a poor servant girl like me.'

'I've never known a young gentleman stay here yet who

didn't interfere with my servants,' Hannah retorted. 'Don't try to lie to me, girl – he's had his way with you more than once, I'll be bound! Watch out he doesn't give you a big belly!'

Minnie giggled, and Monty giggled, and then Hannah giggled too. Below her soft round belly, where the columns of her thighs joined, her fat and hairy pussy seemed to bestow a wink of welcome on Monty, as if to say: *Here's a grown-up pussy for you, not a young girl's tight little hole*. One-Eyed Jack jumped for joy when Monty parted the wet lips before him and burrowed a couple of fingers into Hannah to feel how slippy she was.

'Oh, Monty,' she murmured, 'put it up me, I beg you. I shall die of longing if you keep me waiting any longer.'

'There is no fear of that,' he answered. 'When I saw you on your back being fetched off by Minnie, the sight put me in such a state I very nearly came off in my hand and wet your carpet! I shall flood your pussy with my juices the instant I put my shaft into you!'

'Then do it!' she cried.

'Lord love us!' said Minnie to nobody in particular. 'One minute she's complaining about being raped and forced, and the next minute she's begging him to put it up her!'

With no more ado, Monty placed his twitching shaft to her wet pussy and pushed. He sank into her with the ease of a knife in a pound of best butter, until his bare belly was on hers. She sighed and wriggled her bottom under him, he laid hold of her titties and went at her briskly.

'Oh how delightful a feeling!' she cried, thrusting up her belly at him to meet his strokes. 'Roger me hard and fill me up to the brim – make my pussy overflow!'

The most intense emotions that the human organism

can bear possessed Monty at that moment. He plunged so forcefully into Hannah's hot slit that he reached the climax of voluptuousness very soon and flooded her with his spurting essence. She moaned and sighed and her belly shook under him to the spasms of her coming off.

'Lord, she does love it!' Monty heard Minnie exclaim. 'No sleep for any of us tonight, now she's got the feel of a shaft inside her! Ooooooh!'

He glanced round over his shoulder and saw that Minnie sat with her skirt pulled up in her lap and her hand between her open thighs to finger herself whilst she watched him roger the landlady. Her long moan had announced the moment of her coming off against her busy fingers.

'Well done, Minnie,' said he with an encouraging grin. 'Keep your pussy wet and ready, and we'll have you on the bed again before long.'

'What!' cried Hannah, pushing Monty off her naked body now that she was recovered a little from her culminating spasms. 'Do you think to give the orders here, in my bedroom, to my servant? Do you think that because you took me by surprise and ravished me, this confers on you the right to command me?'

'Hoity-toity!' he replied. 'I mean to start as I shall go on with you, Hannah. That you are by birth the owner of a pussy gives you no privileges other than those I allow you. Pussies are ten a penny, my dear, ten thousand women walk the London streets nightly offering the use of theirs for a few shillings. Privilege comes from the ownership of a male shaft like mine.'

He allowed her no time to complain further but thrust his hand between her thighs before she could clamp them together. He gripped the fleshy lips of her pussy between strong fingers, and pinched them together hard. Hannah gave a gasp of pain, but did not try to pull away from him.

'If I want Minnie to join us on the bed and suck my shaft or lick your pussy, then she shall do so,' he said.

'If this is your attitude toward me, you can go to your own rooms now,' Hannah warned him, her soft round belly squirming in discomfort at the tight grip of his fingers.

'My attitude is one of loving affection and unbridled lust, if you will let it be so,' he told her, 'as it was until you undertook to tell me what I must and must not do. You shall be either my dear female friend on whom I shall bestow continuous sensual delight, or you shall be a pussy I use when the mood takes me. You must choose now.

'I entreat you not to treat me with contempt, Monty,' she said softly. 'You cannot doubt that I wish to be your devoted female friend, with a pussy at your disposal whenever you want it. But leave Minnie where she is – we have no need of her. If you wish your shaft to be sucked, let me do it.'

'What do you say to that, Minnie?' Monty asked the skivvy in the corner chair. 'Do you wish to be made use of, mouth, pussy and the rest – or will you go to your bed and sleep?'

'I'll do whatever you tell me to, Mr Monty,' said the girl at once. 'I'd love to see you poke Mrs Gifford again – it gave me a real thrill to see somebody else besides me attending to her. And if you fancy me giving you a lick-off, just say the word.'

'You're a good girl, Minnie,' said Monty. 'Strip yourself off bare and come here and lie on the bed with us.'

'Ah, I see you mean to insult me!' said Hannah, displeased by his words and sulky of tone. She clapped her thighs together to make certain that Monty was in no doubt of her mood.

'Insult you?' said he, with a laugh. 'By no means! I mean not to insult you, but to roger you unconscious, as you will in a short time find out!'

'Where do you want me, Mr Monty?' asked Minnie, standing at the bedside naked.

Monty grinned at her obliging nature and reached out to touch the soft little pussy between her thin thighs and tickle it for a moment or two.

'Sit here on the bedside,' said he, 'and I will tell you what to do in a minute.

He turned to the landlady, lying in a silent sulk, seized her clamped thighs and wrenched them open. She brought her knees up to protect herself, but he was too strong for her and forced them wide apart so that her belly and hairy pussy lay readily exposed to his whims.

'Put three fingers up her pussy, Minnie, while I hold her,' he said. 'She may have gone dry while we've been talking, and I do so love a thoroughly wet pussy.'

Hannah protested at this new insult to her person, but could do nothing to prevent it. Monty watched in growing excitement to see Minnie's fingers inside Hannah's well-stretched lips, to tease at her pink nub.

'Stop it, Minnie!' Hannah commanded. 'Stop it this minute!'

'Why?' Minnie asked. 'You've made me do you like this two or three times a night since I've been working for you. Tonight was the same – you had me bring you off twice before Mr Monty burst in uninvited and gave you a good tousling. So why are you saying no to me now?'

'I will not be the plaything of a tenant and a servant-girl,' said Hannah with a sighing moan. 'Make her stop,

Monty – you are not a Turk and I am not your harem slave.'

'Scrumptious thought!' exclaimed Monty. 'I've got a book upstairs about a sultan in his harem – jolly exciting stuff, I can tell you. One night I'll bring it down and read it to you – we can try some of it out – what do you say to that?'

'You are a beast!' cried Hannah, 'Oh . . .!'

Minnie's sly fingers had done their work well and spasms of pure ecstasy seized Hannah and made her belly quake and rise as she came off. Immediately Monty was on her, thrusting his shaft into her twitching pussy while her throes still shook her body. To see her brought off had aroused him greatly and he lunged into her slippery split with verve.

'Go on – give her a good poking!' cried Minnie, her hand between his manly thighs to take hold of his pompoms and gently squeeze them.

Hannah sustained his strong lunging with an energy equal to his own, and returned his strokes with upheavals of her belly as eager as any man could wish for. With a cry of bliss, Monty gushed his ardent lust deep into her and she dissolved in joy to feel the sudden flow in her belly, and continued to come off even after Monty was finished and lay gasping on her.

'That's more like it,' said she faintly, when she could again speak, 'there is no need for Minnie to finger me off if you are going to roger me like that the rest of the night.'

This time Monty did not descend from the saddle. He lay on Hannah's belly, his shaft softening inside her but never being taken out. He played with her titties and told her of the deep delight she had given him. Meanwhile Minnie, seated beside him, fingered his knot-hole until his shaft grew strong again inside Hannah's pussy and he recommenced his rogering.

Monty prided himself on being a man of his word. He had told Hannah that he intended to roger her unconscious, and to prove that was more than empty words he remained ensconced on her soft belly between bouts while Minnie stimulated his interest by feeling his pompoms and between the cheeks of his bottom to make his shaft hard-on again. In this way, and by these means, in the space of half an hour he rogered Hannah three times more without ever dismounting, throwing her into noisy raptures at his performance.

After that feat, Monty lay on his back on the bed, his thighs wide apart to cool his pompoms, his limp dangler lolling wetly on his belly. Hannah also lay in languid contentment, her soft belly heaving gently and her legs open. From the plump lips of her hairy pussy a trickle of pearly essence escaped to run down to the bed sheet below as her well-filled belly brimmed over a little. Minnie lay trembling, her head resting on Monty's feet, for she had been so overcome by assisting him to roger Hannah that she had eased her nervous tension by hand at the same time and had come off as many times as had he and the landlady.

The first to recover from the soft fatigue that embraces all creatures in the sweet aftermath of love was Hannah. She raised herself on an elbow to gaze fondly at Monty's well-used shaft, showing her appreciation of its capability to thrill her by touching it fondly and tugging gently at it.

'If only it would stand up again!' said Monty, bestowing a friendly smile on her. 'I would poke you again gladly, Hannah – but I fear my bolt is shot for tonight!'

'Don't say that, my dear!' she cried. 'I want it again!'

Her ardent fingering had little effect, but before giving up as a hopeless task she told Minnie to see if she could achieve anything. With a grin, Minnie rolled on to her belly, took his shaft in her mouth and sucked strongly, all the while tickling his bung-hole with a finger pressed between the cheeks of his bottom. At last the limp little thing began to stir itself, whereupon Minnie tongued it lovingly until it stood straight again as a soldier at attention.

She raised her head to grin at Monty and her clasped hand slid up and down the swollen shaft, making it throb in amorous anticipation of the ecstasy to come.

'That's more like it,' said Hannah, keeping a close eye on the skivvy's progress, 'but stop now, girl – I don't want him finished off before he's properly begun.'

She pushed Minnie aside and took her place between Monty's legs, her hand about his shaft while she planted a brief kiss on the sticky purple head. She stared into his face with a look of deepest affection whilst her fingers circled his shaft and played up and down it until Monty was shaking and straining to fetch off.

'Ah, would you!' she exclaimed. 'I say you shall not! You shall not squirt your last few drops of sap wantonly over your belly, but into my pussy!'

So saying, she climbed over him, with her knees on either side. With shaking fingers she opened the wet lips of her pussy to display the slippery pink inside.

'Look at this,' she commanded him, 'see where your shaft is about to be plunged – in here, into my belly!'

She rubbed the engorged end of his shaft on her wet flesh, and Monty moaned in bliss to feel the sensations.

'You shall not go inside yet,' she said, 'not until you have rubbed my button a while to make me ready again.'

'Oh, Hannah,' Monty murmured, 'how delightful that

feels! I swear you will bring me off like that in another minute!'

'I will not let you cheat me by fetching off on my finger!' said she, seeing the near onset of his spasm.

She sat down hard on his shaft, driving it deep into herself.

'Minnie, squeeze my titties!' she ordered the watching girl, and at once Minnie squatted behind her over Monty's legs and slipped her arms about her. Monty watched with bulging eyes to see Hannah's big titties felt and rubbed, whilst Minnie's face stared at him over the landlady's shoulder.

No more than half a dozen jerks up and down by Hannah on his shaft were required to do the trick. Monty cried out as his hot essence spurted upwards and Hannah shrieked loudly and pumped him dry with her clinging pussy, while Minnie's fingers clenched in the flesh of her titties as if to screw them off. When it was over Monty lay under Hannah exhausted for the moment and she sat panting and perspiring on top of him.

Eventually she was helped to descend from her lofty perch by Minnie's arms round her to lie breathing slowly on her back. Minnie busied herself with her employer's comfort, wiping the perspiration from her belly and under her voluminous titties with a pair of drawers picked up from the floor, before wiping dry her sopping pussy. With the same pair of drawers she attended to Monty's shrunken shaft.

Completely content and worn out, Monty closed his eyes and felt himself sinking into a deep and refreshing sleep. The last thing he heard was Hannah's voice, speaking to Minnie:

'I've never before been poked as many times as tonight!' she said. 'Mr Standish is armed like a veritable

Goliath as to his person, and pussy-struck beyond words! I mean to have him here night after night, until he rogers me to death!'

'He'll wear your pussy out for you, that you can be sure of,' the maid answered.

'I've got to have it again, Minnie,' said Hannah. 'Sit here between my legs and bring me off with your fingers!'

CHAPTER 12
Selwyn Learns About the Female Nature

Two days after Monty's interesting evening in Hannah's bed Gwendolen visited London on her so-called shopping excursion. On this occasion she made no pretence of looking in shops – she took a cab straight from the railway station to Seymour Place and by eleven in the morning she and Monty were naked together in his bed. When she left, most reluctantly and with tears of sorrow at their parting, she had been as soundly done as any woman in the kingdom – five times by Monty's shaft, four times by his fingers, and three times by his tongue.

With sentimental agonies she confessed that she had not been able to find a suitable secret meeting-place in Reading for him to visit. He urged her to keep trying, for his desire for her gave him no rest by night or by day, he declared. Needless to relate, he said nothing of employing his energies on Cecily and Hannah Gifford, not to mention Minnie the skivvy.

Gwendolen kissed him in tearful farewell, vowing to him that the problem would be resolved, and sooner than he expected, for her love for him was too fierce to be denied, and *have* him she must, day after day and night after night. Monty played the sighing lover to perfection and when she had gone, went to bed again to sleep and rest until it was time for dinner.

The very next day, while he was at breakfast in his sitting room, Selwyn burst in waving in his hand a telegram that had just been delivered. It was from Gwendolen to her brother, and its message was brief but shocking – Mr Elliot Fanshawe had passed away in the night, and Selwyn's presence at Reading was urgently required to assist with the arrangements.

'You must be on the next train!' Monty cried, his emotions a mingling of satisfaction that Gwendolen was a widow and a free woman, and apprehension as to the manner of her husband's hasty demise. He suggested accompanying Selwyn to Reading, to comfort his grieving sister, but Selwyn thought that most improper and declared it to be a well-established social custom that a widow must needs abstain from sexual connection for some months.

Off he went, leaving a message to be delivered by hand to the Board of Education to account for his absence from his post for the next few days. He gave Monty his word to telegraph full details of the sad occurrence at Reading the instant he learnt the circumstances. He was as good as his word – in the early evening a telegram was delivered to Monty, and a perusal of it revealed that Mr Fanshawe had suffered heart failure.

The funeral was arranged for Friday, but both Selwyn and Mrs Fanshawe thought it wiser for Monty not to attend. Not that Monty had the least wish to be present – the information that so outwardly robust a person as Elliot Fanshawe had suffered heart failure had caused extreme vexation, for Monty was unable to put out of his mind the deduction that it was by using dear Gwendolen's lovely body for his vile pleasures that the errant husband had overtaxed his heart and met his just desserts.

Nevertheless, jealous as he was, Monty would have liked the opportunity to see Gwendolen and get her alone long enough for a consoling poke or two. Since this was not to be, he set out to find diversions for the next days, awaiting Selwyn's return.

One afternoon he passed with Cecily, playing a lewd game of her devising, in which she dressed fully as a man, whilst he wore female clothing – stockings, drawers, chemise, and frock. By the time they had finished with each other, both declared themselves marvellously well satisfied. On two nights running Monty rogered the landlady in her bed, after Minnie had played her part in appeasing Mrs Gifford's appetite with fingers and lips. Two evenings were spent at Mrs Lee's with Miss Emmy, the first of the month having arrived and Monty's allowance duly paid.

Selwyn remained in Reading after the funeral and was not back at his digs until Sunday evening. As soon as Monty heard him on the stairs, he rushed out and dragged him into his own sitting room, agog to hear all that had passed. Selwyn assured him that Gwendolen was bearing up well and sent her fondest regards.

'No hitches with the arrangements?' Monty asked cautiously,' 'I mean, Mr Fanshawe's passing was a trifle sudden.'

'None at all,' said Selwyn, shaking his head, 'Dr Bowker, the family physician, knew of Elliot's habit of taking tincture of laudanum for his neuralgia and, so as not to distress Gwendolen in her grieving widowhood by causing public gossip, he wrote out a certificate to the effect that Elliot had died of heart failure. I thought that was very considerate of him.'

'Uncommonly considerate,' Monty agreed readily, 'and deuced convenient all round. Is he a young man or an older man?'

He had revised his previous thought that Mr Fanshawe harmed himself by too strenuous a session with Gwendolen's beautiful person, and now was secretly convinced that it was her session with himself that had induced her to mix a fatal dose for her inconvenient husband. Perhaps with the tacit connivance of the family physician.

'I can guess at your thought,' said Selwyn, 'but you do my dear sister a wrong. Never would she take part in deception of that nature! And your speculation that she would ever submit her person to Dr Bowker to gain an advantage – that is unworthy of you!'

'No such dreadful thought crossed my mind!' Monty assured him, although it had been precisely what he had deduced. 'You know I adore her beyond reason!'

'Gwendolen is innocent of all wrongdoing,' Selwyn declared, 'like Caesar's wife, she is above suspicion!'

'Certainly,' Monty agreed, seeing that nothing more need ever be said on the subject of Mr Fanshawe's demise. 'But you have a melancholy look about you, Selwyn. Buck up, old chap, all will be for the best and unless I am mistaken, your next rendezvous with dearest Cecily is tomorrow evening. That will restore your zest for life!'

'You must advise me, Monty,' said Selwyn, mightily agitated, 'something has happened which threatens to destroy all my new happiness with Cecily. I am in the most desperate of plights!'

'Lord!' said Monty. 'What a taking you are in, old fellow! Have a drop of malmsey wine with me and calm yourself. What can have happened to put you in this state?'

Selwyn took the glass of rich dark wine Monty poured for him and related with expressions of dismay the unfortunate incident that had unnerved him. It was at Reading, after the interment of Mr Fanshawe and after the many family mourners had at last glutted themselves on cold beef, pressed ham, cold mutton, eggs boiled hard and sliced, port wine, brandy and bottled beer, and departed. By then it was mid-afternoon and the poor distraught widow had retired with a headache to her room to rest. Selwyn too felt exhausted and went upstairs to lie on the bed until tea time.

'I thought to doze for an hour,' he told Monty, 'but into my mind unbidden came sweet thoughts of my dearest Cecily, and how sublime was our love when I was last at her villa. The curtains were drawn to darken the room to let me rest and this served only to intensify the pictures that formed in my mind. If only you knew how I delight in Cecily!'

'I never doubted your affection for the lady,' said Monty, 'but please go on – what happened to upset you?'

'To continue then, I lay on the bed lost in a sweet reverie of my darling, when of a sudden the bedroom door opened without a knock and in came Gwendolen. She had divested herself of her widow's weeds, and put on a long dressing gown of pale mauve with a lace collar. Her face was pale from the ordeal of the morning and she said she must speak to me, seating herself on the side of the bed. Now to spare myself all the trouble of undressing and then dressing again for tea, I had removed only jacket and waistcoat – and my footwear, of course, and lay with just the bedspread over me. What it was that Gwendolen wished to discuss I never found out, for without a word she dragged the bedspread right off me and in high dudgeon accused me of fetching off in my hand!'

'And had you?' asked Monty.

'No!' Selwyn declared. 'You know that I gave Cecily my word never to allow myself to come off except in her dear presence and with her spoken permission. Do you imagine I would break a vow made in the very peak of devotion?'

'Then Gwendolen was mistaken, and you were able to refute her accusation,' said Monty, a trace of cynicism in his tone.

'Why, no, not precisely,' Selwyn murmured, his cheeks a faint pink for shame, 'the thing was this – whilst I was thinking of Cecily and how I adore her to distraction, I happened to undo my trouser buttons and slip my hand under my shirt to hold my shaft. Not that I had any intention of making myself come off – you must believe me when I assure you that was very far from my mind. In fact, it was to discourage my shaft from twitching and jerking that I held it, to quieten its movements before worse could befall.'

'Quite so,' Monty cried cheerfully, 'I understand perfectly, my dear fellow – but I wager you had the devil of a job trying to persuade Gwendolen of the purity of your intentions.'

'She refused to believe me, whatever I said,' Selwyn replied mournfully. 'She dragged up my shirt and pulled out my shaft – and when she saw that it was stiff she upbraided me fiercely for neglecting a loving sister while pleasuring myself alone.'

'Then there was only one thing for it,' said Monty, 'out with your dolly-whacker and give her a good rogering!'

'Impossible!' Selwyn replied. 'I knew that Gwendolen would be angry with me if I told her I had taken an oath to another woman, and so I did my best to explain that I felt it would be unseemly for a widow to be poked by her brother when she had a lover – to wit, yourself, Monty. I said it would be a betrayal of you, for me to roger her.'

'Good thinking!' said Monty. 'Did that do the trick?'

'Not entirely,' Selwyn answered shame-faced. 'Gwendolen threw a leg over me and knelt upright over my chest, then seized me by the hair of my head and dragged me into a sitting position – it is exceedingly painful to be dragged by the hair, I assure you. Before I could guess what she was about, she had my face pressed against her belly. *Very well*, she cried in a voice that brooked no denial, *if you won't poke me, you shall do me with your tongue, Selwyn, for I mean to be satisfied before I leave this room*!'

'My word!' said Monty breathlessly. 'How did you escape from this compromising situation?'

Selwyn's face blushed scarlet and his eyes were downcast, not meeting Monty's bold stare of enquiry. 'To tell the truth,' said he, 'I was powerless to escape from Gwendolen's demands, try as I might. She rubbed the lips of her pussy against my mouth and repeated that she would not leave before I satisfied her. Thus held captive, I thought it best to do as she wished and so get rid of her quickly. There was no question of breaking my vow to Cecily, of course, either in deed or in word or in thought for, whilst I tongued Gwendolen's pussy, I firmly fixed my thoughts on my darling Cecily.'

'I say! That's devotion far beyond the call of duty, if you ask me,' Monty exclaimed. 'How did you keep your thoughts fixed on Cecily at such a moment?'

'I recalled the sublime moments when you took me to her villa to meet her,' Selwyn declared with pride in his voice, 'and how she stood by the window with her wrapper open to let me see her divine body, while I knelt at her feet and pressed my feverish face between her thighs. You remember the scene, I am sure, though you cannot hope to understand the feelings of love that flooded through me as I thrust my tongue into the pouting lips of her darling pussy.'

'I remember it well,' said Monty, pretending a solemnity he did not feel. 'The force of your emotions in some measure found an echo in my own heart, and I too, burned for Cecily.'

He was not speaking the complete truth, for whilst Selwyn had been lapping between Cecily's parted thighs, Monty had pulled out his stiff shaft and had played briskly with it to the amusement of Cecily, who had watched what he did over Selwyn's head.

'So much the better,' said Selwyn. 'Then you will know what was in my heart when, tonguing Gwendolen, I made myself believe that it was Cecily's pussy I was licking. This brought me great comfort, since I knew myself to be faithful to Cecily, even in this perilous plight.'

'Excellently well planned, my dear chap,' said Monty. 'What then? You brought Gwendolen off and she left you in peace?'

'Something of my devotion to Cecily must have transferred itself to the merely mechanical licking I was giving Gwendolen, for she came off almost at once, shrieking out, *Oh, I'm doing it, Selwyn!* I heard her words with much relief, thinking that she would return to her own room satisfied. But not a bit of it – I had thrown more fuel onto a blazing fire! Before the spasms of her pleasure had faded away, she threw me down on my back and sat herself on my shaft and began to roger me!'

'Hm,' Monty observed thoughtfully, 'but why was your shaft stiff enough for her to get it up her? Surely you did not become aroused by being compelled to tongue her pussy? Considering that Gwendolen was outraging your sworn devotion to Cecily, I would have expected your shaft to be small and soft in dismay.'

'It was because I had been thinking of Cecily whilst forced to satisfy Gwendolen that I was aroused,' Selwyn explained in haste, 'the thought of her alone suffices to bring me up hard.'

'Quite so,' said Monty, with a grin of disbelief, 'and so you had no choice after all but to resume your old game with your sister – is that the long and short of it?'

Selwyn nodded unhappily and asked for Monty's advice as a friend on how best he could explain this unfortunate lapse to Cecily when next he saw her.

'Least said, soonest mended,' said Monty. 'Only a fool tells a woman he desires to poke that he has recently poked another. Say nothing of it and no problem will arise.'

'But that is deceitful!' Selwyn exclaimed. 'I worship Cecily body and soul – she has a right to know of anything that bears on the loving affection between us.'

'You are being unbearably selfish,' Monty said, finding a way to tease poor innocent Selwyn. 'You only pretend this devotion to Cecily – your true devotion is to yourself, I fear.'

'What do you mean?' Selwyn gasped. 'It is a matter of honour and respect to confess my renewed moral weakness to her.'

'What stuff!' said Monty enjoying the game. 'Your wretched little conscience pricks you for conceding too easily when your sister wanted a poke. May I remind you that a gentleman would say nothing of her readily assuaged little urge. To unburden yourself of a peccadillo, you are prepared to blurt all out and make Cecily the most miserable woman alive. Shame on you, sir! Keep your counsel and let Cecily's happiness remain untainted by your moral weakness!'

'I stand rebuked,' Selwyn sighed, 'thank you, my dear fellow, for your eminently sensible advice. No word of what happened to me at Reading shall pass my lips when I am with Cecily. I am glad I have a true friend like you to preserve me from my own foolishness.'

He rose from his chair, dashed a tear of honest emotion from his eye, and shook hands warmly with Monty, who recharged their glasses with his excellent malmsey.

'When may I hope for the pleasure of seeing Gwendolen in town next?' he asked Selwyn. 'I yearn to see her, as you know. Does being in mourning preclude her from shopping trips?'

'I regret that is so,' Selwyn informed him. 'Six months must pass before she embarks on any visit outside her neighbourhood – and it will be a twelvemonth before she next shows herself in town, I believe.'

'Then I shall go to Reading tomorrow,' Monty declared. 'I am burning with desire for her – and she for me, I have no doubt.'

At that, Selwyn looked distinctly shifty, shuffled his feet on the carpet and glanced away from Monty.

'Out with it!' Monty cried, recognising the signs of evasion and deception. 'What are you concealing from me? Has Gwendolen found another love?'

'Lord no!' Selwyn murmured, shame-faced, 'but she let fall something that disturbed me greatly.'

'What was that? Tell me, before I go mad!' Monty exclaimed.

'It was after she had rogered me the third or fourth

time,' Selwyn answered in a whisper, 'she climbed off my violated body and lay down beside me to sleep, her arms about me . . .'

'Third or fourth time!' Monty cried in a voice of thunder. 'Once I could have forgiven, for my darling girl must needs be frustrated without my presence to satisfy her! But three or four times? This was an orgy! You have betrayed me, and you have abused our friendship!'

'For which I humbly beg your pardon,' said Selwyn miserably, 'but it was none of my doing – I swear it! Gwendolen was afire with lust and rode me until I was drained dry!'

'Well then, what was it she said after she was satisfied?' Monty asked, calming himself by breathing deep and slow.

'She said it had been lovely to be done properly again, and not to rely on her fingers to bring herself off,' Selwyn said in an embarrassed mutter. 'Naturally, I was appalled to think my dearest sister would contemplate abusing herself in so very disgraceful a manner. Even now, I cannot wholly believe it – I am of the opinion that she was speaking of what she had avoided by making use of my person, rather than of something she had ever done to herself. Don't you agree?'

His words had cheered Monty enormously. It relieved his mind to learn that his darling girl was fingering herself to quell her natural lusts in his absence. So long as she continued in that way of doing herself he had nothing to fear from a rival. As for Selwyn – she had rogered him because he chanced to be at hand when she had the letch. It meant nothing to her, and Monty entertained no hard feelings towards the supplier of the shaft that had rubbed Gwendolen's itch.

'Of course she brings herself off at bedtime,' he said,

'all women do it if they have no man nearby with a handy shaft.'

'You imply that Gwendolen strokes her pussy to fetch herself off?' Selwyn asked, his eyebrows raised. 'That is a calumny – I don't believe it. The female nature is far more ethereal than that of mere men – I refuse to believe any woman could bring herself to so degraded an act!'

'Help yourself to another glass of wine,' said Monty, 'and I shall return in a minute. There is much for you to learn about female nature, my boy.'

Leaving Selwyn perplexed Monty went down to the kitchen and found Minnie alone, ironing Mrs Gifford's lingerie. She grinned as he came in and winked at him, holding up a pair of white cotton drawers with rose-pink ribbons threaded though the leg-hems.

'All nice and warm from the iron,' she said. 'If Mrs Gifford put them on now, they'd warm her pussy for her! She'd want you up her a time or two, to calm her down!'

Monty grinned back and thrust his hand through the forward slit of the drawers, and then through the rearward slit, until his hand touched Minnie's titties. He fondled them through her clothes and said he was entertaining Mr Courtney-Stoke upstairs and there was a gold sovereign waiting for Minnie if she would join them for half an hour and perform certain actions by way of demonstration.

'Right!' said she, throwing down the drawers. 'Mrs Gifford's out for the evening and cook's gone to church. For a sovereign in my hand you can both do me, one after the other!'

On the way upstairs Monty explained that it was not precisely a question of doing her, but of acquainting Mr Courtney-Stoke with some facts of life of which he was ignorant. By the time they reached his rooms, Minnie understood perfectly well what was wanted of her, and she found the prospect highly amusing.

Monty ensconced her in one of his armchairs and asked her to demonstrate to Mr Courtney-Stoke and himself the matter they had discussed on the stair. Minnie grinned and lay back, parted her legs and picked up her skirts to reveal her drawers. In another moment she had opened them to show her lightly fledged pussy.

'Oh, Mr Courtney-Stoke, I do believe you are blushing,' she said, seeing Selwyn's cheeks turn red. 'Don't make out you've never seen a girl's crack before.'

'He's seen one lovely dark-haired pouting pussy that I know of,' said Monty with a knowing laugh, 'though I won't put a name to it! But you may believe me Minnie, he's been up it more times than you and I have had hot dinners.'

Minnie understood very well whose hairy delight was meant and, seeing Selwyn's blushes renewed, she pulled open the lips of her pussy and stroked inside with her middle finger. The two men stared in rapture at the finger that glided expertly over her uncovered nub.

'You've a most loving touch, the way you play with yourself, Minnie,' said Monty, 'how often do you do it?'

'Why, every night in bed before I go to sleep,' she answered. 'Just like everybody else.'

Selwyn gasped loudly to hear this item of information and his face turned crimson.

'Every night in bed,' Monty repeated for Selwyn's benefit.

'That's right,' she said softly, her thin belly starting to quiver to the tremors of pleasure she was sending through it.

'And you say that every girl does the same – and every

woman, too – she plays with her pussy before she falls asleep?'

'Right you are,' Minnie breathed, her thighs straining wider apart as the sensations of delight grew stronger in her belly.

'Well, I am sure that naughty girls like you rub your pussy off in bed, but surely you don't expect this gentleman and me to believe that ladies of breeding and refinement also handle themselves in this low way?' Monty objected, winking at her.

'Why ever not?' she retorted. 'A pussy's only made of flesh and blood – every one of them's got an itch that wants rubbing regular, and if there's no husband to ease it with his dolly-whacker, it gets done by hand, duchess or kitchen-maid.'

By this time Minnie was far advanced along the pathway that leads to climactic bliss. With the fingers of one hand she held wide the pink lips of her slit, and with the joined fingers of the other she caressed the slippery rose-pink bud that was exposed. She watched the two men through half-closed eyes, and they gaped open-mouthed and red-faced at what she was doing to herself.

'Oh, oh, oh!' she exclaimed suddenly, and her legs thrashed about as she brought herself off in quick spasms.

'By George!' said Monty, 'the little slut's given me a hard she'll have to take care of!'

With that, he threw himself to his knees between Minnie's open legs, and ripped his trouser buttons open with shaking and desperate hands. His shaft leapt out the moment his shirt-front was raised and, without a pause, he plunged six inches of hard gristle into her wet pussy and rogered away for dear life.

'My word!' Selwyn exclaimed, his eyes bulging from

his head, 'how can you do such a thing, Monty? What will Mrs Gifford say if she finds out you have taken advantage of her servant! She will tell you to leave the house at once!'

'Fiddlesticks!' Monty gasped 'Do you think this is the first time I've had Minnie? She's a dear girl, always willing to oblige for a shilling or two, and she enjoys a good poke!'

'No mistake about that!' Minnie gurgled, kicking up her legs either side of Monty as he plunged in and out. 'Give it to me hot and strong, sir!'

In six more strokes Monty reached the acme of sensation and squirted his lust into her quaking belly. She squealed joyfully and humped her belly under him, to extract the very last drop.

'There!' said he with a sigh of content. 'That was a first-rate poke.'

He raised himself from the floor and flopped down beside Minnie, who was lying with her legs spread and a foolish smile of satisfaction on her plain face.

'How about you, my dear chap,' Monty said to Selwyn. 'Is not your own shaft hard-on and ready to roger her? Indeed it is – I can see the bulge down your trouser-leg from here. Get it out and make use of this lovely wet pussy here at your disposal.'

'I cannot!' Selwyn groaned. 'I have given my word to a lady you know of, whose name I dare not mention in the presence of a third party. She alone may release my tension!'

Monty rested an arm over Minnie's thigh to slip his fingers between the lips of her pussy and stroke her bud slowly.

'We are men of the world, Selwyn,' said he. 'Ladies need to be cosseted and fussed over and flattered and rogered – but no man but a fool thinks that promises given with a standing shaft are meant to be kept. The lady you worship will be no worse for our private amusements so long as she never learns of them. Throw off this pious simpering attitude and make the most of what is offered to you.'

Whether it was the force of Monty's words that converted his primness, or the sight of Monty's fingers playing in Minnie's pussy, or her shrieks of bliss as she came off again, Selwyn rose from his chair and knelt between the girl's legs.

'Good man!' Monty encouraged him, taking his hand away from Minnie's thighs. 'Slip your shaft up her and give her a good poke!'

Blushing furiously, Selwyn undid his trousers and hoisted his shirt, to let his impressively large shaft appear.

'My stars!' Minnie exclaimed. 'Look at the size of that! I want it up me!'

'This is against my better judgment,' Selwyn sighed, pausing with his leaping shaft in his hand. 'You are urging me to do a deed I have promised not to do, save with one beloved person.'

'If I recall rightly,' said Monty, 'the promise you gave was not to fetch off in any other woman's pussy. Well then – there is no problem at all here to vex us. Give Minnie a feel of what she is dying for – push it up her. But take care not to fetch off, and then you will have kept your solemn word.'

'Dare I?' Selwyn murmured, as if to himself, staring all the while at Minnie's open wet slit.

'Go on, stick it up me,' Minnie urged him. 'I want to feel it in my belly.'

'It would be impolite to refuse a request so easily

granted,' Selwyn murmured. 'You shall have your wish, Minnie, if only for a moment or two.'

By an act of will Monty kept himself from grinning at this fine example of self-deception. He stared in fascination to see Selwyn set the head of his mighty shaft to the mark and slowly slide its eight-inch length into Minnie.

'Oh my!' said she, her eyes closing in rapture, 'I've never been so full up before!'

'You are a gentleman, Selwyn,' Monty exclaimed, suppressing his laughter, 'you have made the girl happy at no great effort. Stay in her a while and give her a memory to cherish forever.'

'That would be most unwise,' Selwyn gasped, his face becoming redder and redder. 'You are fully aware of my moral weakness – there is no telling to what depths of folly I might sink if I relaxed for one instant the self-control I have learnt from the dear friend you know of.'

'I am astonished at how far you have progressed in so short a time,' said Monty. 'The lady in question seems to have taught you most efficaciously to restrain your natural impulses. You have my congratulations. How long are you now able to contain yourself in this highly commendable way?'

'With my dear teacher I have endured the strongest sensations of sensuality for almost ten minutes before being compelled to surrender my essence,' said Selwyn, his body trembling.

All this time they were conversing, Minnie had been wriggling her bottom surreptitiously on the chair cushion, to transmit to the embedded shaft ripples of pleasure through the clinging flesh of her pussy. Of this Selwyn was unaware, being occupied with his conversation and with the thoughts of Cecily that were stirred by it. The spasm when it came was therefore surprising to him.

'Oh no!' he gasped. 'I will not!'

But he had no choice. His elixir was spurting freely, and in his delirium he rammed in and out of Minnie's pussy as if he would split her asunder.

'You're coming off!' she cried. 'It feels like a fountain inside me!'

CHAPTER 13
Grace Pays a Visit

Parted from his darling Gwendolen by the cruel necessities of the polite conventions, Monty had no recourse for his burning desire other than to summon up in his mind his fond memories of when last she was with him. It had been on her last visit to town, when she had come direct to Seymour Place by cab from the railway station and they had passed the whole day together in bed enjoying the sweets of love.

In this mood of gallant frustration that she was not now with him to repeat their joys, Monty wrote to her a letter in which he expressed his longings for her beautiful person, and he gave ardent promises of rapture without end when next they were with each other. A hot tear of love fell to the page whilst he wrote of his passion, and his hard-on shaft throbbed in his trousers.

The hour was a little after ten in the morning, Mrs Gifford had gone to the market to purchase green vegetables and taken Minnie with her to carry the shopping basket. There was nothing for it, Monty concluded as he sealed up his letter, but to take out One-Eyed Jack and ease his heavy burden of desire by hand. Yet even as his hand fell to his trouser buttons and his eager shaft bounded in anticipation, he heard a light tap at his sitting-room door and went to investigate, walking as stiffly and awkwardly as if he had a rolled umbrella under his shirt.

His visitor was, he was surprised to see, his sister Grace. She wore a new frock of chocolate brown with a green-braided jacket to match and a bonnet with artificial flowers. Monty kissed her on both cheeks and drew her into his cosy sitting room to a seat on the sofa. She removed her bonnet and gloves and began a lengthy explanation of needing to visit an Oxford Street store for something or other and, being so close to his dwelling, she had decided to drop in for a moment on her dear brother.

Monty waved away her explanations, took her hand and placed it over the bulge in his trousers.

'No excuses, Grace,' said he with a smile, 'tell me truly why you came here this morning.'

Her cheeks reddened a little at his very open approach, but she took her courage in both hands and spoke out.

'Some words you spoke to me when you were last at Putney have been running in my mind ever since,' said she, a tremor in her voice betraying her nervousness. 'You claimed that we had the same hot nature, you and I. You were pleased to inform me that it was my duty to this nature to let you satisfy me as often as possible. Do you deny your words?'

'Lord no!' Monty sighed, and his shaft jumped underneath her hand. 'That was the day I poked you six times before tea.'

'Yes,' Grace whispered, her eyes modestly downcast and her cheeks a pretty pink, 'and perhaps you may also recall that I enquired of you if a brother had any right to make use of his sister in so lustful a manner.'

'I say now what I said then,' Monty replied. 'Only by obeying the urges of our nature do we find happiness. Under your hand lies all the proof required to convince you of my right to poke you whenever I choose – a stiff shaft. Do you still doubt me?'

'No,' said Grace, a trifle hesitantly, but with sincerity in her tone, 'I have come here to tell you that I have given much thought to your claims and I accept them completely. It is my duty to submit myself to you in all things, for I am persuaded now that a brother must take precedence over a husband. You may satisfy me whenever you will, dearest Monty.'

With that, she undid his trouser buttons from top to bottom, pulled his shirt up to his belly and clasped his hot and hard shaft in her hand. With a grin of understanding, Monty spread his legs apart and she fingered One-Eyed Jack lovingly. Monty sighed with delight at the pleasurable sensations and he soon had her skirts and petticoats up over her knees, her legs apart and his hand in her drawers. His deft fingers played lightly over her curly-haired pussy and teased the soft lips, to coax them into opening themselves.

'How delicious a touch you have!' Monty gasped. 'For one who has never been allowed to handle her husband's shaft, you have learned the skill with commendable speed!'

'The skill is yours, dearest, in teaching me,' said Grace, a soft gleam of affection in her eyes.

While they were thus pleasantly engaged in provoking sensual pleasure by feeling each other's privities, Monty was nothing loth to explore his own emotions and motives. To this end, by a feat of imagination, he pretended to himself that the parted thighs and bush of brown curls that lay under his hand were not his sister's, but dearest Gwendolen's.

By dint of closing his eyes tight, he was able very nearly to deceive himself, and he found that his pleasure was greatly augmented by this flight of fantasy. It was not that he would have rather had Gwendolen to feel than Grace – that was not the point at all. It went without saying that because he loved his darling Gwendolen to distraction there was the most tremendous delight in feeling her pussy and then poking her. That aside, he had ascertained at Putney that it was also a source of very great delight to finger Grace and then roger her.

By the exercise of his imagination, it was as if he had both of his dear charmers to play with at the same time, and when he spoke he was not altogether sure to which lady his words were addressed – whether Gwendolen or Grace. Not that it made much difference, for words had ceased to be of any importance in the welter of emotion that swirled through him and through her.

In this delicious way and by these exciting means, Monty came to an understanding of what moved him. At Putney, on the sofa, he had shot his sticky essence up Grace's pussy and given her to experience spasms of true bliss until she collapsed under him of exhaustion. Lying in contentment on her belly, he had at that time drawn the conclusion that the sensations of rogering a sister were heavenly in the extreme – unquestionably far more delicious than with any other woman he had poked, including his darling Gwendolen!

This conclusion seemed to him strange. Fond as he was of his sister, she could not match Gwendolen in the beauty of her face and figure. Neither she nor Gwendolen could match Cecily for sheer delicious lustfulness, and none of the three could match thin-shanked Minnie in lewdness. Nor could any of the foursome – Grace, Gwendolen,

Cecily or Minnie – hold a candle to Hannah Gifford in her insatiable enthusiasm for sensuality.

What then was a chap to make of all this? Only this, Monty decided – that the most delightful woman in the world was the one he happened to be rogering at any given time, whether that was any one of his four darlings, or little Miss Emmy at Mrs Lee's poking academy, or even a buttered bun up against a wall behind Paddington station, The best pussy in the world was the one you were up at the time.

This abstruse point of philosophy settled at last, Monty gave himself up to the thrills running through him. Grace in all her willingness to please him rubbed her clasped hand up and down his straining shaft. His heart beat faster to feel the moment coming ever closer when his hot elixir would spurt from him in hard spasms of ecstasy. In the very nick of time he restrained Grace's hand by seizing her wrist.

'Dearest girl!' he gasped out, 'let us not waste this first precious emission – I mean to fetch off in your pussy, not in your hand – and you shall shriek in delight to feel me gushing into you!'

She sighed tremulously to hear his bold words and her pussy became wetter yet to his touch. To impress upon his dearest sister the strength and power of his manhood, Monty stood up, gathered her in his arms, and carried her into his bedroom. He deposited her on her back on the bed and sat beside her on the edge, leaning over to smile into her eyes, while his ever-busy hands felt up under her clothes. Grace tried to return his burning gaze, but some of her self-assurance had ebbed away now she found herself on a bed with her brother and her eyes closed in modesty when he put his fingers into her drawers to stroke her pussy again.

This did not content him for long, and Grace gave a nervous little laugh as he untied the string of her drawers and pulled them down her legs and cast them aside. She gasped when he took her hand and pressed it to his hard-swollen implement. She held it in the palm of her hand and it throbbed under her touch, until her eyes grew round at the wonder of it. She grasped the quivering length firmly again, as she had in the sitting room, and stroked it up and down.

Her clothes were turned up to her waist as she lay, her head on the pillow, so that Monty could lean over and press a kiss on her soft bare belly. Emboldened by the open affection he displayed, Grace opened her eyes and saw that his handsome face was flushed with powerful emotion, and that his eyes gleamed brightly while he stared at her uncovered pussy. Then in a sudden movement his face was between her naked thighs and his hot tongue lapped at her in a deliberate repetition of the sweet caress that had banished all her fears and doubts when at Putney he had first done this to her, to persuade her to let him roger her fully.

'Dearest Monty . . .' she whispered, her backside wriggling for joy on the bedspread.

His warm tongue penetrated her, licking and pulsating, until it found her hidden button. At that lewdest and most intimate of touches, Grace shrieked faintly and came off at once. Monty laughed to see how intensely he had moved her with so slight a caress and flung himself between her legs and over her belly. A moment later she felt his hard shaft thrust into her, prying her wet flesh open to reach deep into her belly.

'O, yes . . .' she moaned, and jerked her loins up and down in a frenzy of desire, working at his embedded shaft to make it gush out its elixir into her.

'Yes, Grace my dearest girl!' Monty gasped i response, and plunged up and down in short fast thrusts. Both felt the tides of lust rising ever higher, threatening to overflow the bounds and drown them in the sensations of pleasure. Grace pressed her mouth to Monty's in a frantic kiss, and his body jerked wildly to the sudden gush of his essence into her wet pussy.

'Monty, Monty!' she cried, to each throb of his shaft inside her. 'That's lovely, Monty – I can't stop coming off!'

For fully a minute she shuddered and moaned beneath him, even though One-Eyed Jack had long ceased to spurt, before she was satisfied and lay in a half-swooning limpness, sighing in deep satisfaction.

When she had sufficiently recovered herself to have the power of speech restored, she threw her arms about Monty and told him certain things which had come into her mind.

'Oh Monty – when at Putney I felt you kiss my pussy and tongue it, it was so very delightful that I knew nothing like it! To think I have reached the age of twenty-eight years and have been a wife for five years, and never until you did it to me last week had I any inkling that this exquisite pleasure existed and could be within my reach!'

From which Monty deduced that his sister's husband had been decidedly lax in his attentions to her. But then, according to Grace's account of her marital connections, only on the rarest of occasions did Arthur put his shaft up her.

'I must return the compliment,' Grace continued. 'Forgive me if I am clumsy at this, Monty, but this will be the first time I have tried to do it.'

As she was speaking, her ardent gaze was fixed on his

shaft, which lay limply in the gaping opening of his trousers. She took it in her hand, marvelling at its dwindled size and eager to restore it to its manly six-inch length. Whilst engaged in raising it to its former magnificence, she asked a question.

'Monty, my dear – when I first entered your sitting room this morning, your shaft was already stiff inside your trousers. Why was this – won't you tell me? Were you perhaps thinking about the person with whom you are in love, your dearest Gwendolen?'

'Clever girl,' murmured Monty, watching his shaft growing in Grace's hand. 'To be frank with you, as you deserve of me, my longing for Gwendolen was hot upon me. I was missing her dear presence and yearning to take her in my arms.'

'Ah, then there is no doubt left that you have had her,' said Grace, 'though you insisted to me that you have not yet had the enjoyment of her body. That I refuse to believe, in view of the evidence of your shaft being hard-on when you thought of her.'

'I cannot tell a lie,' said Monty, who told lies as often as it suited him to do so, 'I have visited her at Reading and she allowed me the inestimable privilege of rogering her! I dream every night of that divine experience! But cruel Fate keeps us apart – Gwendolen has suffered a bereavement in the family and cannot receive me at home, or travel to London.'

'My poor boy!' Grace murmured in sympathy, her hand sliding up and down his now hard-on shaft. 'You dream of her in bed, do you say? Then you must wake each morning with a sticky nightshirt, I fear. Let me comfort your dear lonely shaft!'

She brought her face down to it, and in another instant her tongue had darted out to touch the purple head which had grown shiny with passion. Monty sighed when she drew it well into her mouth, holding it with her lips whilst her tongue lapped at it briskly. To further Grace's sentimental education, he twisted himself about on the bed until his head was between her bared thighs and explained to her that this was the sixty-nine position.

Grace knew nothing of such refinements, of course, for Arthur had shown her but the one position for marital love, and that not often. Nevertheless, strange though it seemed to her at the beginning, she soon took to having her pussy licked while she sucked at Monty's shaft. Their spasm came together, he gushing his thick juice into her mouth, his tongue thrust deep into her to bring her off boldly.

Afterwards they at last undressed, Monty down to his shirt, Grace down to her chemise, and lay in each other's arms to rest a while from their delightful efforts and gather their strength to renew them. Monty raised with his sister the matter of her husband's shortcomings in the bedroom, and if it had always been so with him. For instance, during their long courtship and year-long engagement to be married, had Arthur made the least attempt to feel her titties or put a hand up her clothes?

'Never once,' said Grace sadly. 'On my bridal night I was a virgin, as is proper, but Arthur had not even tried to give my bosom a feel through my clothes. But for one incident that I myself precipitated, I would have judged him a neuter and with regret broken off the engagement.'

'Tell me of this incident,' Monty pleaded, his hand under her chemise to stroke her warm belly. 'What did you do to him?'

'Promise not to laugh at me,' said Grace. 'It was a somewhat shameful stratagem to find out if Arthur was at all susceptible to female charm. Soon after our engagement was announced, and I had enjoyed no more than a chaste kiss or two on the cheek from my new fiance, we were staying with his parents in Wimbledon. One sunny afternoon, when Mr and Mrs Austin had gone out in the carriage to visit friends . . .'

'You seized the Heaven-sent opportunity and invited Arthur to your room, where he found you lying on the bed clad only in a chemise and drawers!' Monty interrupted her.

'You're quite wrong,' said Grace. 'Arthur challenged me to a game of croquet on the lawn. I would happily have sat indoors and canoodled with him, but there we were, knocking silly balls about on the grass. A thought came into my mind, and at once I acted upon it! When my turn came next to play, I swung my mallet hard at the ball, and let it slip as if by accident from my hands. It flew through the air and stuck Arthur a blow, as I had intended, where his legs join.'

'By George!' Monty exclaimed. 'You hit him in the pompoms with a croquet mallet! But this would incapacitate him!'

''It did,' Grace agreed. 'By the aid of the gardener and cook we got him upstairs to his bed, where he lay moaning. I sent the gardener for the family doctor, and bade the cook bring me a bowl of warm water and some towels.'

'Great Heavens – surely you were not so audacious as to attend to his pompoms!' said Monty with a grin.

'He fussed and said how improper it was when I had the cook unbutton his trousers and pull them down his legs, but against my plea of medical emergency he had no defence and he was too much in discomfort to resist strongly. I wrung out a towel in warm water, turned up his shirt front and laid it over his . . . pompoms, as you call them. Arthur blushed scarlet to think I'd seen his shaft.'

'And the cook too,' said Monty.

'The impertinent creature was staring and grinning openly at this revelation of Arthur's person. Very soon it began to stand hard under the towel, which I removed to dip again in the warm water, so obtaining a full view of his endowment.'

'I would have given ten guineas to witness the discomfiture of Arthur Austin!' cried Monty. 'What then, dear Grace?'

'His shaft began to tremble after a time, and from this I was able to form the guess that his crisis was near. I sent the cook downstairs for more warm water and touched my hand to the wet towel over dear Arthur's twitching shaft, *to see that the water was not yet too cold* I told him. Then I slipped my hand under it for a moment, *to make sure that it did not lie heavily on his bruising*, I explained. Purely by accident my hand made contact with a length of hard and twitching flesh – I gasped – Arthur moaned – his legs shook! I felt a warm gushing over my hand and knew that he was coming off. This gave me an assurance that he would be properly capable of the act of love when we were married. As indeed he is, although he chooses to use this ability all too seldom.'

'My, my!' said Monty. 'I would not have thought you capable of so devious a scheme, dear Grace.'

'Now, I have confessed to you the full extent of my youthful transgressions, and in comparison with yours they are nothing,' she answered, her hand under his shirt to rub his shaft slowly, 'it is your turn to disclose the follies of your youth to me. Did you ever, during the years when we were growing up, ever take a fancy toward me?'

'Lord yes!' he exclaimed. 'Well I remember an afternoon when Mama had taken you out somewhere and Papa was dozing under his newspaper in the garden – I stole into your room and opened the wardrobe to feel your frocks and press them to my face to catch the faintest trace of the warm fragrance of your body. My shaft stood hard-on in my trousers and, greatly daring, I took from the laundry basket a chemise and a pair of drawers you had worn the previous day. I laid the chemise on your bed, and slipped the drawers into it, as if you were wearing both and lying on your back for me.'

Grace was blushing crimson to hear how her garments had been made use of, years before. She jerked fiercely at Monty's stiff shaft and squeezed it hard as if to crush it in her palm.

'I let down my trousers and rolled up my shirt, turned back the chemise and rested my bare belly on your drawers,' Monty continued in a voice that trembled with emotion, 'I slid my shaft into the slit of the drawers, pretending to myself that it was your virgin pussy I was penetrating.'

'Oh Monty – stroke it now!' Grace cried, 'Your words have set me on fire and I must come off!'

His fingers were in her wet pussy at once, to tease her warm and swollen bud while he completed for her the tale of his use of her undergarments long ago for his pleasure.

'I lay face down on the bed,' said he, 'sliding my shaft into the slit of your drawers so that it rubbed on the inside. I was in Heaven, my mind overflowing with pictures of you, my dearest Grace, lying beneath me to receive my rogering. Then in gushes of sheer bliss I shot my hot sap into your drawers with such feelings of delight as if I'd shot it up your maidenly pussy.'

'Oh, Monty!' Grace sighed, her legs shaking as her emotions grew ever stronger under the stimulus of his fingers fluttering inside her. 'To think you did me in your mind and I never knew of your interest in me!'

'It was more than in my mind,' said he, 'it was also in the drawers you had worn, for when I returned them to the laundry basket they were soaked through with my emission.'

'Oh, Monty . . .' Grace said again, her voice hardly audible now that she was on the brink of coming off, 'I'm glad it was nice for you . . .'

'So nice that I repeated it every time you were out and I had the chance to creep into your room, my dearest girl,' he told her. 'Over the years I rogered every pair of drawers you ever wore and left the white stains of my passion on them.'

'Oh!' she shrieked, coming off at last, and her belly bucked upwards against his busy hand.

When she was calm again, he rolled her onto her back and lay half over her while he kissed her face fondly, and asked if she too brought herself off with her fingers when she was a girl. She blushed and would not give him an answer, from which he was certain that she did. With a grin, he reached under the pillow her head lay on and brought out the book he had left there the night before. Undoubtedly Minnie had seen it when she made the bed that morning, and perhaps read a little of it.

'What is your bedtime reading?' asked Grace in all innocence of the existence of literature such as this.

'A story of schoolgirls,' said Monty with a laugh. 'I shall read a short passage of it to you, dear Grace, for it makes the point for me. Listen to this:

Jennifer flinched away from the stern look of authority on the coldly beautiful face of Miss Harriet, who stood glaring at a sheet of drawing paper she held in her hand.

'Explain this if you can!' Harriet cried, flinging the paper at the trembling girl. 'Is this your vile work? Answer me!'

It was one of the sketches Jennifer had made from life that morning outdoors. For her model she had taken the gardener's assistant, Dickie, a fair-haired lad. Her sketch depicted him in the vegetable garden, sitting on an upended wheelbarrow. Jennifer was talented with her pencil and it was a good likeness. The offence lay in that Dickie was shown with a hand thrust under his gardener's apron and a blissful smile on his face.

'Well?' Harriet demanded ruthlessly. 'Have you lost your tongue, Miss? Do you deny that this obscene sketch is your own work? Speak – I will have an answer.'

'The sketch is mine,' Jennifer admitted in a quavering voice, her pretty face flushing bright scarlet with shame.

'And what is this boy doing?' Harriet asked in an ice-cold voice. 'Why is his hand under his apron in that disgusting way? What is he doing to himself?'

'I don't know, Miss Harriet,' said the unhappy girl. 'When he sat like that for me to draw I thought that he was scratching himself. I could see his hand moving under the apron.'

'Do not play the innocent with me!' Harriet said harshly. 'I have been in charge of girls like you long enough to become acquainted with their tricks and schemes. Confess it now – you provoked Dickie to handle his private parts. Your sketch shows him at the very moment of sensual spasm, when he fetched off in his trousers!'

Jennifer thought she would faint away with shame. She stared at Miss Harriet, her pale lips moving but no words emerging.

'I thought as much!' said Miss Harriet, a cruel smile on her face. 'You are ashamed now that you have been caught out! And well you might be! Explain to me, if you can, how you came to be acquainted with the habit of self-gratification in boys?'

Jennifer burst into tears and hid her face in her hands.

'You understand the shocking gravity of your offence,' said Miss Harriet, 'and you well know the punishment for it. Bend over and raise your clothes behind.'

Terror stilled Jennifer's sobs, but she had no thought of not obeying the stern school mistress. She bent forward and with trembling hands lifted her frock.

'Untie the string of your drawers and drop them to your ankles,' was the next command of Miss Harriet. Jennifer did as she was told, so baring the soft round cheeks of her bottom for chastisement.

'Ten of the best!' cried the tormentor, and her flat whale-bone implement thrashed across Jennifer's tender cheeks making her scream for mercy.

When it was over, she ordered Jennifer to turn and face her, and get down on her knees. The chastened girl's face blushed as red as her bottom to observe that Miss Harriet had raised her own clothes to her waist, to expose her soft white drawers and stockings. With a firm hand she opened wide the slit and showed to the kneeling girl, without the least evidence of modesty or shame, her large and dark-haired pussy.

'It is my duty to make sure you understand properly what is involved in the act of self-gratification,' said Miss Harriet, her voice animated as her fingers prised open the soft lips of her own plump pussy. 'Of the habits of boys there is nothing to be said, but what young ladies do to themselves in private is of the greatest importance. Observe where I am touching with my finger, Jennifer,

this is the most sensitive spot of my person – are you aware of that?'

'I beg you, Miss Harriet, do not continue further!' Jennifer exclaimed, her face redder than ever.

'Do not be insolent!' said Miss Harriet, pulling open wider yet the lips of her pussy. 'Before our lesson is finished you will be thoroughly familiar with the many possibilities and the delights of sensuality. Put your tongue to the rosebud I have bared for you and let me feel you lick it.'

Monty broke off his reading, delighted to see Grace had gone a dark red in the face with her emotions. Her belly was quaking under her thin chemise, and her bosom rose and fell rapidly to her breathing. She implored him to lie on her and poke her hard to quell the storm of furious passion he had raised in her with his lewd book. He smiled at her in the most charming way, and told her that if things were that desperate with her, then she must relieve herself with her fingers.

'No!' she exclaimed, sounding as if she would swoon at the immodesty of his suggestion.

To encourage her, Monty slid off the bed, pulled her round on it until her legs dangled over the side towards him, then turned up her chemise above her titties. He stood between her knees, and pulled his shirt over his head, so that Grace imagined that he had relented and spread her legs wider to be mounted. With a chuckle, Monty took his stiff six inches in his clasping hand, and rubbed up and down in a brisk rhythm.

'Ah, you beast!' Grace moaned, her head rolling from side to side on the bed. 'To subject me to this indignity! But I have no power to restrain myself . . .'

Monty grinned down at her, his hand sliding up and down to see her pull open the wet lips of her pussy, to expose her firm nub and flick her fingers over it. In this manner they played with themselves, she staring at his straining shaft while he manipulated it, and he staring at her open pussy as she stroked it with nervous flicks.

'Monty – you beast – why didn't you make me do this before?' she gasped. 'In the past I've only done it alone, with feelings of shame – I had no idea that it would be so delicious to do it for you! The sensations are heavenly – now I know that I shall do it for you very often while you stand and watch me!'

'And I love to watch you playing with yourself while you see me playing with myself,' he responded eagerly, his hand moving all the faster as the crisis approached.

Only moments later, his creamy essence spurted out in a long curve over her, splashing on her pulsating belly and trickling down her sides in warm rivulets. Grace squealed in delight to watch the throbbing gushes, and feel the wetness on her skin, and with quick fingers rubbing in her slippery pussy she came off to a convulsive climax of lust.

CHAPTER 14
An Old Friend Reappears

By the first post on Thursday morning there arrived for Monty two letters, one of them with a Reading postmark and the other with a London mark. They were waiting for him on his breakfast table when he rose, propped against the toast rack. Naturally, it was the one from Reading that Monty's eager hand seized upon first, to have news at last of his beloved Gwendolen. It was contained in a thick square envelope, which he pressed a score of times to his lips in devotion, before using the butter knife to open it.

The letter in Gwendolen's firm, round and elegant handwriting was brief, but it stirred his deepest emotions.

My dearest boy,

A thousand, thousand thanks for your darling letter! You ask if I remember the joy and transport of being in your arms – ah, how it torments me by day and by night that I am prevented from enjoying that dear bliss! My charms, such as they are, are for you, darling Monty, and never can there be another since I have tasted with you the utmost delight that humankind may aspire to this side of Heaven! Only one other has ever penetrated to the innermost portion of my person – Selwyn – and of him you know all there is to know! As for my late husband Elliot, he never showed any interest in the treasure of mine that inspired your letter to me, but preferred a meaner route to his pleasure! I burn with impatience for the time when I shall be reunited with my dearest, and promise you faithfully that you shall not rise from the bed where we plight our troth until your manly shaft will no longer stand hard-on, and I lie prostrate and swooning before you from your mighty ravishing! May it be soon!

Your own loving Gwendolen

Secured to a bottom corner of the letter by a pin was a small dark-brown curl of hair. Monty caressed it with a fingertip, his heart pounding in his breast for joy that his darling girl had thought to send him this token of her love and affection – a curl clipped from her warm pussy! The thought flung him into so profound a reverie of love and devotion that his shaft stood thick and swollen and strong under his dressing gown, it being Monty's custom to postpone dressing until after his breakfast.

While he raised the letter to his lips and pressed a delicate kiss to Gwendolen's pussy curl, Monty slipped his other hand in his dressing gown and grasped his throbbing shaft through the thin material of his nightshirt. He sighed in joy when he felt how long and hard One-Eyed Jack had grown – and with every good reason, for Gwendolen in her letter was promising him hours of bliss when they met again! Ah, the ecstasy that would be his – lying on her bare belly, to fill her pretty pink slit to overflowing!

Sitting at the breakfast table, where the porridge was going cold under its cover, Monty crushed the letter to his lips and trembled through all his limbs with powerful emotion. One-Eyed Jack jumped in his hand, and Monty pulled his nightshirt up to his waist. His clasped hand gripped One-Eyed Jack tightly while he addressed him in terms of affection and optimism:

'Well may you stand hard and twitch,' said Monty, staring at the uncovered purple head of his shaft, 'for there are words of hope and encouragement for us from our darling Gwendolen – and more than words! Here is a silky little curl that grew on the pussy you love! What do you think of that, eh?'

One-Eyed Jack jumped for joy in Monty's grasp, demonstrating his approval very clearly. Monty's hand slid up and down the straining shaft, a vision of Gwendolen in his mind's eye – dear Gwendolen naked on a bed, lying on her back with her legs apart to make him welcome in that plump dark-haired pussy of hers.

'She misses you,' Monty sighed to his straining shaft, 'she longs to feel your solid six inches inside her. She yearns for your hot gush of love in her pussy! You may feel very proud of yourself that so beautiful a charmer as Gwendolen takes true delight in being rogered by you.'

Under the influence of Monty's affectionate fondling his hot shaft had grown to its fullest size and thickness and Monty smiled down at it in warm regard.

'Tell me what you feel for her,' he requested One-Eyed Jack. 'The same devotion as I do, I am sure, coupled with lust and a tireless desire to roger her.'

His enquiry was answered without delay. One-Eyed Jack bounded furiously and hurled a raging flood of passion into the air.

'Ah, yes!' Monty gasped, to the spurting of his shaft. 'You adore her and you display the manner of your adoration to me in the most unmistakable manner! So be it then – this is what you shall do to Gwendolen the instant she and I are reunited – I give you my word!'

During the time that One-Eyed Jack was calming himself after his demonstration of passion, Monty spoke to him in terms of warm comradeship, promising him most faithfully that he should soon enjoy all the delights of Gwendolen's beautiful body – not only her dark-haired pussy but also the bliss of fetching off up between her soft titties, and in her hot mouth, under her delicate armpits, and in various other delicious parts of her person. One-Eyed Jack heard this with great satisfaction, and after a twitch or two to show his appreciation, he curled up to dream sweetly of the delights in store until the moment came for him to unleash his strength yet again.

Only when his shaft had reverted to limpness and contentment did Monty think to open the second letter that lay on his table. He feared it might be a bill from his tailor or wine merchant, but it proved to be far more interesting than that. The envelope contained the briefest of notes – only two lines of writing – below which there stood for signature but a pair of initials.

Monty – I shall wait for you at three o'clock at Mrs Lee's and have much to tell. Keep my secret – tell no one of this!

NC

There could be no doubt who had sent this message – Naunton Cox, whom Monty thought to be taking refuge in Paris from the misfortunes that had befallen him for becoming interested in a Church of England vicar's wife on a train to town – a journey which had ended at Clapham Junction Station when he was caught in the very act of coming off in her hand. Evidently he had returned in secret to London. It would be a pleasure to see the dear fellow and hear of his adventures amongst the Frenchies.

The setting of the meeting place at Mrs Gladys Lee's in Margaret Street turned Monty's thoughts unerringly towards his favourite occupant of that house – namely, dear Miss Emmy, the seventeen-year-old with golden hair and lovely titties. So long did his reverie dwell upon her and how well he had rogered her at their last meeting, that Monty's shaft awoke again and stood hard-on, in spite of its recent tribute to darling Gwendolen.

It was Mrs Lee's very well-known custom to open her house to gentlemen visitors with guineas in their pocket at two o'clock each afternoon, thus affording to herself and the young women under her protection the whole of the morning to themselves. If any lecherous gentlemen required the use of a female commodity before lunch then he must look for it elsewhere and not in Margaret Street. In dire necessity he could take a hansom cab to Covent Garden market, where the flower girls made themselves available from four in the morning.

There was nothing refined about them, and who could expect it for the shilling or two they charged? Not that a man in urgent need is fussy, and the market girls would stand readily against a wall and raise their bedraggled skirts to bare a pussy for the accommodation of a paying guest. Nor were the men who went to Covent Garden for relief of their letch of good class, or so said Mrs Lee, whose considered opinion it was that a gentleman did not require female service before noon.

'I see,' said Monty, when she explained her views to him over a glass of brandy in her parlour, 'and to what do you attribute this, if I may enquire?'

'In society,' said Mrs Lee, 'a gentleman rises early and goes out to ride in the park. He has no time to take an interest in poking until later in the day.'

'But it is a well-known physiological fact,' Monty objected, 'that a gentleman wakes in the morning with a hard-on stand. It cannot be dismissed as of no significance, as you would appear to do. For the married there is no problem in this – he simply rolls on top of his dear wife as she lies sleeping beside him, and wakes her with a morning poke. The unmarried have no such useful recourse to hand – what are they to do?'

'You have answered your own question,' said Mrs Lee with a coarse chuckle, 'their remedy is readily to hand. They make use of their own five fingers, or summon a servant to perform the task for them.'

'Quite so,' said Monty, who had paid Minnie to bring relief to his stiffness on many a morning, 'a willing maid-servant is a boon and a blessing.'

'And the ruination of my business!' Mrs Lee retorted. 'Maid servants are in general stupid and soon find themselves with a big belly and are turned out in the streets without a reference and in disgrace. The titled gentlemen who honour my house with their presence do not demean themselves to poke servant girls, that I can assure you of, Mr Standish.'

'But you said a moment ago that a servant is summoned to the bedside to unburden them of the morning stand!' said Monty.

'I meant their valet,' she replied. 'A gentleman's gentleman is trained in the art of slipping a hand into the bed to bring off his master with a delicate touch in the early morning, even before he is fully awake and ready for his tea. I fear you are not acquainted with the customs of the upper classes.'

'I confess that I am not,' said Monty, 'and to be truthful, I am surprised by what you have told me. Is this general, do you suppose, or is it the whim of one individual you know of?'

'I am given to understand that it is universally in vogue in good society,' Mrs Lee replied, 'and I have heard this from the lips of three lords, a marquis and a duke, who have honoured my girls. Naturally, the valet wears white cotton gloves when he performs this duty, in order that the aristocratic shaft is not in contact with common flesh.'

'Except when it rogers your girls,' Monty pointed out.

'That is different,' said Mrs Lee, 'for in the conjunction of shaft and pussy, there are no distinctions made of aristocratic and common. In the act itself all are considered to be of equal worth, as when our ancestor Adam rogered Eve, before divisions of class had arisen.'

'This is all most interesting,' said Monty, 'and I am your debtor for enlightening me as to the daily duties of valets in noble households. Now, if we may reach our usual arrangement about fee, I will take my leave and go upstairs to present my compliments to Miss Emmy.'

He had arrived at Mrs Lee's house not at three o'clock, as he had been bidden by Naunton Cox, but immediately the front door was opened to visitors, at two. His intention was to first pass a pleasant hour in poking Miss Emmy before Naunton arrived.

'That will not be possible, I regret to say,' Mrs Lee said to him with a shake of her head. 'The desirable Miss Emmy has gone to Limehouse today to attend her father's funeral. But there is a new girl since you were last here – a darling little creature named Miss Arabella. She is only sixteen, and of a beauty that has thrown Lord Granston into a perfect rapture – at the sight of her titties he shot his noble roe in his trousers and needed a large glass of brandy to revive him before he could continue with her!'

'Is she fair or dark?' Monty enquired.

'Her hair is as black as a raven's wing and her eyes as dark as a starless night,' said Mrs Lee in a fine poetic frenzy. 'An hour with her will bring you all the delight of half a day with any other of my girls.'

'His Lordship's accidental spillage is not a recommendation,' said Monty thoughtfully. 'He is surely one whose valet fetches him off before he stirs in the morning. Miss Arabella sounds to me like a chimney-sweep's wench from your description.'

'It is unworthy of you to dispraise the girl before you seen her,' Mrs Lee told him. 'I'll tell you what I'll do, since you are one of my regulars and a favourite of mine – instead of the five guineas I'd ask anyone else, you shall enjoy the dear girl for only three. I can't say fairer than that, can I?'

'Two guineas,' said Monty.

'You're a shrewd bargainer, Mr Standish,' said the old bawd, 'but I like you – very well, you shall have her for two!'

Monty handed over the money, and Mrs Lee escorted him up the stairs and knocked at the door of the front bedroom. Without waiting for a response, she turned the knob and nodded to Monty to go in.

'A gentleman to visit you, Arabella dear,' she called from the doorway. 'Be pleasant to him for he is a friend of mine, and a handsome young fellow.'

The door closed behind Monty who stared at the girl who lay on the bed. She wore only a chemise and drawers – no stockings or stays – and his heart lurched in delight at the sight of her. At Mrs Lee's voice she had turned on her side towards the door, disclosing to Monty's sight her smooth bare shoulders and, down the loose front of her chemise, the plump soft roundness of her titties.

Her long and softly waved hair was as black as Mrs Lee had promised, making Monty at once speculate whether the curls that grew between her legs were of the same raven hue. He introduced himself to the lovely girl whilst crossing the room to the bed, where he took a seat on the edge and gazed down at her in warm admiration. She gave him her hand to hold between both of his – a dainty little hand with a tender palm and slender fingers. He imagined those fingers curled about his shaft, which at once reared itself upright in his trousers and stood quivering.

'Dear Miss Arabella,' said he, 'you are even more lovely than Mrs Lee was capable of informing me. I beg you will enrol me on the list of your devoted admirers from this moment on.'

'How kind you are,' she murmured, her jet-black eyes glowing with affection, 'I hope you will come and see me often now that we have made each other's acquaintance.'

'You may rely on me,' he assured her, 'and I trust that you will admit me to your confidence in a matter that is giving me some little puzzlement.'

'And what might that be?'

'Why, it is this, my dear – are your nether curls as blackly beautiful as the hair that graces your pretty head?'

'You must judge of that for yourself,' said she, and slid her legs apart on the bed. Her delicate fingers drew open the slit of her cotton drawers, and there in full sight lay one of the prettiest playthings Monty had ever set eyes on. Framed between deliciously creamy white thighs, her thicket of curls was as black as the Ace of Spades! Monty breathed out in a long and ardent sigh of desire at the very sight of it, and pressed his hand to his trouser-front to hold his wildly shaking shaft still.

'Oh, not you too!' Miss Arabella exclaimed, her dainty hand resting on a thigh so that her fingertips just touched the pretty pink lips of her pussy. 'Have you come off already?'

'You need have no fear,' said Monty. 'I am no effete lord who shoots off his essence into his shirt-front before ever he gets it near a girl's pussy, let alone up it.'

'Are you quite sure of that?' she asked with a smile.

She sat up on the bed and opened Monty's trouser buttons with a skilled hand, pulled up his shirt and felt between her cool fingers the hardness of his shaft.

'How it leaps in my hand!' she cried, her fingers gliding up and down its length. Monty sighed in delight and put his hand into her drawers to play with her warm pussy and part the lips to find her proud little bud and tease it gently.

'And does it match up to your expectations?' she enquired.

'Oh, Arabella – I declare that you have the prettiest pussy I have seen for a very long time,' he murmured, his belly quaking to the spasms of delight her fingers on his shaft sent rushing through him.

'And you fully intend to roger it?' she asked with a smile.

'Yes . . .' he sighed, 'yes . . .' and at that very instant his sap gushed out of his leaping shaft under the ministrations of her busy hand. She laughed and drew out his pleasure to its limit then, when he spouted no more, released his sticky shaft and lay back on the bed again.

'I love a good rogering,' she taunted him. 'Why do you delay? Push your shaft up me and do me hard!'

'So that is your game, you minx!' said Monty, astonished by how easily and quickly she had brought him off. 'Two can play at that, my girl!'

His hand was in her drawers, his fingers thrust deep into her moist pussy, rubbing her pink nub until her back lifted off the bed and she moaned in climax. Before she recovered from that, a resumption of his stimulation caused her to gasp and throw her legs about, and in another minute he brought her off again. By then his shaft was standing hard-on once more and, even as she spread her legs wide to be fingered to yet another climactic spasm, Monty threw himself on her and pushed One-Eyed Jack deep into her slippery split.

'Ah, so you do mean to roger me after all!' she gasped. 'I had put you down as another lordling's son and heir who lacked the stamina for poking, and needed to be brought off by hand!'

'Then you mistook your man,' Monty grunted as he poked her fast and hard, his hands up under her chemise to grasp her soft titties and squeeze them. They rose and fell to the swift pace of her agitated breathing and she rolled her bottom from side to side beneath him whilst he ravaged her with sensations. She came off with a little shriek, her hot belly pressed so tightly to Monty's that the jet-black curls about her pussy were twined into the chestnut-brown curls round the base of his plunging shaft. Monty moaned in heavenly bliss and flooded her clinging pussy with long throbbing spurts.

After that, Arabella wanted him to stay with her and repeat their pleasures but Monty begged off, saying with truth that a friend was waiting for him at this very moment. She extracted a sincere promise from him that he would return to her soon and give her another taste of ecstasy. Monty adjusted his clothes decently, kissed her *farewell* and went downstairs. He found, as he fully expected, Naunton Cox in Mrs Lee's parlour, conversing with her while he finished her bottle of brandy.

They wrung each other's hand and slapped each other's back in the joy of their meeting. Monty suggested they should repair to the Cafe Royal to crack a bottle of Napoleon brandy by way of a celebration, but Naunton explained that he dare not be seen in a public place for the police had his description. Mrs Lee's alone seemed to him a safe haven.

'Then I'll leave you gentlemen to talk,' said Mrs Lee, rising to her feet. 'I'll send another bottle in for you.'

They thanked her for her kind hospitality, fully aware that they would be required to pay for it, and she left them alone.

'Lord above, Naunton – why are the police looking for you?' Monty asked. 'And why have you come back from Paris so soon?'

'You recall my telling you of that infernal bank manager who burst into the carriage and discovered me with Louise?' said Naunton. 'Thwarted of his prey at the time, when we both gave him the slip, the damned busybody wrote a nasty letter and sent it to my aged uncle at Effingham – the one whose heir I hope to be! In this letter the wretch blabbed all he had seen and gave it as his opinion that I am not a suitable person to inherit uncle's property and investments when the Grim Reaper pops down to Effingham! The frightful cheek of it! What a bounder this Bramley is, to go sneaking on a chap like that!'

'Great Scot!' Monty exclaimed. 'He should be horse-whipped! Is there anything I can do to help?'

'I've already revenged myself on him,' said Naunton, a savage grin on his handsome face. 'I crossed the

Channel yesterday and reached London by the boat train that set me down at Victoria station in the early evening. I concealed myself in the station buffet until eight o'clock, when I knew that Bramley the bank manager would out of his house in Clapham . . .'

'Wait!' said Monty, 'How could you know that? You have been in Paris since the ghastly day Bramley found you fetching off with the vicar's wife.'

'I am not without influence,' said Naunton, mysteriously. Then taking pity on Monty's bewilderment, he revealed that from Paris he had been in touch by letter-post with Minnie!

'She's a useful girl to know and she'll do anything for me,' said Naunton. 'Many is the poke I gave her when no other slit was available to me. Have you had her yourself, Monty?'

'As you say – she's handy in those otherwise lonely moments,' said Monty. 'Particularly in the early morning, when a fellow wakes up with a standing hard-on. But were you aware during your residence at Mrs Gifford's that Minnie's domestic duties include her bringing off the landlady by hand every night at bedtime?'

'No!' Naunton exclaimed. 'Who'd have thought it! You have truly astounded me. How did you get it out of Minnie? It must be her deepest secret?'

'I got it *out* of her at a time when I had it *in* her,' Monty answered, 'and to cure Hannah of her Sapphic tendencies, I went to her room at bedtime and had her enough times to assuage her curious urges and give her a rattling good night!'

'Damn me!' cried Naunton. 'You've been busy since I left! But to get back to my story, through Minnie I found out when my hated bank manager attends his Lodge Meetings. I made my way to his house and the servant showed me into the sitting room when I told her I was a colleague of her master. As I had intended, Mrs Bramley was alone, passing the time with embroidering. She went very pale when she recognised me but my tale was that I had come to apologise humbly to Mr Bramley, and I gave a fine appearance of being disappointed when she told me he would not return home before eleven, or even later.'

'You are a sly devil, Naunton,' said Monty, in admiration. 'I have no doubt your golden tongue was able to persuade her that nothing untoward was taking place in the railway carriage, and that she mistook what she saw that day.'

'Not at all!' his friend declared. 'The contrary, in fact. I explained that I was at the time head over heels in love with the lady she and Mr Bramley found with me when they entered the carriage at Clapham Junction but that family reasons prevented us from marrying. On the day in question I was escorting dear Louise to London to care for her paralysed mother and we knew that we should never see each other again. What Mrs Bramley and her husband had witnessed was the natural expression of a profound love Louise and I felt for each other.'

'By George – did she swallow it?' asked Monty.

'An interesting choice of words,' said Naunton with a grin, 'for as you will remember what Mrs Bramley – whose given name is Flora – had observed was dear Louise swallowing it! Take my word for it, Monty old sport, when a woman has had a good look at your shaft in a condition of full erection, she indulges in fantasies of it and is like to want to see it again. Flora had seen mine not only stiff but at the instant it was pulled out of Louise's mouth as I came off. No woman could forget that, or the trickles down Louise's face. As we sat talking

I could see Flora's agitation growing as she rehearsed the scene again and again in her mind's eye. I observed her covert glances down at my trousers and the trembling of her legs. In short, I need do nothing at all but sit there and let Flora see me and remember – and in remembering she became more and more excited.'

'But this is fiendish!' Monty exclaimed. 'You had her!'

'Simplicity itself,' Naunton agreed. 'At the right moment I whipped out my hard-on shaft in front of her and she uttered a long sigh. I left my chair to kneel at her feet and raise her skirts. Her legs opened like a pair of cabinet doors and I had her drawers gaping wide and my shaft up her in a flash.'

'You told me that Mr Bramley was middle-aged,' Monty reminded him. 'Was Flora not above the age of desirability also?'

'She is not yet forty,' said Naunton, 'and many a good tune is played on an old fiddle, my boy. I poked her sitting in her armchair to the best come off she'd ever had in her life, then laid her on the sofa and rogered her three more times. When the time came for me to go before Bramley returned, she implored me to visit her every day, in the afternoon when her husband is at the bank. Needless to say, I shall not do so, for my revenge is now complete.'

'But why are the police looking for you?' asked Monty.

'A small miscalculation on my part,' Naunton confessed. 'I pawned my gold watch in Paris and there being no clock in the Bramley parlour, I lost track of the passing of time. As I left by the front door, the bounder Bramley was coming in! A look passed between us on the doorstep and from my expression of triumph he guessed what I had been doing! He chased me for at least half a mile down the road, shouting vile imprecations and waving his walking stick at me in a threatening manner. But I am fleeter of foot, and made my escape.'

'And the police?' Monty asked.

'A news item in the morning newspaper reports a break-in at a house in Clapham last night, with the abuse of females and the theft of valuable property. The householder is named as Alfred Bramley, a bank official. I am certain that in his rage he lied to the police about my presence in his house and demanded my arrest on these monstrous charges. So I shall remain here until time for the evening boat train, then go by closed cab to the railway station to slip out of Old England yet again.'

'What about your uncle at Effingham?' Monty asked. 'Has he cut you off as a result of Bramley's sneaking ways?'

'Thank Heaven, no,' said Naunton in great relief. 'Uncle Bart was a goer in his day, it seems, and he wrote me a kind letter in Paris to congratulate me on pulling it off with a woman on a railway train – a feat he had more than once attempted, but had never achieved.'

''Then there was no need to seduce Bramley's wife, since his evil plan had miscarried,' said Monty.

'Yes, there was,' Naunton retorted. 'I wanted my revenge and I had it. I have written to my uncle with the full facts, and I am sure he will be proud of his nephew when he reads that I have exacted vengeance on my persecutor. He enclosed a twenty-pound note with his first letter – I have every hope he will do the same again when he hears of my double achievement last night.'

'Double? What do you mean by that?'

'After I had shaken off Bramley, I rested for half an hour in a low drinking den in Vauxhall. It was there that I penned the letter you had from me this morning. Whilst

I refreshed myself with a glass or two of gin, a thought struck me with the force of a thunderbolt – if I had revenged myself so pleasantly on Bramley by poking his wife, then why not his daughter too?'

'Has he one?'

'Most certainly – a plump girl of sixteen. When Bramley took me by surprise in the railway carriage, his whole family trooped in behind him and caught me in the act of coming off. There was Flora and her three children – of whom the girl is the eldest, and two boys. With a renewed thirst for revenge in my heart, I waited for an hour and then returned to Bramley's home. It was silent and dark and locked up for the night, but I effected an entrance by means of a scullery window. Upstairs I prowled the dark passages and pressed my ear to doors, till I located the room shared by Bramley's sons, and the one next to it in which his daughter slept alone.'

'What a fearful risk you ran!' Monty exclaimed. 'If you ever are captured by the police you will be convicted of a serious crime and sent to Dartmoor prison to break stones.'

'I slid into Hermione's room – for that is her name – put on the gaslight at half-full and woke her with a kiss,' Naunton continued. 'She recognised me at once, and the same forces were at work in her as in her mother – she had seen my shaft at full stretch on the train, and the image remained in her imagination to excite her. Believe me, dear old chum, all it took was three or four minutes persuasive talk by me and her nightgown was up round her neck and I was sucking her titties.'

'You are a perfect devil!' said Monty, his eyes shining with amusement. 'She was a virgin, I make no doubt.'

'Quite so,' Naunton confirmed, 'but willing to be

relieved of her virginity by the shaft she had seen in action elsewhere. I bared it for her and she fondled it with such enthusiasm that I fetched off in her hand. After that nothing would satisfy her but to have it up her! She spread her chubby thighs wide for me and I lay on her fat belly. I brought my shaft to the mark and pressed it slightly between the lips of her pussy. Shudders of delight passed through Hermione's tubby body and with a dear little smile she whispered, *I know it may hurt, my darling, but I must have it up me*. She heaved up her bottom to meet me, and with no more ado, I gave a good hard push and broke through her maiden membrane. The dear girl winced but she made no outcry. I did her with caution that first time and she came off most voluptuously the instant she felt my gushing cream inside her. Before I crept out of the house in the light of dawn I had rogered her thrice more, and she had developed a strong liking for it.'

'Where did you go then?' Monty asked, from curiosity.

'As it happens,' said Naunton, 'I have for some long time now been acquainted with a young married woman at Battersea and I took myself by cab to her house. Her husband is employed by the Gas Light and Coke Company and departs for his place of work at half past six every morning. I lurked opposite until I saw him leave the house, then presented myself to Matilda. She was very pleased to see me after so long an absence abroad and she made me most welcome. After I had told her of my pursuers and given her a good poking in the manner she prefers, she allowed me to sleep until it was time to come here to meet you.'

'And what, pray, is the manner she prefers?' enquired Monty.

'Sitting on the kitchen table, stripped down to her

stockings and drawers,' Naunton explained, 'her legs clamped tight about my waist as I stand between her knees and do her slowly. I find it fatiguing to roger in the standing position, particularly at the third time of coming off, but in the circumstances, it was needful to keep Matilda sweet by falling in with her desire to be poked upright. Naturally, after I had restored my energies in sleep, before I left her I insisted on throwing her down on her back and doing her the proper way.'

'We have some hours until you leave for the railway station,' said Monty with a grin, 'I intended to suggest to you that good use could be made of them upstairs here with a newcomer to Mrs Lee's – a charming young creature by the name of Miss Arabella. Between us we could roger her royally – but I fear you have so exerted yourself with Mr Bramley's women-folk and your married friend Matilda that you have no strength left for poking.'

'You do me an injustice,' Naunton replied at once. 'My sleep, after I had done my duty by Matilda's hot pussy a time or two, refreshed me completely and I am ready for another bout. Your account of Mrs Gifford's tastes has whetted my appetite and I owe Minnie a guinea or two and a good poke for her assistance. Miss Arabella can wait for some other time – let us take a closed carriage to Seymour Place now and together give maid and mistress the rogering of their life until it is time for me to depart.'

'By all means,' said Monty, ready to oblige his old friend whatever he proposed.

'Mrs Gifford, as I recall, has a large pair of titties under her clothes,' said Naunton, 'Are they a good feel?'

'When her stays are removed, her titties are heavy though slack and pendulous,' Monty informed him, 'But they are warm and soft – ideal for wrapping round your shaft and fetching off between. We can take turns at doing that, while the other makes use of her pussy at the same time.'

'Capital!' cried Naunton.

CHAPTER 15
Lovers United in Bliss

In the week that followed Naunton Cox's clandestine journey to London to wreak vengeance on the person who was trying to ruin his life and prospects, Monty received yet another letter from his darling Gwendolen. This was of a strikingly different tone to the first, written not in the yearning of thwarted passion, but in confident hope and expectation. It was delivered in the midday post and the postmark showed that it had been sent that morning from South Kensington.

At the sight of his dearest girl's handwriting, Monty kissed the envelope and tore it open with a trembling hand. Within he found a missive that was brief and to the point:

My darling boy,
Our love has triumphed over all adversities! Come to me at the above address! Hasten!

Your own loving Gwendolen

The address at the head of the page was in Brompton Road. Monty put on his hat and hurried along Seymour Place to the cab rank, and was on his way within minutes of reading Gwendolen's note. His brain whirled in speculation – what could this address be at which she awaited him? The house of a friend, perhaps? Not that it mattered in the least – she was in town and would soon be in his arms! Yet it seemed to him strange that Selwyn had said nothing of friends in South Kensington, nor of a visit by his sister to London.

The house, when Monty was set down outside it, appeared very respectable and well-kept. He bounded up the steps and rang the doorbell with a light heart, his hat at a jaunty angle. A maid opened the door, a pleasant-faced woman of thirty, and enquired his name. When he told her, she stepped aside for him to enter, saying that Mrs Fanshawe was expecting him. She conducted him upstairs to the drawing room, announced him and withdrew. With a racing heart and outstretched hands, Monty stepped forward to where Gwendolen stood by the piano. From head to toe she was dressed in the deep black of mourning.

She ran to meet him and was in his arms in a trice, her lips to his in a burning kiss and her belly pressing hard against him. Monty's arms were about her in a loving embrace and while the kiss continued, his hands slid down her slender back until he was kneading the cheeks of her bottom through the silk crepe of her dress.

'Yes – take me!' she cried. 'I have dreamed of this moment night after night! Make my dream reality, my dearest Monty!'

With no thought for the time of day or fear of interruption, he pressed her down on the sofa and laid her on her back. She trembled and her beautiful face flushed pink, and she implored him to be swift and put her out of her sweet suffering. On his knees at her side, Monty turned up her skirts over stockings as black as jet to find to his astonishment that she was wearing thin black drawers!

This was by no means the first time Monty had rogered a young widow but never before had he seen black underclothes. He ran his hand over the fine material, feeling up between her legs, and Gwendolen smiled at him and asked did he not find her drawers stylish?

'They are utterly delightful,' he said, 'though I must admit it is what they conceal that gives them their *bon ton*!'

'They shall not conceal anything an instant longer than you choose,' said she. 'Take me however you will, my dearest!'

Monty's trembling hand had parted the slit of her drawers to bare her treasure for his attentions. The piquant contrast of jet-black crepe juxtaposed to her creamy white belly made him gasp loudly in admiration, and his hard-on shaft throbbed and leapt in his trousers. Then, with a hoarse cry of ardent desire, he bowed his head and pressed his mouth in a burning kiss to Gwendolen's pouting pussy.

'How many times I have dreamed of this blissful moment!' she exclaimed. 'How man nights I have lain awake in the torment of love, wet with passion!'

She reached down and jerked so hard at Monty's trousers, to open them and release his straining shaft, that all the buttons were torn loose and rolled under the sofa she lay on. One-Eyed Jack leapt out from under Monty's shirt at full stretch and eager for the fray. In a flash, Monty sprang to his feet, threw off his jacket and loosened the knot of his necktie, preparing himself for the pleasant exertions to come.

The moment that Gwendolen saw that he was ready for her – his straining shaft in his hand, its purple head bared for action – she spread wide her legs with deliberate slowness. The effect was extremely arousing – Monty stood motionless and hardly able to breathe as he watched her black-drawered thighs moving apart on the cushions. The slit in the raven-hued crepe gaped open to the full, revealing to him her dark fleece, the delicate white hollows of her groins, and the fleshy groove of her pussy.

Monty groaned in delight and got on the sofa with her, on his knees between her thighs, his swollen shaft sticking out over her belly like a signpost showing the way to pleasure. He was running his clasped hand up and down it, aroused almost to the point of delirium by the pink-lipped pussy held wide open for him by the position of Gwendolen's legs.

'Put it in me before you fetch off over my drawers,' she said with a sigh of longing.

Monty obliged her at once, flinging himself onto her heaving belly and guiding himself into her with an eager hand. Even as he started to slide into her with a strong push and felt the warm wet cling of her pussy about his hot shaft, he knew that he had been away from his beloved too long. He was trembling on the very brink of coming off without even a single thrust! He shook passionately, transmitting to her his desperate condition, so that she smiled and said softly, *Love me, Monty, love me*!

Thus urged by his darling, Monty continued with his upward progress and pushed slowly into the depths of her warm wetness. The sensations were so prodigious that he fetched off at once, spouting his frantic desire into her.

'Oh yes – you are mine!' Gwendolen sighed as she felt his hot pulsations in her belly. 'Mine, mine, mine!'

She raised her legs and wound them about his waist to hold him fast, then moaned in ecstasy as his hard and gushing shaft reached her ultimate depths. He writhed on her, continuing to pour his youthful virility into her in fast spurts, while she lay squirming beneath him, uttering little cries of triumph.

'Yes, you are mine, Monty, mine!' she panted. 'You love me with all your heart and soul! I feel it in your coming off.

He thrilled to her words and emptied his tumultuous passion into her quivering belly. When at last he was calm once more, he lay beside her holding her in his arms, his lips pressed to her soft cheek, while he assured her of his undying devotion.

'When I felt your rapture gushing,' said she, 'the sensations aroused in me were so sublime that I understood for the first time the force of those lines of poetry by Mr Matthew Arnold in which he speaks of the awareness of life's flow.'

'The lines to which you refer do not spring readily to mind,' murmured Monty, his hand right up her clothes to feel her soft titties. 'Remind me, if you will be so good.'

'With all the pleasure in the world. This is what Mr Arnold said on the subject:

A bolt is shot back somewhere in our breast,
And a lost pulse of feeling stirs again.
A man becomes aware of his life's flow,
And hears its winding murmur, and he sees
The meadows where it glides, the sun, the breeze.'

'How true, how very true!' Monty sighed. 'And now I come think of it, there are some other lines by the same poet which have always struck me most forcibly.'

'Recite them to me, I beg you,' said Gwendolen, and her small warm hand clasped his limp shaft.

Monty collected his thoughts for a moment, then launched into the little-quoted lines of strong sentiment:

'A life time of wet dreams my strength to drain
I gladly would endure and not complain,
To gain possession of my darling's charms
And pass an hour of bliss in her soft arms;
My trembling hand to feel her snow-white breast
While tongue and lips make free with all the rest!
I hear her lusting sobs, her eager sighs,
To feel my hard-on shaft between her thighs,
My hairy pompoms dangling down below,
And swinging in between those cheeks of snow,
As in her slit I thrust with might and main,
And feel her heaving belly quake and strain,
Until my passion gushes hot and fast,
And she comes off, and tranquil lies at last.'

'Yes!' Gwendolen cried. 'The yearning of the lover is well expressed in these lines, and the satisfaction that comes from a good rogering!'

'To Monty's surprise, she freed herself from his embrace, rose from the sofa and went to the grand piano, smoothing down her clothes before she sat at the keyboard and raised the lid to play. He sat up and put his feet on the floor as the strains of *Come into the garden, Maud* sounded through the room. A moment later he stood at his darling's side, his hand on her shoulder and his limp shaft dangling loose from his open trousers, while he raised his pleasant tenor voice in song to her melody:

'All night have the roses heard
The flute, violin, bassoon;
All night has the casement jessamine stirred
To the dancers dancing in tune;
Till a silence fell with the waking bird,
And a hush with the setting moon.'

Whilst he sang he watched Gwendolen's nimble fingers over the ivory keys and wished they were playing on his shaft, which at the suggestion twitched a little in sleepy approval. Gwendolen seemed almost to read his thoughts, and paused a moment or two in her playing to turn her head and bestow a tender little kiss on One-Eyed Jack as he swung close to her.

Monty warbled the next stanza as the piano resumed its music:

> '*Queen rose of the rosebud garden of girls,*
> *Come hither, the dances are done,*
> *In gloss of satin and glimmer of pearls,*
> *Queen lily and rose in one;*
> *Shine out, little head, sunning over with curls,*
> *To the flowers, and be their sun!*'

He saw Gwendolen's bosom heaving with emotion under her black mourning garb and, stirred by the thought of her white titties beneath that sombre crepe silk, he serenaded her with a stanza not sung round the piano in mixed company:

> '*Sweet rose with the rosebud hid twixt your thighs,*
> *Come with me, lie down by the stream,*
> *For feeling and licking and hot lustful sighs,*
> *And all the long thrills of love's dream;*
> *Be wet, little pussy, be open, my prize,*
> *While I fill you brimful with my cream!*'

'Oh!' Gwendolen exclaimed. 'Are they the words of dear Lord Tennyson?'

Her hand took an affectionate hold on Monty's strengthening shaft and tugged him round to stand with his back to the piano. She stood up and raised her clothes in front to reveal to him again her thin black drawers.

'Then in the immortal words of our revered Poet Laureate, my pussy is wet and open for you, my darling,' cried she, parting wide the slit of her drawers to show him that she spoke only the truth. Monty stared down open-mouthed, to see her fingers stretching open her dark-curled slit, and he sighed in deep joy when with a dainty hand she took hold of One-Eyed Jack, now at his full six-inch length again, and slipped his swollen purple head inside her.

'Gwendolen – how delicious that you want to be rogered again so soon!' Monty sighed in delight.

His arms were round her waist and his hands laid flat on the plump cheeks of her bottom to squeeze them through her dress. Gwendolen pushed slowly forward against him and, looking down, he observed how his shaft stretched her pussy wide open as it slid in. She placed her small hands on his shoulders and leaned forward to kiss his mouth while she pressed her belly to him. Her hot kiss and the movements of her loins set Monty's blood racing faster in his veins.

'You are mine, my dearest one,' he babbled, feeling his shaft jerking furiously of its own accord inside her, 'every darling sweet part of you – your darling face, your darling eyes and mouth, your darling soft titties, your darling warm belly and thighs, your darling pussy . . .'

'No, Monty,' said she, with a soft, loving smile. 'It is you who are mine. I told you that – you cannot have forgotten.'

'What difference is there?' he sighed. 'I am yours, you are mine, my darling girl . . .'

With the loving smile still on her beautiful face, Gwendolen started to roger *him* with thrusts of her belly against his, as she pressed close.

'The difference is nothing you need trouble yourself with, my dearest,' she said, her voice becoming tremulous as the thrills running through her grew stronger. 'Let me concern myself with the subtleties of such matters – all you need do is to remain in readiness to roger me whenever I tell you, day or night!'

At her confident words, Monty felt the sap begin to surge up his shaft and in another second it would fill her pussy with a delirium of sensation! He grappled her to him with hands that clenched on her bottom and thrust up in her to the very limit. Then, with a long gasping moan of heavenly enjoyment, he gushed his copious flood into her belly.

'More, more, more!' Gwendolen cried.

At this he realised that she had not yet achieved her moments of ecstasy and was waiting for him to carry her up to a climax of bliss. His shaft had ceased to spurt but she maintained her vigorous thrusts against him until the moment came, and with a long moan she shuddered and thrust her tongue into his mouth. When at last her tremors of delight were over, she sank limply down from his arms until she sat on the piano-seat.

Monty sat beside her, and raised her clothes to her waist yet again to pull open the wet slit of her drawers. With pride in his beating heart he saw the traces of his passion – his white essence trickling down the insides of her soft thighs from the loose lips of her pussy.

'Gwendolen, my dearest girl,' he whispered in her ear, whilst he stroked her slippery thighs with languid fingers, 'I hardly know whether to say that I rogered you then, or you rogered me, for in the joys of our coming off it seemed to me that we were united as one flesh. Did it seem like that to you, my angel?'

'Dear sweet Monty – do not speak so foolishly,' she

replied, 'I rogered you, my dear, and made you come off very nicely.'

'Not so,' he returned fondly, 'for I brought *you* off.'

By way of answer Gwendolen stood up, holding her clothes up about her waist, turned herself round to face him and sat down astride his thighs. She took his soft and sticky shaft in her fingers and rubbed the head slowly up and down the soft moist lips between her black-clad thighs.

'We will have no misunderstanding between us as to which of us is going to roger the other from now on, my dearest,' said she. 'Since there appears to be some question in your mind as to what precisely occurred when we were standing up together, I shall enlighten you now we are sitting down.'

Although he had only just fetched off, the sustained sight of Gwendolen's jet-black silk drawers, coupled with her soft, slow rubbing of One-Eyed Jack against her wet pussy, aroused Monty almost at once. No sooner was his shaft at full stretch again than Gwendolen raised herself from his lap, held it to the mark and sank down on it, impaling herself neatly.

'Now, my precious boy,' said she, 'I am going to roger you – so do not pretend otherwise after you have come off.'

With that, she threw her arms about his neck drew his face to hers, and kissed him and sucked his tongue whilst riding up and down on his embedded shaft. Immediately Monty's head began to swim as if he were drunk on the best brandy, and he clasped Gwendolen by her slender waist and abandoned himself utterly to the blissful sensations that rolled through him like a tide of the mighty ocean.

She, too, was enjoying the most divine thrills, he was aware – and from her broken gasps and the little spasms that shook her body, Monty knew that his darling was about to come off! His heart pounded for joy in his breast and he sighed his passion into her open mouth. His eager hands were under her clothes and inside her black drawers, stroking her warm thighs and belly in divine rapture. Her rise and fall on his shaft became brisker as her excitement gathered strength towards a crisis, forcing his penetrating shaft deeper and harder into her.

The bliss became too overpowering to bear! Monty gasped out in broken little words his eternal love for her and gushed his passion into her massaging pussy.

'I've brought you off!' she cried. 'Admit that you've been soundly rogered, Monty!'

'Yes . . .' he sighed, as his love and desire spurted into her, 'yes, my darling girl, you have rogered me . . . I admit it with pride and delight . . .'

On hearing his words, Gwendolen at once attained the peak of sensation. With One-Eyed Jack right up inside her she shook to the throes of her own coming off, uttering cries and moans and shuddering continuously in ecstasy. When at length her pleasure was completed she sat half-swooning against Monty, her head on his shoulder, her body shaken from time to time by little tremors.

'I must rest a little,' she whispered. 'Help me to the sofa.'

To demonstrate to his beloved that his manly strength was at her disposal in all possible ways, Monty rose to his feet with her in his arms and carried her across the room. He stretched her out at full length on the sofa, and would have pulled down her clothes to cover her endearing young charms – but she with a sweet smile asked him to remove her drawers.

With shaking hands he did as his darling bade him, and on her soft white belly and dark-haired mound he planted a score or more of kisses. She instructed him to remove her frock and by raising her bottom and then her shoulders, aided him in getting it off. Like her drawers, her thin chemise was of finest black silk, completing her mourning attire.

Was this all for the sake of a husband for whom she felt no love and no respect? Monty pondered the question while he slid her black stockings down her white legs, so rendering her completely naked. This for a husband who shot his elixir in the wrong orifice and cheated her of her conjugal pleasures? The thought was absurd – the purpose of this beautiful black finery was to sensually arouse the beholder, namely himself.

'Put your back to me for a moment,' said Gwendolen.

She sat up on the sofa, her full round titties swinging to her movement. Monty bowed his head to press a kiss to the pink bud of each, then obeyed her, wondering at her intentions. Then he knew – he felt his wrists drawn together behind his back and bound with one of her stockings. Even while his mind ran wildly on this new development, Gwendolen put her black drawers about his face and tied them behind his neck, covering his mouth and nose but allowing him his sense of sight.

He turned towards her and she lay on her back once more, her legs slightly parted to show her plump and pink-lipped pussy to best advantage. Above his jet-black gag Monty gazed at her with eyes filled with devotion. The scent of her warm flesh lingered on the thin silk, mingled with the Lily-of-the-Valley perfume she had dabbed on her drawers. Monty's head swam with giddiness and desire as his limp shaft grew long and thick yet again to this stimulus.

'Now do you doubt that you are mine?' she asked with a smile that sent a thrill of ecstasy through him.

Her hand played with his shaft, coaxing it skilfully to ever greater size and strength.

'Everything is mine now,' she told him. 'Poor Elliot left me a great deal of money and property, I have discovered. I never knew he had so much, for we lived modestly. The house down at Reading is mine and I have decided to let it out to rent. This house we are now in is mine for as long as I wish, for I have taken a lease. I mean to live in London now, not in Reading.'

Monty's brown eyes were misty with emotion as Gwendolen held his hard-on shaft and stroked it with tender fingers.

'Best of all,' said she, 'you are mine, and I shall roger you by day and by night, my dear. You will give up your rooms and move here to live with me, before bedtime tonight.'

Monty nodded his agreement and his shaft nodded in her hand, as if also agreeing. Gwendolen raised her knees a little and invited Monty to mount her. He did so awkwardly, lacking the use of his hands and arms. She guided his standing shaft to her moist split and he pushed it in.

'Oh!' she exclaimed, as he thrust home to the hilt. 'Bliss, pure bliss, my dear! How I adore this rogering!'

With an arm round his neck, she kissed his mouth through the black silk of the drawers that gagged him.

'Oh!' she exclaimed as he thrust home to the very hilt. 'Oh, Monty dearest boy, what a superb shaft you have!'

Even while she spoke, he felt her slender legs closing over his back like a steel man-trap, thereby increasing his state of helplessness. She began to move herself beneath him, thrusting her hot loins up at him with fast and nervous little strokes, in effect sliding herself along his embedded shaft and back. At once he responded, as would any virile young man, but Gwendolen clamped her legs tighter round his middle and her arms around his back. She held him with his belly tight to hers.

'Be still, Monty!' she exclaimed sharply.

There was little else he could do now, held fast as he was by her, except to lie still while she had her way with him from below. On top of her he might be but there was no doubt at all in his mind that he was the one being rogered, not his dearest Gwendolen. It did not matter – the outcome would be the same as if he were the active partner and she were the one being poked.

Monty's passions rose in a throbbing crescendo towards their eventual summit, and he stared down tenderly at the face under his. Gwendolen's dark brown eyes were set in a stare, her mouth was open in a victorious smile. It was obvious that she derived an unnatural and yet thrilling pleasure from compelling him to submit to her in this way. Her pussy thrust up and down beneath him, the velvet flesh rubbing along his wet and jerking shaft with a hot remorseless desire. Her climactic moments were tardy to arrive, but when at last they did, their intensity was such as to fling her into throbs of bliss.

Spasms of joy flitted across her beautiful face, while her arms squeezed him so tightly to her that the breath was forced from him. Her back arched off the sofa to ram Monty's shaft in her to the uttermost depths, and the sensation was so thrilling that he fetched off instantly. He could feel her pussy sucking at his shaft, draining it of every drop of his essence.

'You are mine, Monty!' she moaned, 'mine to have and hold!'